The
Goliath
Bone

MIKE HAMMER NOVELS
BY MICKEY SPILLANE

I, the Jury

My Gun Is Quick

Vengeance Is Mine!

One Lonely Night

The Big Kill

Kiss Me, Deadly

The Girl Hunters

The Snake

The Twisted Thing

The Body Lovers

Survival . . . Zero!

The Killing Man

Black Alley

The Goliath Bone

Mickey Spillane
with **Max Allan Collins**

An Otto Penzler Book

Harcourt, Inc.

Orlando   Austin   New York   San Diego   London

Requests for permission to make copies
of any part of the work should be submitted online at
www.harcourt.com/contact or mailed to the following address:
Houghton Mifflin Harcourt Publishing Company,
6277 Sea Harbor Drive, Orlando, Florida 32887-6777.

www.HarcourtBooks.com

Library of Congress Cataloging-in-Publication Data
Spillane, Mickey, 1918–2006.
The Goliath bone/Mickey Spillane;
with Max Allan Collins.—1st ed.
        p.   cm.
"An Otto Penzler Book."
1. Hammer, Mike (Fictitious character)—Fiction.
2. Private investigators—New York (State)—New York—
Fiction.   3. Goliath (Biblical giant)—Relics—Fiction.
4. Relics—Fiction. 5. Terrorists—Fiction.
6. Extremists—Fiction.   I. Collins, Max Allan.   II. Title.
PS3537.P652G66   2008
813'.54—dc22   2008010091
ISBN 978-0-15-101454-5

Text set in Fairfield Light
Designed by Lydia D'moch

Printed in the United States of America

First edition
A C E G I K J H F D B

For Jane
of course

The
Goliath
Bone

Chapter 1

The snow had stopped. Barely an inch of it had come down to cover the icy sheet that made New York City shine with strange new prisms of light. The temperature was twelve degrees below freezing, and it wasn't going to get any warmer. Traffic barely moved, and a lot of it was pinched against curbs where they had slid earlier. Nobody bothered to stay with their vehicles. Sitting shut up with an engine going was inviting trouble, and with all the lights on outside the bars in the adjoining blocks, it was a night to play until it thawed or somebody came and got you.

I had enough of being parked on a bar stool, brushing off the half-drunks and the chippies who were making the most of a bad night on the street. I paid my tab, nodded good night to the bartender, left a full Scotch and soda for the doll baby who was trying to give me a rush job, and went outside.

Damn, it was cold.

I buttoned up the old pile-lined trench coat and snugged the belt around my waist, glad I wasn't on a job where I'd need the .45.

This time it was in a belt holster on my right hip, accessible through my pocket. Nothing was happening, but the precaution of keeping my hands stuffed in my coat wouldn't be a noticeable gesture. Everybody else had their hands in their pockets, too.

Across the street a battered sedan was parked, a gypsy cab, the hood and top under a layer of snow. The front wheels were angled out and the distance from the car in front of it was enough to make sure it wasn't trapped. The windshield wipers had kept the snow off.

Briefly, there was a dark blur of a face in a rear window—up front, the driver, a guy in a stocking cap, was bored and slumped behind his wheel; but behind him, the blurred face slowly scanned the sidewalks before sinking back into the darkness.

Whoever this passenger was, he'd been sitting there for over an hour freezing his ass off, waiting for something to happen. And paying a cabbie for the privilege.

I had seen too many nights like this on streets like these. There is an atmosphere that goes along with it, like smelling smoke from a fire a long way off. There was nothing you could put your finger on, but the years of living under the shadow of violence gave me an alertness I never tried to shrug off.

Something was going to happen.

Two drunks came out of a bar trying to sing. One got as far as the curb and threw up. The sight and smell of it caused the other one to make it an upchuck duet. Then they both argued about which way to go, decided to head toward the dull glow of Sixth Avenue, and lurched off.

A fat guy carrying a couple of packages came by, and when he waddled past, I stepped out, went about ten feet, and stepped into a doorway beside an abandoned old store.

Nothing was happening. But it was getting ready to. I could feel it. Pat Chambers of Homicide always told me that's what cops felt. Old cops. Real street cops. He always said I should have stayed one instead of taking the money road of being licensed to play the cop game for big and private bucks. Guys like me weren't supposed to have those weird feelings, like having little people crawling up along your spine and making funny noises in your ears.

Something was happening, all right. It was under way. I was buried in the shadows and had pulled the glove off my right hand. My fingers crept to the liner opening in the pocket where they could slide around the butt of the cold 1911 model .45 caliber Army Colt Automatic that had six in the clip and one in the chamber.

All I had to do was clear the fabric of my trench coat and thumb the hammer back.

Across the street, a dingy late-night diner disgorged a pair of mildly gassed-up college kids who took a long time figuring out where they were. Taxis weren't showing, so the Broadway glow waved them to head that way and they shuffled off, kicking up the snow ahead of their feet.

I took my thumb off the hammer of the Colt.

Thirty feet down toward the bright lights, a door opened, and the glow of a Chinese restaurant spilled out onto the sidewalk, making a rainbow of colors from the red and green lanterns inside. The noise was muffled, but it had to be a popular place, happy with laughing sounds and even the faint rattle of dishes.

The pair that stepped out were also of college age, well dressed and sober. The girl had her blonde hair mostly stuffed under a stocking cap and wore a fur-trimmed suede coat; the boy had on a Western-style sheepskin coat and no hat at all. The boy was carrying a tubular brown-paper–wrapped package that was three feet long or more and a good six inches thick. His hand held it at the bottom and the other one clasped it firmly to his chest. A musical instrument, maybe? If so, a precious one to this kid.

I didn't know what, but something was going to happen. The needles along my spine were beginning to probe into my skin.

I heard the car door open and saw, from the rear of the gypsy cab, a bronze-faced figure emerge in hooded navy sweats, loping across the street and falling in behind the two kids, whose backs were to him. The couple disappeared down the stairs of a subway station. The hooded figure, lagging perhaps a dozen feet behind, followed them.

I moved fast but I didn't run—I might have slipped and broken my tailbone, and maybe, just maybe, I was wrong. Maybe there was a good reason for some asshole to sit in a gypsy cab for God knew how long waiting till a couple kids left a bar with a bulky wrapped package and headed for the nearest subway station. . . .

The stairs were empty by the time I got there, but as I headed down, hand on the .45, I knew damned well I *hadn't* been wrong. I couldn't just feel it, I could *hear* it. . . .

Panic has its own sound. It hisses with a terrified breath full of wild fear. It stumbles and makes strange animal noises of knowing something deadly is right behind you.

But this panic came toward me, its panting a harsh rasp, tripping on the steel steps, creatures fleeing from a dark nightmare. Here I was trying to catch up with them when the two kids were suddenly scrambling back up at me, eyes wide but not seeing me, running jerkily my way, only their eyes directed past me toward the freedom above, on the streets of New York. So close. So close . . .

The oval-faced, blue-eyed young man was half-dragging the terrified dark-eyed little looker behind him, his arm bent, holding her by her wrist, clutching his bulky package with his other arm. Then the girl slipped, nearly pulling the guy down with her, and he almost dropped the package, trying to hang on to her. It was only a momentary pause before he got her to her feet, and for an instant I saw the contorted, frenzied expression as she turned her head for a terrified look over her shoulder.

Their pursuer was right behind them, running silently on rubber-soled shoes, the gun in his hand ready to pump slugs into the backs of the kids and in two more seconds, it would be done.

I grinned because I already had the .45 out and in my fist, the hammer thumbed back, and nothing bothered me because this was no cop after a couple of young offenders, not with that silencer on the snout of his piece, and when he paused for that fraction of a second to aim, my .45 slug tore the rod right out of his hand and in that fleeting moment, dread bit into him like a lightning flash that contorted his face, and he spun to get away from this sudden nightmare.

But his feet didn't hold him.

He tripped, made a waltzy spin and his echoing yell was stifled when his head smashed against the metal-tipped stairs and his body made squashy sounds in its mad tumble, the head pounding out drum notes until it split, and all was quiet. Then he was too far away and I could barely hear the blood dripping.

Down below, the heavy thunder of a train going by on the express tracks tolled a death knell like the kettledrums in a Wagnerian opera.

So far, nobody else had come up the stairs.

On the landing just behind me, the two kids were waiting, not knowing which way to go. I put the .45 back in the leather and held up a hand, indicating they should stay put. They exchanged glances that said neither saw any better option.

Then I took out my cell phone and called Pat Chambers's number at home.

The captain of Homicide took it on the third ring; not bad for a guy nearing retirement. "Mike! Do you know what time—"

"Since when do I call this time of night to shoot the shit?"

A long sigh. "Since never."

I told him to get a squad car to the subway station immediately. No details. Just do it. I broke the connection and turned to the kids. They were huddled together, shivering, the boy managing to cradle both the girl and the bulky butcher-paper–wrapped item.

Down below, a BMT local rumbled into the station and rumbled out again. Nobody came up the staircase. It was a lousy night to travel.

The young couple looked like cross-country runners at the end of the race. Their white pluming breath was uneven, their faces wet with sweat despite the cold, their eyes a silent signal that panic lay right behind them. A killer had stalked them and had almost ended the chase. Now they were looking at me like maybe I was another killer, and they weren't wrong.

I said, "I'm a licensed private investigator." As I told them, I flashed my wallet and let them see the state ticket behind the plastic. They didn't breathe any easier, and the girl's lower lip was quivering with fright.

"The cops'll be here in a minute or two," I told them. "You kids in any trouble with them?"

Swallowing hard, the girl shook her head.

The young guy said, "That . . . man . . ." His head jerked toward the body on the lower stairway. ". . . was following us all day. . . . It started at the university."

"You college students?"

Between heavy breaths, he said, "Graduate students. NYU. Our parents teach there."

"At this time of night?" My voice had a sour note.

He shook his head, sucked in his breath and added, "That guy 'accidentally' bumped into us on Broadway, about pushed us under a bus. That was when we got through traffic and thought we'd lost him."

"Who was he?"

There was no answer.

Then the girl asked, "Could we hire you?"

"Can you afford it?"

The boy was nodding even as he hugged that unwieldy item. I indicated the package. "Is that something you stole, son?"

"No! . . . But I . . . I'd rather talk to you about it than the police."

So I hustled them out onto the street and down the block to my car and put the girl in front and the boy in back and got the hell out of there. Pat knew where to find me.

We'd gone maybe a block when the boy said, "Thanks, mister."

"No sweat."

The girl said, "He could have killed us."

I got the boy's eyes in the rearview mirror. "He was aiming at *you,* son."

With one motion, the pair gave each other a quick, introspective look that said it was happening all over again, and before they could make any excuses, I asked, "How many times?"

Without any discussion, the girl said, "Three." Then her eyes opened wide and she half-whispered, "How would you know about that?"

Both sets of eyes were on me now. There were no expressions on their faces at all. For a moment they seemed like rabbits under the dark muzzles of a shotgun, not knowing whether to run or just die quietly.

I said, "All I did was step out into a situation I've seen before. Trouble seems to have an aura about it. It was the way a car was parked, wheels out, not crowding the car in front, windshield wipers keeping the glass clean. It was a guy wearing a hooded jogging outfit in the wrong weather."

The girl frowned. "That's all?"

"That's enough. You know what kind of area this is?"

The boy murmured, "Not really."

"This is Sugartown," I said. "Hookers' heaven. An easy place to pick up some crack or pot or some heavier stuff, if you have a thick wallet."

"We don't use those things," the girl told me. Her voice was irritated.

Half-smiling, I jerked a thumb at the bulky brown-wrapped item and said, "Then that baby's not a bong?"

The boy knew I was kidding, and said, "We went to that restaurant to meet a friend."

"Did you?"

". . . Yes."

"Who *was* he? Or was it a *she*?"

There was no answer.

At the corner, I turned left, went a few blocks, cut over cross-town and while I waited at a stoplight, called my secretary Velda, and told her to get over to the office.

"A little late for office hours, isn't it?" she asked, a tiny edge in the purr of her throaty voice.

"It's a case I stumbled onto."

"What happened to not taking on any more cases this month?"

"This won't interfere with our plans, doll. I promise."

"I love you, anyway."

She clicked off and so did I.

There had been no other questions from Velda. Maybe it was the tone of my voice, but she had been in on enough kill scenes to know that something had gone down the hard way.

Behind me, the boy shifted the package in his arms to a more comfortable position and leaned back against the cushions. Finally he said, "Were we dumb asses to hop into your car like you told us to?"

I shook my head. "Not if you want to stay alive."

"Where are we going?"

"In ten minutes, we'll be at my office. My secretary's apartment is nearby, so she'll meet us there."

"Your secretary," the girl said, trying to understand what that was about.

A pair of squad cars came screaming past, fearless in the ice and snow. I knew where they were headed, so I didn't look back.

"She's a PI, too," I said. "Licensed and carries a concealed weapon when she's on a job. If you don't like the way this goes down, we'll call it quits right away. Then I'll turn in a full written report to the New York City Police Department, who you can tell all about that package you're holding."

The two of them suddenly stiffened and glanced at each other surreptitiously before staring out the windshield at the snow, which was coming down again, my wipers working overtime.

Unconsciously, the boy seemed to pull his ungainly package closer to his body. His fingers tightened against the wrappings, and there was an odd rasp to his breathing.

And this was where it was, I thought. That feeling I had that meant something ugly was brewing. That a car ready for an instant takeoff wasn't in a normal stance. That a guy was dressed wrong for winter. And now an assassin was dead, but there would be more attempts, better calculated. They would allow for oddball possibilities such as an itinerant interloper breaking up an artfully contrived plan.

I parked in the building's basement garage, and the three of us went up to the eighth floor. For the first time, some of the tightness had gone out of them and their eyes held only questions, not abject terror.

The kids were quiet, their bodies touching each other for mutual comfort. I was half a head taller than the boy and a whole head over the girl and had a good fifty pounds on the male. It had been a full day since I had shaved, and since I wasn't all that pretty to begin with, I knew what the kids were wondering: Had they traded one tight spot for a tighter one? What kept them fairly calm was the fact that this was an old but well-maintained office building, refurbished and nicely outfitted, and not a likely place for unsavory characters. Like me.

We got off the elevator at the eighth floor and I steered them to the office numbered 808 and when the boy saw the inscription on the door that read MICHAEL HAMMER INVESTIGATIONS, there was a sudden constriction in his shoulders and his eyes flashed toward me momentarily.

I wasn't supposed to see that, but I got it.

The lock opened soundlessly and I pushed the door open, my hands gently ushering the pair in ahead of me. A momentary touch of apprehension made the boy's arm tighten around his package again, and it stayed that way until he saw Velda sitting behind her desk, the lamp beside her dramatically highlighting her face and the sleek darkness of her hair.

There was something of the past about her that could take your breath away, the soft pageboy curl that heightened the width of her shoulders, the fullness of her stature, the lush wet redness of her mouth.

When you've worked with a doll like Velda as long as I have, you'd think a woman, no matter how luxuriantly beautiful, would be just another attractive fixture in a wood-paneled office. She downplayed that beauty in tailored suits, which also concealed the short-barreled .38.

But the boy who hugged that wrapped package almost dropped it when he got a load of this statuesque, dark-haired beauty who was old enough to be his mother, though I doubted he was thinking of her that way.

When she smiled, the boy's arm seemed to loosen around the package he was holding. Velda knew what she was doing, all right. She had been jarred out of bed, but had made a showgirl's quick change and had gotten to the office in record time, ready to cope with any emergency that had popped up.

Velda beamed at our clients in a kind, reassuring fashion, took their coats and hung them up in the closet, saying, "Pat called. Fit to be tied. You seem to have left a crime scene again."

The two kids exchanged glances, the girl mouthing, *Again?*

"It's a bad habit," I admitted.

Velda said, "He said he'll be over here in half an hour."

"Gives us some time," I said, nodding.

She got up and opened the door to my inner office and waited until the two kids had gone in, then brought up the chairs for them in front of my desk. She brought her own chair up around beside my desk, halfway between me and our young new clients, and crossed her legs. The boy's eyes couldn't help themselves, and the girl gave him a look.

So they were a *couple,* then . . .

Couldn't blame him—she was an attractive girl, with short dark-blonde hair, lovely brown eyes, and little or no makeup, one of those young women who make no effort to attract a guy's attention and give you whiplash, anyway.

When everybody had settled, I said, "Crazy night, huh?"

There was no answer. But their eyes asked questions.

I leaned forward on the desktop. "Mind if I record this conversation?"

The boy, that brown-paper mystery in his lap with his hands on it protectively, said very quietly, "Why?"

"Because we left a dead man back at the bottom of those subway steps. We want an accurate account of what happened. The best time to get it is right now."

This time the boy's eyes narrowed slightly. "*You* shot him."

I shook my head slowly. "No, I didn't. I shot the gun out of his hand, and the clumsy fool tripped and fell down the steps."

The pair gave each other a fast glance.

I said, "You know who I am, don't you?"

There was a slight change of expression as he told me very warily, "I saw the name on your door."

"Isn't that where it should be?"

"I don't like . . . coincidences."

"Like how?"

"You're . . . a private investigator, right?"

I nodded. "You hired me, remember?"

"But you're . . . Mike Hammer—the guy who makes the papers?"

"Sometimes," I agreed. I let my eyes drift to the wall where all my legal documents were framed. One plaque was for winning a small-arms competition with some pretty big shooters. A few headline stories were on display, too.

"Are you already taping?" he asked suddenly.

"Sure," I told him. "Why not?"

"We didn't give you permission yet!"

"Tough," I said. "Listen, hiring me doesn't make what happened tonight go away—or mean I don't need to know what's wrapped up in that package. I can only help you if you level with me."

"Help us how?" the girl asked.

"Help you with the cops. Help you not get killed. That kind of thing."

The boy frowned, then sighed. "What do you need to know?"

I said, "Look, this isn't official. You don't have to tell me anything, but right now I'm one big part of your story, and we'd better get everything straight before a cop comes walking through that door. *Then* it will be official."

"Okay," he said. "So ask."

Behind them, Velda said, "Let's start with names."

All business, my Velda. You'd never know these kids threatened to spoil our plans. We'd been engaged for longer than most people are married.

And we were set to fly to Vegas this weekend so she could finally make an honest man out of me.

"My name is Matthew Hurley," the boy said, "and this is my stepsister, Jenna Sheffield. But our names aren't as important as *his* . . ."

Matthew Hurley placed the big brown package on my desk.

"His?" I asked. "What's his name?"

"Goliath," Jenna Sheffield said. "That's *Goliath* . . . or anyway, what's left of him."

Chapter 2

"Let's hear the story," I said, peering across the bulky butcher-paper–wrapped package. "We don't have much time."

Matthew sat forward, blurting, "*My* father . . . and *her* mother . . . are professors at NYU."

The way he separated his father from the girl's mother caught my attention.

Jenna noticed it, too. "Be *nice,* Matt," she scolded. Then, her eyes moving from me to Velda and back again, she said, "My mother was Matt's father's assistant. She still is; they've worked together for many years."

"What's their specialty?"

"Dead languages," Matthew said. "After studying the Dead Sea Scrolls for over six years, they finally decided to go to Israel for some on-site research."

Velda's brow was tight with thought.

I said, "Aren't your folks in with some pretty fast company there? Most of the religious world looks upon those scrolls as if they're community property. I understand there's a lot of red tape to go through to even get close to the originals."

Jenna nodded. "But the university provides impeccable credentials, and finances. Plus, our parents managed to . . . well, grease the way somehow." She caught me frowning a little and added, "Not bribery. It's just that the brains of the world seem to have a peculiar relationship—one day they'll ask for a favor back."

Hoping to cut out the nonessentials, I said, "Where do you two fit in? Just along for the ride?"

"Sort of," Matthew said evasively.

"Do you like Israel?"

His boyish grin was disarming. "It's not exactly Aspen or Vail, or spring break in Florida. But Jenna and I have a healthy respect for history ourselves—our majors are both in that area, and we assist our parents, as grad students—so the Israeli kind of sun and sand was just fine with us. Anyway, somebody had to look out for Jenna."

She gave him a kidding poke with her elbow—yeah, they were a couple, all right.

I tried tearing a few pages out of the script. "So you both got bored and took off on a trip somewhere, a little getaway. Someplace not too hairy with bandits and buzzards, but a spot on the map you could tell stories about when you got home. That it?"

They both nodded.

"So," I said, "where did you go?"

Jenna leaned forward in her chair. "We had a Land Rover and all sorts of equipment, including GPS."

Things sure had changed. Global-positioning instruments on vehicles now could tell you within inches where you were on the surface of the earth. What the hell, kept a guy from having to ask directions, didn't it?

"We had plenty of gas and food and water," Jenna was saying.

"How about a gun?"

She shook her head. "We aren't political or militaristic or anything. Not us, *or* our parents."

"Go on."

Her expression grew thoughtful. "You know anything about the Scriptures, Mr. Hammer?"

"I got the 'eye for an eye' part down," I said. "I'm kind of fuzzy after that."

"Does the phrase 'low plain of Elah' mean anything to you?" she asked.

"Not unless it's a stop on the Long Island Rail Road."

Her big brown eyes stared me down, unblinkingly. "One of the greatest military battles in the history of the world was fought there in the Valley of Elah."

I could see Velda's tiny expression of puzzlement, and since I wasn't following this, either, I kept my questions to myself and let the girl talk.

"A huge battle line was drawn up, armed warriors at the ready. The generals were right there at the front, surveying the enemy, and the enemy had something really special to look at—a weapon so huge nothing like it had been seen before and the very sight of it terrified the whole army. That enemy stood behind that weapon absolutely convinced they'd be the victors in the battle about to take place. That their weapon would lead them into a wild and bloody victory over the opposing force."

Quietly I said, "That weapon couldn't have been explosive. Both sides would have lost."

"Oh," Matthew said, "it wasn't explosive."

"Yeah?" I waited a moment and asked, "Who was fighting this battle, anyway?"

"The Israelites were on one side," Matthew said, "and the Philistines on the other."

Nothing in the Six-Day War covered this, I thought.

"And what was this weapon?" I asked.

And both kids looked toward the brown-paper–wrapped package sitting in front of me like a great big sack lunch I hadn't gotten around to unwrapping.

Velda, as usual, was way ahead of me.

"Goliath?" she asked, knowing.

They nodded in sync.

"Goliath wasn't a weapon," I said. "He was just a man."

Velda said softly, "I know a man who some have considered to be a deadly weapon."

"That was before I got my AARP card," I said. "Listen, I know this can't be some stupid college prank, not with bullets flying, but convince me I'm not wasting my time here on some idiot—"

"Goliath," Matthew said firmly, sitting up straighter, "was a man, all right—a man who stood ten and a half feet tall."

"He'd do great in the NBA," I allowed. "Head above the basket. So I assume there's a point to all this?"

But Matthew answered with his own question: "What *happened* to Goliath, Mr. Hammer?"

I remembered the story, all right. I didn't get kicked out of Sunday school till I was ten. "David nailed him with a rock out of a sling. Close enough?"

"Dead on," Matthew said, smiling a little. *"Then* what happened, Mr. Hammer?"

"Beats me."

"Then David took Goliath's sword and lopped off the giant's head and held it up for both sides to see." Matthew had his hand up in the air as though he was holding Goliath's head up by its hair himself. "What do you think happened next, Mr. Hammer?"

"You're doing fine, son."

"Seeing their supposedly invincible giant defeated by a little brat with no armor, and just a slingshot, well, it threw the Philistines into one hell of a panic. They turned and ran like crazy, because the whole Israelite army was coming after them in a wild charge that was going to wipe them off the face of the land."

He painted the picture well; and it was some picture to imagine. Matthew's enthusiasm made it seem as real as live video coverage, and even Velda's head bobbed with satisfaction.

But he was holding something back.

I said, "Finish it, kiddo."

"What do you suppose happened to Goliath then?" he asked.

"Not much, I'd guess. Not much going on in your head when a kid like David has it in his hands."

"But what happened after *that*, Mr. Hammer? What happened to the body?"

"Well . . . I guess the whole goddamn army ran over him in the charge. Trampled the son of a bitch."

Matthew gave me a satisfied grin; he was coming out of his shell—he *did* have a taste for history. "You guessed right, Mr. Hammer. They tripped right over that monstrous 'weapon'; they stepped on it, stomped on it, with enough feet to drive the remains right into the soil. When the rout was over, just the head was left, and the remains of the big guy were only a muddy puddle in the dirt. Vultures and insects took care of the edible bits. Goliath was dead. Goliath was gone. Goliath was only a memory."

Jenna wasn't squeamish. She'd been taking Matthew's story in with not just interest, but pride.

Now I was leaning forward on my desk, cradling my chin with my fingers. He had a punch line left, and I wanted to hear it.

"Apparently, everything got eaten or taken away by scavengers," he said. He paused and his eyes partially closed. "But they didn't get all of Goliath."

"Yeah?"

Jenna, her hand in Matt's, nodded toward the lumpy brown package between us on my desk. "Matt found the rest."

"The bone," I said. I gazed at Matt over his find. "And how did you manage that, Matt?" The answer had to be a beaut.

It was.

Jenna went on: "We were camping on the plain. It was night and Matthew had to put out the campfire, so he took our small shovel to cover it up, but do you know what he did first?"

"Peed on it?" I asked. I'd put out my share of campfires myself when I was a kid.

Velda smirked at me, but Jenna had a startled look.

Then the little blonde turned to Matthew. "You finish the story. You found the thing."

Matthew said, "I dug the shovel in, hit something hard, started to dig around it and, when I turned the flashlight on it, saw it was really big, incredibly big . . . and a sort of dirty white color. It was long and round, and when I had it uncovered, and lifted it up, I saw what it was. *A bone.* One great big bone that had knobs on both ends and must have weighed forty pounds. For a moment there, I thought I'd found a fossil bed with the remains of a T-Rex."

"What changed your mind?"

"The size. It was about three feet long, too short for a T-Rex femur. It was a mature specimen, so it wasn't an adolescent critter, either."

"How did you know?"

"Well, I didn't right then . . . but when we had cleaned it up, the evidence was clear."

I nodded. "You show it to anybody?"

"No."

"Then how *did* you know?"

He shrugged. "Advanced biology in college."

I was studying him. "But something happened out there at your encampment, didn't it? Something that made you pretty jittery?"

The two kids gave me the smallest look of astonishment and nodded hesitatingly. I didn't question them. I let them spill it out themselves.

Jenna's tongue flicked out and wet her lips. One hand gripped the other and she pressed both against her stomach. She didn't like what was about to be said.

But it was Matthew who said it: "Our parents knew we were in a part of the world filled with animosity toward Western Civilization. Doing historical and archeological research in the Middle East, post–September eleventh, is inherently risky. When I called my father on my cell and said I'd found an oversize human femur in the plain of Elah, he didn't have to have the significance spelled out. He wanted us out of there."

"And you headed right back?"

"No. Dad wanted us to have protection, so he sent another Land Rover after us, and the driver followed our GPS right to us."

"How long did that take?"

"Maybe an hour. The driver was an Arab native. He was the only one they knew who was familiar enough with the route we took, and the terrain. Bryan, one of Dad's colleagues, an old student of Jenna's mother, came along."

"What happened?"

"They helped us pack the thing. We were wrapping the bone in some burlap when the Arab saw it, and his face lit up like a lamp. He began chattering in his own tongue. I kept saying that this was a T-Rex bone, but he kept shaking his head and jabbering."

"Later we figured out," Jenna said, "that *he'd* figured something out."

Matthew nodded gravely. "Suddenly our Arab driver quieted right down. Twice he looked at a map in their Land Rover and I could just tell something was going through his mind."

"And now you know," I said.

"Now I know," he said. "That guy may have been working as a driver, but he was an educated man—a history major at his country's only university, I found out later. A lot of them have educations over there, but no place to use them—doctors, lawyers, teachers, rocket scientists, and no place to earn a buck."

I nodded. "And your history-major driver figured out you had latched onto Goliath's bone right away?"

"That I can't be sure. But at least he'd spotted a fossil find, a find that could make a fortune for somebody."

"End of story?"

"No. Before we left the country, our educated Arab driver was found dead on the city's edge. He'd been tortured, then murdered.

Robbery was the official motive. My father had paid him hand-somely enough to make that vaguely credible."

"When did somebody first try to steal the bone from you?"

The two kids shot glances at each other, then gave me that creepy look that said they wondered if I was a mind reader.

Jenna told me, "Somebody broke into my room while we were at supper, the night before we left Israel."

"But you didn't have the bone there, did you?"

"No. We'd already packed it and had a friend ship it out for us. It was labeled ANIMAL REMAINS FROM ANCIENT TRADE ROUTE — FOR UNIVERSITY STUDY."

"Nobody challenged that?"

Jenna shook her head. "In that part of the world, education is a big thing. That word 'University' can be a magic pass."

I nodded toward the massive wrapped package. "If you sent the bone to your folks at NYU, what's it doing on my desk right now?"

"We didn't dare have it shipped from or to our parents. Anything and everything that people like my parents take out of the Middle East is gone over thoroughly. The argument would have been made that the artifact we found was the property of the Israeli government."

Velda said dryly, "That argument could be made, yes."

Ignoring that, Matthew said, "So we sent it to a friend of ours, another graduate student at the college who's also a teaching as-sistant at the university. She took it home with her—that's why we were in that area where you spotted us, Mr. Hammer. We met our friend at that Chinese restaurant in Sugartown. We'd just picked the package up from her before you came to our aid."

Jenna said, "Mr. Hammer—should we be scared?"

I sighed, leaned back in my chair. "You kids were targets tonight.

But after we get this package delivered to your parents, the heat may come off."

Velda said, "It's not you two that they want—it's the Goliath bone."

Matthew brightened. "So we're in the clear?"

"Hard to say," I admitted. "My guess is your late educated driver back in the Valley of Elah reported you to his buddies . . . buddies who eventually killed his ass. Now you two are entangled in an international situation, in the shadow of two towers that aren't there anymore. You two, and Goliath."

"Damn," Matthew said softly. He gazed at me earnestly. "This is . . . big, isn't it?"

"If the contents of this plain-brown-wrapper package are real? Gigantic."

"Like Goliath," Velda said.

Her eyes had clouded up and she sat there half-lidded, letting the facts go through her mind. They were the same things I was thinking. Out of the blue came a world crashing down. The corners were beginning to crumble and we were all racing to prop it up, but the slings and arrows of outrageous fortune were coming at an unsuspecting populace from strange angles, and nobody knew which way to duck. The anthrax scare had quickly followed the first attacks, white powder delivered in envelopes. Courtesy of idiots or enemies? Nobody knew. The world situation bred copycats, and now we were faced with a ten-foot giant from another time.

In the quiet of the night, we all heard the elevator reach our floor and the door snick open and shut automatically. The footsteps on the tiles in the corridor were determinedly audible, marching, not creeping, coming our way.

Jenna seemed alarmed, but before Velda even got out of her

chair, Matthew said, "You mentioned that the police were coming here, didn't you, Mr. Hammer?"

I grinned. "I like the way you stay on top of things, son. That'll be Captain Chambers right now."

"Captain Chambers?"

"Of Homicide."

Velda was up and had the door open before Pat could knock. The big rangy guy in the rumpled off-the-rack suit looked ten years younger than he was, which didn't mean he looked young. His eyes, not surprisingly, went to the ungainly oversized brown-paper package on my desk. But he said nothing about it.

He politely took off his hat, nodded to Velda and me, and let his eyes drift to the kids. I made the introductions, Pat flipping out his police shield so they could see it, and the city's most decorated detective pulled up another client's chair and eased down on it.

The gray eyes glanced at me knowingly. "Having kind of a long day for a guy your age, aren't you, Mike?"

"Hell, buddy, they're all long in this game."

"Not in mine. Not anymore." An eyebrow lifted. "You got me up out of bed."

"Tough. We left a dead man in that subway station. He won't be getting up again, period."

"Oh I know. I just came from there, touched bases with the squad before coming to the source. Seems the guy wasn't murdered, Mike—he fell. Losing your touch?"

I said nothing. The gray eyes never left me.

"Or maybe you aren't. The slug caught the guy's rod in firing position and mashed the action so that his shot never went off." He let a slow grin play around his mouth. "You do that, Mike?"

I didn't deny it. "Velda can take a statement from me and I can sign it right now, if that'll make you sleep better when you climb back in your jammies."

He pretended he didn't think that was funny. "Oh, we'll get around to your statement, Mike." Then he grunted a gruff laugh. "But don't sweat it. Calling it in immediately took the curse off, and you not knowing whether or not the guy had a partner with him explains hustling these two out of there."

"You *have* learned a thing or two over the years."

"The media may see it different. They may pick up on you being the rescuing agent here and do a piece about your exploits back in the old shoot-'em-up days. You always did make for good press."

"Getting good publicity never hurts, Pat."

"What do you need it for? You and I are both facing imminent retirement."

"Speak for yourself."

"You really think attracting attention makes sense when you're coming up against an organized mob like this?"

"Mob hell, Pat. John Gotti's dead now. Sammy the Bull's back in the slammer. Who's that leave to play footsie with?"

Pat's grin wasn't attractive. "This is a new kind of mob, Mike. The kind that might have been out of your league even before you qualified for the senior discount. That kid you killed—make that *helped* to kill himself—he's enjoying himself right now."

"Yeah? Doing what?"

"Hanging out with forty virgins in the afterlife. Get my drift?"

I got it.

Pat's eyes lowered and fixed upon the wrapped package sitting like an abstract centerpiece on my desk. The heavy butcher's paper that was used for wrapping had been worn in spots, and there were dirty smears where hands had held it tightly for a long time. The heavy cord that tied it had come loose in places and had been hurriedly retied.

It sat there, a thing completely out of place in that office, shaped so that nobody could say positively what lurked beneath that wrapping.

A man was dead in the subway station. But I didn't kill him—his fall did. All I did was shoot a rod out of his hand when he was about to commit murder. He'd been after something . . . and it wasn't money.

"Okay," Pat said. "I'll bite. What's in the package?"

This was addressed to Matthew, who didn't look at Jenna this time, nor did she look at him. But his hand was grasping hers now, and that told its own story.

Matthew Hurley said simply, "A bone."

Pat frowned as he studied the strangely shaped parcel.

"No rag," I said to him. "No hank of hair, either."

He frowned at me impatiently. Then to Matthew he said, "Pretty big bone, isn't it?"

"Yes, sir. Pretty big."

I said, "Maybe they have a big dog. Pit bull, maybe."

Pat glared at me. "They have a pit bull, all right." Then to the kids: "What is it . . . an artifact of some kind?"

The two bobbed their heads.

"An old one?"

Again they bobbed their heads.

I loved to watch cops play Twenty Questions.

"How old?"

The boy said, "We don't know yet."

I could think of a hundred better questions to ask, but Pat was the pit bull now and couldn't let it alone. "A hundred years?" When nobody answered, he upped the ante. "A thousand?"

"More," Matthew said. "We were . . . delivering it."

Of course Pat should have asked them where they were delivering it to, but his one-track mind wouldn't let up. "Okay, so you have an ancient artifact." The old hardness came into his tone. "You mind showing it to me? Or do we have to go downtown, like they say on TV?"

I said, "I don't think they say that on TV anymore, Pat."

"Shut up, Mike. How about it, kids?"

"It shouldn't be opened until we deliver it," Matthew said, petulance in his tone.

Jenna touched his arm. "It'll be a bone here as well as it is down there. If Captain Chambers wants to see it, why not? Open it, Matt."

"No! We promised!"

"Hold it!" I raised a traffic-cop palm. I let ten seconds go by, then swiveled half a turn in my seat. "Who does it belong to?"

The kids exchanged startled glances. Then Matthew said, "Right now it's ours."

"Then if you don't want to unwrap that birthday present," I said, "my good friend here can't make you."

Pat was watching me close. "Right now it's yours," he said to them. "Whose *was* it?"

Matthew flicked another glance Jenna's way, then asked, "How do you mean that?"

"Did somebody own it *before* you?"

This time Jenna offered an answer. "It's a little difficult to explain . . ."

I said, "It wasn't stolen, Pat."

Jenna said, "It *did* belong to somebody else, once."

Pat's eyes flared. "Then you *did* steal it?"

"No," Jenna insisted. "We found it. At an approved dig."

"Nothing illegal about it," Matthew put in defensively.

Pat's eyes narrowed. "What is it, a fossil you kids unearthed? You think it's valuable?"

The two glanced at each other again, with a kind of little-kid-ashamed look that brought Pat forward on the edge of his chair.

"That thing isn't . . . *human*, is it?" Pat's eyes were anything but narrow now.

With a bare nod, Matthew affirmed it.

"Well"—Pat was flustered—"*who* did it used to belong to?"

This time Matthew simply shrugged and answered, "You wouldn't believe me if I told you."

But his stepsister clutched his arm and said, "Tell him. You better tell him, Matt."

In the silence, the office clock was making audible clicks, louder than it had ever made before.

Finally Pat said tightly, "Yes, Matt. Tell me."

His tone flat, Matthew said, "Goliath."

What passed felt like a minute and I was starting to wonder how long Pat could stretch it out when he finally asked, "Goliath who?"

"I never caught the last name," Matthew said sourly.

"I'm not dumb, kiddo," Pat said, his upper lip curling. "I get the supposed connection. It's an artifact. And I remember the Biblical story of a man called Goliath."

"Not just a 'story,'" Matthew said.

"And you're saying"—Pat pointed an accusing finger at the un-gainly butcher-wrapped package—"that that's the remains of this historical personage?"

"Possibly," Matthew said.

"And somebody walking around today is dead tonight, because of . . . *this*?"

"Possibly," Matthew said again.

I finally had to break into the conversation. "Pat, there's been an incident, not a *murder*—"

Pat cut me off: "An uptight DA could throw a nasty rope around this one, buddy."

"This is an election year, *buddy*," I said. "You think our esteemed DA's going to tangle himself up in an accidental death of an Arab stalker with a loaded shooter in his hand, chasing a couple of kids whose parents are top university people? Maybe he'd enjoy having to deal with me being on the scene, stopping the guy, a notorious old-time private eye half the public thinks is already dead? And as icing on the cake, he'll have an atrophied leg of a dead giant to swing around. . . . Should be a fun election cycle."

Pat knew I was right. He pawed the air. "Come on, Mike. Can it."

"Sure," I said with a shrug. Velda was watching me from across the room, wondering where this was going. Wondering where *I* was going . . .

That was when I noticed Jenna, half-raising her hand up to wiggle her fingers, like a student in class. It was a tiny gesture, but Pat saw it, too, and looked straight at her. He didn't say anything— he just waited until Jenna got the message from his eyes and finally she blurted, "I was shot at today."

Matthew moved his chair closer to Jenna's, and slipped a supportive arm around her.

Pat, sitting forward, said, "But you weren't hit, obviously? Right?"

"Actually . . . I was."

Everybody else in the room, Matthew included, made a jagged chorus: *"What?"*

"Not me! My purse. It hit my purse. But I didn't figure out what had happened, until later."

I said, "Silenced shot."

Jenna held up her heavy leather handbag, turned it over to show us where the bullet had hit it, then fished inside until she brought out a metal cosmetic compact with a nickel-sized dent in it.

Pat reached out and gently took the compact away from her. Just as gently, he rolled it around in his palm, then said, "Most likely a .22 slug."

I said, "The gun I shot out of that punk's hand was no .22."

"Right, Mike. It was a nine-millimeter of foreign make. Which means . . ."

But he didn't finish the sentence and neither did I, not wanting to tell these already-traumatized kids that the guy I'd stopped on those subway stairs wasn't the only shooter after them.

Nonetheless, Matthew and Jenna traded terrified expressions, while Velda took a more businesslike approach. "Wouldn't even a .22 slug have torn up that purse a little more," she asked, "or even penetrated it?"

Meaning Jenna should at least have been wounded.

Pat reached out and took the handbag from Jenna. "Mind if I take a look?"

Jenna shook her head.

Pat withdrew a small metal ring with three keys attached. The teeth on the keys were bent back, and he nodded. "You have any-thing important in here?" he asked her.

Jenna shook her head again. "Just the usual junk."

"Will you tolerate a cop's curiosity and let me poke around in here?"

Pat was a stickler; he knew without a warrant he needed permission.

"Go ahead, Captain."

"Mike, you and Velda witness this." He stood and shook out the contents of the pocketbook onto the desk not far from the brown-wrapped package. Jenna hadn't lied: the typical female junk. But that wasn't what Pat was after.

From the bottom of the now-emptied purse, Pat's fingers brought up two tiny pieces of metal. One was sharp and copper-colored at its bent tip.

Pat's eyes caught mine. We had both seen bullet fragments a lot of times before. And we both knew how close this girl had come to buying it.

"When did this happen?"

The question was aimed at Jenna, but Matthew answered it. "Just as we were coming out of our hotel today, maybe around four? We were just getting into a cab. The snow was coming down hard. When I went to take Jenna's hand, because it was slippery on the sidewalk, I saw another cab pulling in—"

Pat snapped, "What kind was it?"

"Blue or black or something."

"Not yellow?"

Matthew shook his head. "No. Definitely not yellow. Why, what difference does that make?"

"That was a gypsy cab," Pat told him softly.

"So?"

"So they don't usually pick up that far downtown. They'll drop you off, but not pick you up. They have no medallion . . . privately owned transportation."

I said, "That cab could have been a backup to the shooter, or maybe even the source of the shot."

Both kid's faces turned pale.

And I hadn't even pointed out that their subway shooter had emerged from another gypsy cab.

Jenna said, "Why would anybody shoot at us?"

Pat shrugged. "Maybe you had something somebody wanted."

Matthew frowned, shaking his head. "But we didn't have anything . . . except . . ."

"An old bone," Pat finished for him.

Pat took a cell phone out of his jacket pocket, hit speed dial, then mumbled into the receiver. He got up and paced around the room while muttering into the instrument. Twice he slowed and paused in front of the wrapped package and stared at it absently. Then he paused and gave it a hard stare, as if he were trying to see through the brown paper, seemingly letting all the implications of the affair sink into his mind. Finally he nodded twice at the air and clicked off and pocketed the phone.

To Matthew and his stepsister, Pat said, "We're keeping this officially quiet for now. No arrests, but I'd appreciate it if you'd all come down to headquarters so we can get the details on paper and verified."

Velda asked, "No arrests?"

"No. No Miranda questions. This is all voluntary."

He was halfway out when he said, "Meet you down there. You know the address."

"Pat!"

He paused.

"What came up, buddy?"

Pat half-whispered, as if this were so hot even he shouldn't hear it. "They got a fast ID on the dead guy. That portable fingerprint unit gave a plus on a possible terrorist who's been suspected of being in the country illegally for several years."

Then Pat was gone, and the office fell deathly silent.

Finally Matthew, holding his stepsister's hand, asked, "Do we need an attorney, Mr. Hammer?"

"No," I said. "You need me."

Three hours later the pertinent details of the "subway affair" were seemingly cleared up. Witnesses had been contacted who corroborated our stories, the time periods before being in the subway station all held tight and the only foul ball was the assassin with the silenced gun. No positive ID was found on him, but in his pocket he had twenty-seven loose cartridges for his foreign-made rod and two dollars and sixty cents.

Matthew Hurley's wallet contained $116, his stepsister's had $339, and there was some loose change in her jacket pocket.

So the answer came easy. The impoverished terrorist had spotted a couple of well-heeled kids and went after them. Circumstances seemed to be all in his favor. His prey had headed through heavy snow toward an all-but-deserted subway station, where two small *sputs* from his rod would lead to a ten-second search of their clothes, and snap! he'd be in business again. Out the exit doors and good-bye.

Only I was the high overhand beanball pitch in the game. Like they used to say in the Army, "Tough shit, slobbo."

The pair of bored night-beat reporters who were there took everything down in a laconic manner. One looked up from his pad and said, "How did you get mixed up in this, Mike?"

We were in the reception area off the bullpen near Pat's private office.

"Just lucky, I guess."

"Bullshit," Richie said. The old reporter flipped his pad shut and grinned at me. "You know how many times you've been in a shoot-out? Aren't you a little long in the tooth for this, Mike?"

"John Wayne stayed in the saddle till he needed a toupee and a girdle. Me, I got my own hair and a belly harder than a lap dancer's heart. Next question."

But Richie kept the needle in the same groove. "Nine shoot-outs that I can count since I came on this job. And you'd been at it a while."

"So I'm not a kid anymore."

"But you're still a good shooter."

"I practice."

"Then how come you didn't knock the guy off this time?"

"We hadn't been properly introduced."

Old Richie just shook his head and grinned again. "I hear you're finally getting married."

"Where'd that come from? Since when is my marital status newsworthy?"

Richie made a wry face. "You're pretty damn famous, old man. News of you and that long-stemmed beauty of yours finally getting hitched goes around the barn in a hurry. How does that dame stay so hot at her age, anyway? She got a portrait aging in the attic or something?"

"You crossed the line a couple questions ago, Richie."

"It's just, Mike . . . I kind of hate having to write up this scrawny little subway piece about a guy with *your* history."

A voice said, "Tell 'em, Mike."

I turned and saw Pat Chambers at my side. Police personnel aren't supposed to do some things. They don't give up details easily. They protect their own premises with wolflike tenacity. They don't take easily to reporters even when the newshounds are backing them.

So when Pat Chambers, Captain of Homicide, gave me that odd look that expressed nothing but said everything, and stated quietly, "Tell them who the shooter was, Mike," I knew this was going to be bigger than old Goliath himself.

So did the pair of graveyard-shift reporters, print men—no TV cameras had responded to this chickenshit story, even if the name "Mike Hammer" that used to mean so much was smack dab in the middle of it. Hard to describe just how tired, old, seen-everything eyes could snap open like they had just spotted the *Titanic* floating to the top.

There was something else, too. They *knew* it. They could *feel* it. The one thing they always wanted—the *Big Story*—was about to be dropped right in their past-their-prime laps.

I said, "The gunman was a suspected terrorist. Illegally in the United States. Known to the authorities."

Both reporters looked at Pat and his face was calm. He said, "I can confirm that."

It took almost ten seconds for Richie to find his voice. "Something's screwy here."

"Check it out," Pat suggested.

"*Where?*"

"Try the Feds."

"Aw come on, Captain," the other reporter blurted. "They're clamsville."

Pat shrugged. "We've provided you with the details. The terrorist was broke and tried to do something about it. That's what it looks like, anyway."

Very softly, Richie said, "In this country, terrorists aren't broke. There are enough religiously motivated lunatics loose to keep guys like this well funded and damn highly motivated. They have unlimited funds from sources overseas, and all kinds of cash from their money-laundering resources right here!"

I said, "Should I be taking notes?"

The reporters cursed at me, and Pat raised a hand. "All you get tonight."

When the pair of reporters had scooted, I told Pat, "They won't leave this thing alone—you know that."

Pat wore a Cheshire cat smile. It was a look I'd seen before, dating back to his early days in Homicide. "Good. We're going to need all the hands we can get on this thing. The media covers a lot of bases we can't reach, so if we can call in a few favors, let's do it."

I asked him softly, "What do you know that I don't, Pat?"

Pat looked over at a desk where Velda was talking earnestly to the two kids; he lowered his voice. "Interagency communications are pretty fast these days."

"Yeah, I know. It's gotten better."

"We'll have some big answers in a matter of hours."

"You going to tell me, Pat?"

"If it's public information, sure."

"Thanks a bunch, pal. Didn't I get a hold of you right after that guy got splattered?"

"Good to see you living up to your civic duty, Mike. You do realize who those kids over there are, don't you?"

I shrugged. "Brother and stepsister. His father married her mother. Both grad students at NYU."

There was a subtle twist at the corner of Pat's mouth. "That's not what I mean—Hurley, Sheffield? Do anything for you? Top scientists in the academic field. Both have been considered for the Nobel Prize. Sound familiar?"

I shrugged. "Nasty incident, clean subjects."

Pat's head bobbed slowly. "Delicate situation."

"Why 'delicate'?"

"Well, for one thing, there's a wild man in it."

"Named Goliath?"

He gave me a grin that also dated back to early Homicide days. "Named Hammer."

Chapter 3

This time Richie and his pal surprised me. The next morning's papers, under those two knowledgeable bylines, just picked up the official police reports on the subway affair. With all the action going on in the sand hill of the Middle East and the rash of suicide bombings in the Israeli-Palestinian sectors, one New York subway shooting wasn't much of an event at all.

But I knew they hadn't dropped it. Oh, they'd dropped a hat on it, all right, shelved it, to wait for the right moment. They had the oddity of a corpse in this suspected terrorist, dead by accident but with a bullet-damaged foreign rod near his limp hand. And they had a gun-toting Good Samaritan in the middle of it who used to be big news back when crime was really organized and needed some good old-fashioned wiping out.

So Richie and his friend would simply wait for more truth to spill out. Some things were just too big to hide. Even the Atlantic Ocean couldn't hide the *Titanic,* right? And man's footprints are still on the moon.

The only newsworthy surprise that hadn't been mentioned by Pat or me was the name of the guy who used to stride around on that leg those kids brought home.

If that's who it was.

Far as I was concerned, a big bone was just a big bone. I wasn't convinced yet that it belonged to the biggest bad boy of them all.

Pat had played the game with no pretense. No charges were filed against the kids, and he let them call their parents and arrange for a reunion at NYU, where the couple researched and taught. Just to keep it clear and clean, the conversations were on speakerphone, with a few detectives listening in with half an ear because the call was being recorded, anyway.

Now it was a new morning. The sun was battling the cold and a thaw was setting in that would soon turn the white city gray. Sun splashed in the window and painted my desk gold.

I was in my swivel chair drinking coffee and gnawing a dough-nut, both purchased at a corner joint since Velda was not around to nurture me. She'd taken the two kids under her wing last night. And her wing included a .38 revolver and an attitude worse than mine, so they were safe enough.

Right on time, Pat shambled into my office. I'd bought him a java, too, but he avoided doughnuts on general principles. He was wearing that fedora of his that was as out of date as my porkpie hat, but he also wore a faint expression of satisfaction. He dropped into the chair across from me and tossed the fedora on my desk.

"The Feds gave up a positive ID on the shooter." He tented his fingers and grinned at me through them.

"Who was he, exactly?"

"An Iranian college student on an expired student visa."

I sipped the hot liquid. "A college kid out to hit other college kids. Nice."

"Not so nice. That terrorist connection still sticks. We have a name and possible link to a suspect in the 9/11 attacks."

You stand at the heart of New York City and look east to where the twin monuments once stood, gargantuan edifices that reached into the sky, proclaiming wealth and power and hopefully indicating peace. There's an oddball silence there now, not the absence of noise, but the stillness of sounds that people make, like laughter and satisfaction. As they go by that once-busy avenue that housed the magnificent businesses of the world, they avert their eyes, their voices become subdued but, if you listen real close, you can hear someone swear at the bastards who tried to murder a city. It's an empty space now, but someday the snakes who live for destruction across the ocean in their own empty spaces of sand and caves would meet the snapping teeth of the avengers.

"Mike? Mike, you went away there, for a minute. You okay, buddy?"

"Sorry, Pat. I was just wishing I could lay my hands on Bin Laden's throat."

"Take a number. Anyway, the suspect your shooter was connected to was just a hanger-on, the Feds say."

"Hanger-on how?"

Pat shrugged. "Suspect lived on the same block as one of the 9/11 accomplices."

"Any record?"

"Beat up his wife twice." Pat made a face. "Some people from that part of the world have an attitude toward women that makes me sick."

"So do some people born here."

"Mike, I'm not painting all Muslims from Middle Eastern countries as—"

"It's their own zealots who are doing the painting, Pat." I grunted. "Damn, that's a war that's never going to end, is it?"

"Give it another couple thousand years."

"Or till Armageddon comes."

His eyebrows hiked. "You don't have to say that like you're looking *forward* to it." Pat got up. "So what do you say we go pick up Velda and those kids, and get ourselves a college education?"

"A little overdue where I'm concerned, don't you think? But they say you're never too old to learn."

Pat slapped on his fedora. "Mike, you've *always* been too old to learn."

The sprawl of NYU in Greenwich Village included a certain six-story glass-and-steel building with glass doors and an anonymous feel where the parents of Matthew Hurley and Jenna Sheffield did their work.

Matthew and Jenna were dressed as before. We hadn't given them a chance to pick up a change of clothes. Matt in his Western-style sheepskin coat hugged the brown-paper package like it was his child. Jenna in her fur-trimmed suede coat had her arm in his. Brotherly and sisterly love, my keister.

Velda and I were in our matching trench coats. Pat said the sight of us was cute enough to make Santa Claus puke. His top-coat was a heavy-duty woolen deal, but the point was, these kids and that bone couldn't have had more firepower backing them up short of a SWAT team.

Even with our IDs, all that hardware made the security checkpoint an endurance test. The armed guard at the metal detector passed Pat through fast enough, and he knew who I was, all right. But he had his orders and he played them right. Before he had to ask, I eased my .45 out of the shoulder holster, thumbed out the clip, and jacked the live round out of the chamber.

The other two full clips I laid on the little table beside the blued-steel rod, initialed the sheet he held out, and shook my head when he asked me if I was carrying an ankle piece. Hell, the metal detector would have picked it up if I'd had it. What kind of slob did he take me for?

Velda had to leave her gun behind, too, with only policeman Pat approved to carry in these hallowed halls. There was a time the looks those guards sneaked at Velda would have offended me. Now I felt kind of proud, a doll her age perking up a couple youngsters like that.

Matthew and Jenna escorted us to the elevators where we dropped down a floor and came out into a concrete vault of a corridor marked by metallic doors every twenty feet or so, with no handles, no key locks, and no hinges. Whatever was behind those shining slabs had to be pretty damn private and very damn expensive. Everything seemed state-of-the-art electronic and those doors had to slide into the concrete bulwarks to open.

Velda and Pat fell in behind us as I walked alongside Matthew and Jenna.

I asked the kid, "Nice place to go to school?"

Matthew, clutching the bulky package, nodded solemnly.

"You're still a grad student here?"

He nodded. "Jenna and I are just finishing up. We don't have many hours left, but we're still helping my father on his projects."

His father, I noted. *Not his "parents."*

I asked, "Helping how?"

"Sorry, Mr. Hammer. It's a limited-access situation."

Nice to have the confidence of your clients.

"Where down here do your parents work?"

Jenna responded for her brother, since his hands were full with the bulky package, and pointed down to shining steel double doors at the end of the hall. "That's their domain down there—the Antiquities lab."

That sounded like a place where you went in and cooked yourself up some antiquities.

"And that's where the bone will find a home?"

Matthew picked up the ball. "Yes. Under very tight security."

He wasn't kidding.

The four of us stood inside a circle painted on the floor in front of a gleaming door reflecting distorted images of ourselves back at us while a strange humming seemed to engulf us. I knew we were being photographed or scanned or some damn thing, but never spotted a lens. For five unsettling seconds, a tingling sensation ran across my body that had nothing to do with my own nervous system. I knew Matthew, Jenna, Velda and Pat were feeling it, too, but I made no remark since I realized the two kids must have known what it was.

When that stopped, the door slid silently on metallic tracks into the wall and, when we had gone on through, closed again soundlessly. A chill hit us immediately, well-suited to the stainless steel and glass surroundings, an area that looked more appropriate to a hospital than an instructional center. Nobody made a move to get out of their winter coats, and I was halfway surprised our breaths weren't pluming like outside.

A faint chemical odor wafted through the chamber to complete the medical identification, and somehow I connected it with the morgue down at the old Manhattan Center.

A balding thirtyish male attendant in a starched blue smock with a tag that said BRYAN led us around the small cluster of laboratory tables to the far side of the room, where a tall man and a small woman in white lab coats were going over brittle-looking documents with foreign-looking script encased in clear Mylar sheets and spread out on the steel countertop.

The big man turned with a broad smile and came toward us holding out his hand. "I'm George Hurley, Mr. Hammer, Matthew's father."

I wasn't surprised he recognized me. I've been in the media enough. And I surely recognized him: Eerily, he and his wife might have been Matthew and Jenna several decades later, each having a strong facial resemblance to his and her biological offspring.

He gestured to the beautiful woman who remained back at the counter with the documents, though her attention was on us now. She was a petite and, even in the drab lab coat, shapely specimen of what a woman in her late forties might turn out to be with a little luck and the right genes. Her eyes were large and dark brown, her short, curly hair a golden blonde that shimmered under the glare of the laboratory lights. If this was a university professor, maybe I should have matriculated.

"And my wife, Charlene . . ."

She nodded and beamed at us. Her daughter beamed back, but Matthew's face stayed blank, I noted.

As I shook George Hurley's hand, I introduced Velda as my

business associate. She was more than a secretary now, but I wasn't sure it was relevant to mention we were engaged. Or were my eyes too full of Charlene Hurley to remember that right now?

I introduced Pat, who came forward and did the official bit. He held out his shield, flipped open his police ID folder, but said, "Don't let the 'Homicide' designation spook you—I just came along as a bodyguard for that bone your son is lugging."

Pat and our host shook hands.

"We're both doctors," George Hurley said, as his wife stepped forward to shake hands all around, too. "But we'll all get confused if you don't just call us 'George' and 'Charlene.'"

"Fine, doc," I said, and that made the big man smile. I liked him already. For a brain, he was unpretentious.

Charlene Hurley, at her husband's side now, fig-leafed her hands and said, "My daughter told me on the phone that you saved her life, Mr. Hammer. And Matt's."

"I intervened during a holdup attempt," I said. "I was glad to help."

"Well, I hope you know we're very grateful."

George Hurley said, "And I understand our two favorite lab assistants have hired you to assist them . . . and us? . . . in the matter of this incredible discovery of theirs."

"They have," I said.

With friendly skepticism, Charlene asked, "What *sort* of help, Mr. Hammer?"

"Make it 'Mike.' Let's not get ahead of ourselves, okay? I think Matt here is going to fold up if he doesn't set that darn thing down."

Hurley laughed embarrassedly and went to his son. "Mike's

right, Matt—what are we doing, letting you stand there like the UPS man at the front door! Here, son . . . over here."

Father helped his boy move the precious package to a metal examination table where the three-foot–long object in crinkly brown paper could rest.

We all walked over to the table, crowding around like kids under a tree on Christmas morning and with the same wonderment and expectation. Velda was at my side, and Pat and Charlene Hurley were opposite us. The two kids were at one end of the rectangle of shining steel and George at the other. With latex-gloved hands, he used a little surgical knife to cut the strings, then with no ceremony at all he ripped the paper off the contents.

And there it was.

Time hadn't seemed to have eroded it.

Animals hadn't seemed to have nibbled on it.

It was blanched white and silky dry with the spidery traces of age lines and the smooth but gentle curvatures of natural bone formation. And for some reason you knew what it was right away: a human thighbone. The ends of the structure made an immaculate display of engineering, this development into a device that fitted one bone against another with cushions of ligament lubricated with natural fluids thousands of times more efficient than petroleum distillates, a design that no man could possibly duplicate.

And it was huge!

It had joined hip to knee in a man so big he simply *must* be that champ who went down for the count with an underdog's creek rock in his forehead ages ago.

Hurley's eyes were wide and glittering, but then I suppose that was true of all of us. He asked, "What do you think, Mike?"

A little grin touched my lips. "Goliath was one big sumbitch, all right."

Matthew said, in a small, quavering voice, "Then you're convinced, Mr. Hammer? This *is* Goliath's bone?"

"I can't say it isn't. I wouldn't mind hearing a more educated opinion than mine."

Charlene asked, "Do you realize what this means, Mr. Hammer? . . . Mike?"

I said, "My education was a little more mundane than you and your husband's . . . but I get the picture."

George's eyes left the bone and looked at me. "Are you sure, Mike?"

For a few seconds I thought about it, then said, "Planes are flying into buildings, anthrax spores are showing up in the strangest places, we've gone to war against Afghanistan and Iraq, with Iran waiting in the wings . . . and now your kids have found a bone. Damned big one, too."

Charlene's eyes were on me. Everybody's eyes were on me—I'd trumped Goliath with my little speech.

The beautiful scientist said, "This artifact can do more to set nation against nation than planes flying into buildings, anthrax scares, and intercontinental wars can accomplish."

"It's only a bone," I reminded her. "It's been buried up until now."

"Just the point," she said. "From out of nowhere, appearing through the mists of time . . . it has emerged."

That might have sounded silly to me if I hadn't been gaping at a femur twice the size of a normal man's.

"Emerged from the mists," Velda's voice echoed, soft, almost prayerful, "like a *sign* . . ."

"Sure," Pat said. "But of *what?*"

I said to the two doctors, "Tell me . . . this bone has to be authenticated, right?"

They nodded as one.

"How?" I asked.

George Hurley said, "First we check it for age, with the carbon-dating process. Relatively speaking, this should not be difficult. Unlike dinosaurs, for instance, this specimen is relatively recent. Of course we'll X-ray it and identify it as a bone, a human bone."

Charlene Hurley picked up the thread. "Generally we would say the size was due to a condition called acromegaly, a disorder where a person never stops growing. You have seen this in circus giants, for instance. Their death usually occurs at an early age."

"Rondo Hatton in the horror movies," I said. The two kids were gawking at me. "Before your time . . . and this bone here doesn't smack of what Rondo had?"

George Hurley shook his head. "It has all the earmarks of being a natural formation that had fulfilled its growth. If the muscular development equaled that of the bone, in life this person would have been very remarkable. I could well see how he would terrify even an entire army."

I couldn't stop the smirk. "Just one guy?"

Charlene Hurley said, "Put him in great and elaborate armor, give him a spear whose wooden shaft was like the beam of a loom, and the blade the size of an anchor on a thirty-five–foot power-boat . . . then see what you've got."

"I didn't know science used metaphors to make their case."

"The Bible gives an even better description," her husband said.

They were making me dig back into Sunday-school days again. "Didn't the Israelites have archers and spear throwers?"

Charlene shrugged. "Nothing would have penetrated the body armor on this giant. He could walk into an opposing army like Patton with his tanks, and behind him was his own multitude of bloodthirsty Philistines as eager to kill as the Nazis behind Hitler."

"And little David's little rock did him in."

The lady doctor smiled gently. "So the Good Book says."

Metaphors and Scripture. Not what I expected in a research lab. "So what else does the bone show scientifically?"

"Very little," she admitted, "but it apparently had lain these many years in a dirt formation that acted as a preservative, completely coated and sealed with a mud that had unusual properties halting disintegration of bone material. The flesh and sinew around it went back to dust, naturally, but the bone itself? That remained inexplicably intact."

"How unusual is that?" I asked her.

But her husband responded. "Not that unusual at all. Natural mummification has been seen quite often. The old wrapped bodies in the Andes, for instance. The body of the iceman found nearly intact after thousands of years." He stopped suddenly and squinted at me. "Am I boring you, Mr. Hammer?"

"Absolutely not," I said. "You've painted a vivid picture."

At my side, Velda said, "Someone needs to paint a picture of the ramifications of this . . . thing."

She was pointing at the huge bone with an accusatory finger. She alone seemed to find it, in some fashion, repellent.

George Hurley nodded solemnly. "Your associate, Ms. Sterling, is right, Mike. This find opens up a Pandora's box of political and religious conflict. We are dealing with factions here that include zealots of the most dangerous kind."

I grinned at him. "Philistines, doc?"

He managed a smile. "An outdated term, but the factions I refer to include those descended from Goliath's, shall we say, home team. Unfortunately, their progression into the lifestyle of modern civilization has often been stymied by a refusal of some to adjust and adapt their cultures to the modern world. Some still live in caves or primitive quarters. Some exhibit social codes that put our teeth on edge."

"If I said that, doc," I said, "in my own inelegant way, I'd get branded a bigot."

This time Charlene Hurley responded. "In our profession, we don't condemn the faiths of others. We are scientists who study the past. But as people? As Americans? We can make certain observations that I don't believe are ethnocentric. Consider offshoots of their societies that practice female circumcision—a horrible, brutal surgery that prevents a woman from experiencing the pleasure of sex. Generally it is done with no antiseptic methods and under no anesthesia. Other places completely subdue their women like bagged potatoes, in head-to-foot wrappings with no privileges outside of serving their husbands in whatever they demand."

I gave Velda a sideways glance. "I want a girl just like the girl . . . ?"

Velda said, "It's not funny, Mike."

"No. It isn't." *But some people laugh so they don't cry. Me, I laugh so I don't tear the head off some sick son of a bitch.*

Charlene added, "There are many millions of women caught in that trap."

I gestured to the off-white chunk of history on the metal table. "Hey, I'll be glad to vote against all that. But what does Goliath have to do with it?"

For a few seconds, nobody said a word.

Then George Hurley said, "The Arab world has had many heroes throughout their history, from Mohammed on. But of late, the only visible heroes the Arab world has had are Bin Laden, Arafat, and Saddam. They had charisma, financing, and some kind of satanic desperation that got them followers who thought death bought them a free pass to heaven."

"Where does our freshly-dug-up bone come in, then?"

His shrug was casual, but his unblinking eyes were not. "This could be their symbol, perhaps. Their Liberty Bell. Their Alamo."

I had to laugh. "This old paddy-whack bone?"

"Yes," he said firmly. "Proof of a great hero of their supposed forefathers."

"Hell," I said, "the bozo got clouted by a rock and died! Little David cut his head off to boot."

"Nonetheless," he said, "Goliath was their hero, and heroes never die. He was over ten feet tall. He scared the opposing army into immobility."

I shook my head. "I think you've got it wrong."

George Hurley had the expression of a clubbed baby seal. This doc and his wife had spilled more education than I ever had. And here I was doubting them. Out loud.

I nodded toward the big bone. "That's a symbol, all right. It's a symbol of Israeli strength and power. If anybody's going to want to carve that into a Liberty Bell, it's our Jewish pals."

Charlene Hurley's eyes had tightened. She was looking at the ancient artifact with something no longer clinical. Respect, maybe.

"But, doc, you're right as far as it goes—the Arab world would love to get their paws on this puppy. To *destroy* it. It's an embarrassment to them. They'll want to keep it out of Israel's hands."

Pat grunted. "Mike Hammer, Authority on the Middle East. I'll be sure to book you on Fox News."

Velda said to the scientists, "You can't confirm through your tests and research that this *was* Goliath. It's not like you have his DNA on file."

"True," George Hurley said. "But the circumstantial evidence already appears overwhelming."

"But there's no possibility of saying for a historic, scientific certainty that this was Goliath's thighbone."

"No," Hurley admitted.

"Nuts," I said. "Once a religious authority proclaims this as Goliath's bone, then it'll be Goliath's bone. And the game will be on. Hell, it already is."

Nobody said a word. They all wore the same noncommittal expressions, seeming to examine me through an invisible microscope. I flashed a glance at Matthew and Jenna and they were both looking at me in the same curious way.

Deciphering their silent faces wasn't too hard, but I was going to let them tell me what they wanted themselves.

Finally, George Hurley said, "I believe I see why Matthew and Jenna need your help—they'll definitely need protection."

"That's why they came to me," I said with a shrug.

"Yes," the father agreed. "But this is far from a normal bodyguard situation. Right now the circumstances are extremely . . . hostile."

"Hostility's a part of every bodyguard assignment, doc. Interesting root word, don't you think, hostile? It applies to highly aggressive actions. Actually, *warlike* actions."

Pat muttered, "Warlike actions like flying a loaded passenger plane into the World Trade Center and the Pentagon, you mean?"

"Yeah. That kind of warlike."

George Hurley's eyes drifted to the great femur laying exposed on the table. "You're saying everybody in the Arab world, in particular Israel, is going to want to claim this."

"Or *take* it." I let out a half-laugh. "Of course, they'd have to get it first, and I'm thinking security is pretty tight around this joint."

George Hurley merely nodded, but that nod had the confidence of Fort Knox in it.

"First thing I'll suggest," I said, "is you don't let the government in on this secret."

"Mike," Hurley said, "the government backs our research through the university, and—"

"Swell, only I don't give a damn. They have bums up there who would leak it out in a minute to corner a few extra votes. If that granddaddy of all bones ever came under government protection, it'd go the same way the atomic-bomb secrets did."

Velda asked them, "How many people in the university know about the Goliath bone?"

"A good number are aware," George Hurley said, "that we're looking at a potentially important ancient artifact. That kind of word travels fast on a campus."

"But," his wife put in, "that's as far as it goes. The name 'Goliath' has, to the best of my knowledge, not been breathed by anyone outside this room."

Jenna spoke for the first time since the unveiling. "Except in Israel. Some people back there must know."

I nodded to the girl. "And there was that student friend of yours who helped ship that artifact home to start with."

She answered me with a thoughtful nod, too. "But she never knew what was in the package she was carrying for us."

"That driver who saw the bone before you got it out of there," I said, "he was killed soon after, remember?"

Matthew said, "Yeah, but he must have talked to somebody. That has to be what got him killed. Any kind of a major archeological find from that area could easily be worth a person's life."

"Which may explain," I said to the kids, "why a gun-wielding Arab terrorist tried to nab that package last night. Like I said, the hunt is already on." I turned to the parents. "Do you think trained agents could get in here?"

George Hurley shook his head. "Only five of us have access to this room—Charlene and myself and the kids, plus our assistant, Bryan."

Their blue-smocked associate was working at his desk at the other end of the room.

Charlene was saying, "All areas leading to this lab are covered by armed guards. Total security reaches to the front door. People entering here are photographed four separate times by remote TV units."

I frowned. "Why so much artillery and spook gear? What is it you do here, anyway?"

George Hurley said, "We can't discuss that, Mike. Let me say this: The federal government demands this level of security . . . and provides it. In our custody are many pieces of information we have uncovered that the government wants to keep totally secret."

"Nobody swore *me* to secrecy," I put in.

When George Hurley smiled, I knew what he was going to say. "Whether you like it or not, Mr. Hammer, from this minute on you will be carefully monitored."

I smiled back. "Then that makes me one of the inner circle, doesn't it?"

"In a sense, Mike. In a sense."

Pat got into it. "We were told that you both were in Israel doing research on the Dead Sea Scrolls. Can I ask why?"

George Hurley fielded the query. "It is a subject we're keenly interested in, Captain. To date we've published three books on the subject—not bestsellers, but respected works used extensively by students in the early stages of researching the subject."

"You both speak Hebrew?"

Charlene Hurley nodded and said, "Aramaic, too."

"Plus several other languages," George Hurley added.

"Are you well known in Israel?"

This time both nodded. "In academic circles we are," George said, having to work to sound modest. "My wife is Jewish, and spent some time in a kibbutz just out of college. So she feels very much at home in Israel. I'm a lapsed Catholic, by the way—we're a two-person ecumenical council."

Charlene added, "Just in case you're wondering, Captain, we're not politically motivated in the least. We have the same interest in current events as the next person, but we are more interested in the politics, the civilizations, of the past."

I said, "For a lot of countries over there, the past and the present are one and the same. To us they can seem pretty damn pathetic with their dress codes and bird's-nest beards and the crummy way they treat the female gender, but they don't come tougher-minded when it comes to political philosophy. Every day they have the whole world wondering what's going to happen next."

Pat said to the parents, "You make any enemies while you were overseas?"

George Hurley shook his head. "The only enemies we make in our field are jealous colleagues and rivals at other schools." He frowned, not angry but confused. "Why would you think we'd made enemies overseas?"

"Because you're rich. Rich, influential American citizens poking your noses in around the Middle East."

"I would hardly define us as 'rich,' Captain," Hurley said. "And our contacts in our Middle Eastern work are all academics. We had no other interests on this trip other than to study the Dead Sea Scrolls under the tutelage of more knowledgeable persons than ourselves."

The silence lasted a few seconds; then Charlene Hurley said softly, "I understand the possible conflict this discovery brings into all our lives. But why ask about 'enemies,' Captain Chambers?"

Pat told her, "This investigation is classified as an attempted murder—we believe the shooter last night had an accomplice, still at large. Your kids need to stay wrapped up tight until we get to the bottom of it."

Charlene was shaking her head. "But with the bone safely in the university's hands—"

"In *your* hands," I pointed out. "How would you respond to kidnappers who offered you your kids back in exchange for that hunk of bone over there?"

Matthew and Jenna traded startled looks.

"Mike's right," Pat said. "The TV commentators and the news-hounds will soon be getting into this thing, and'll start to give out their own suppositions, which they're bound to do with big names like yours and Mike's here in the mix . . . not to mention a dead Iranian terror suspect with a high-powered foreign gun in his hand. It'll be a media circus, and the Hurley family'll be the center-ring attraction."

Calmly, George Hurley let his breath out and asked, "What do you suggest we do, Captain?"

"Don't tell anybody I said so," Pat said, "but hiring Mike Hammer to help you out is the best thing you could possibly do." He swung toward me. "Quote me, Mike, and I'll say you're a damn liar."

"I love you, too, buddy," I said with a grin.

Charlene Hurley asked, "Should we get a lawyer at this point?"

"Your prerogative, of course," Pat said, "but if you can keep things quiet a little bit longer, I'd appreciate it."

That was almost the end of the discussion. I asked for copies of their résumés and their assistant's, and before we left the cold chamber, I had a four-inch–thick packet of information in a manila envelope.

"We appreciate what you're doing for us." George Hurley held out his hand again.

I was shaking it when I said, "Don't thank me till you've seen the bill."

Charlene said, "I read an article in the *News* that said Mike Hammer never takes a paying client. You're just a guy who sticks up for the underdog."

"There may be some truth in that," I admitted. "Otherwise I wouldn't still be working when most guys my age are playing shuffleboard. But I'm fine with the Hurley family helping me build my belated retirement plan."

Just before we stepped into the corridor, the small, lovely Charlene Hurley touched my arm and gazed up at me with brown eyes that wouldn't stop. Suddenly she reminded me of someone, though I couldn't think who.

"Do you have any children, Mike?" she asked.

"No."

"You're lucky. Because nothing hurts more than the thought of your children suffering or dying. You *must* help Jenna and Matthew, Mike. You *will* help them?"

"Goliath himself couldn't stop me," I said.

Chapter 4

The university had a special car for us. It was a three-year-old limo with a driver whose weather-worn face said he was a retired police officer or an old Army MP. I knew damned well he was carrying some iron under his arm, and felt fine about it. When Velda and I sat down in the backseat, his eyes met mine briefly in the rearview mirror before he readjusted the shoulder sling, and I caught his tight grin in the glass. Hell, he knew I was packing, too. Always nice to run into a fellow lodge member.

Matthew and Jenna slid in and sat facing us and after noticing the lack of knobs on the doors, Matthew gave me a look.

"Only the driver can open those doors," I told him.

"Why?"

"Ask the driver."

But he didn't.

Velda said to them both, "I understand your remaining college hours are as lab assistants to your parents."

"That's right," Matthew said, and Jenna nodded.

"Good. Until further notice, this driver and this driver only will escort you to and from the research facility. Times and pickup spots will be specific or you'll trigger a full-on security breach."

"Ms. Sterling," Jenna said, shaking her head. "We're just grad students. We've *delivered* our package."

But Matthew answered his stepsister's question: "If somebody grabs us, where would that leave my dad and your mother?"

Again, the boy made an odd distinction, setting Jenna's mother to one side.

The Hurleys owned an apartment building in Brooklyn, where a recently vacated flat had been made available to the kids. While the parents lived in a spacious apartment in Greenwich Village, Matthew and Jenna needed the kind of protection that Velda and I could better provide under those more controlled conditions.

We sat quietly for the first part of the ride, the two kids as ghostly pale as the snowy city visible through the limo's smoked windows. We were just heading onto the Brooklyn Bridge when I sprang it on them.

"Maybe we better discuss the elephant," I said.

Both kids frowned, but it was Matthew who bit: "What elephant, Mr. Hammer?"

"The big gray bastard sitting in the middle of the room."

They both shook their heads, not following. I didn't intend them to. I just wanted their attention. But Velda knew, all right.

I said, "When you got your pocketbook shot up yesterday, Jenna, you and Matt were exiting a midtown hotel. What were you doing checking into a hotel, anyway? You presumably have rooms at your parents' place."

They exchanged nervous glances.

Then Jenna said, "Actually, we don't have rooms at their apartment anymore."

Matthew said, "They took over our bedrooms for home-office space years ago. Since our freshman year, I've been in a frat house and Jenna stayed in a dorm."

"Why didn't you go back there, then?" I held up a hand to stop the excuses. "Don't tell me you don't have rooms there anymore, either, or any such baloney. You checked into a hotel for the same reason as all normal healthy young unmarrieds in love. To be together."

Beside me, Velda sat with those lush legs crossed and with a smile going that could not have been more sly if she were a cat with a canary's tail hanging out of its damn mouth. Meantime, those kids were blushing like crazy.

I laughed. "Hey, it's okay. Incest doesn't hurt, as long as you keep it in the family."

Velda elbowed me. "Mike!"

"Okay, okay. Look, you two don't share any blood relatives. You're both what, twenty-one, twenty-two? Nobody's judging you."

Matthew's face had gone from beet red to onion white. "Please, Mr. Hammer," he said, leaning forward, his hands clasped pleadingly, "if our *parents* ever found out . . ."

"Well, they must be blind. But lots of parents are. Listen, I'm way past my job description here, giving you advice for the lovelorn. But you two need to hold hands with your heads held high. If your parents can't handle it, that's their damn problem."

Now the kids were smiling in relief, first at us, then at each other. And they took my advice, or at least part of it, and grasped hands.

"You see this beautiful woman sitting next to me?" I asked. "I was in love with her long before you two were born. There were reasons we waited this long to get hitched, but let me tell you—

none of them were any good. If I had it to do over, I'd be celebrating an anniversary with some precious metal attached, not postponing a quick weekend elopement."

Jenna, wide-eyed, asked, "When were you *supposed* to get married, Mr. Hammer? Ms. Sterling?"

"This weekend," Velda admitted. "We had plane tickets to Las Vegas."

"Oh, I'm so sorry. . . . It's *our* fault. . . ."

"Don't worry," Velda said. "I took out flight-cancellation insurance. This isn't the first time he's asked me to marry him, you know."

That made them laugh, and maybe I was the one blushing now. But you can't prove it.

It was a nondescript brick building on a quiet side street whose scrawny trees were plump with snow. I got out, had a talk with the doorman, gave him some pointed instructions, then went back and gathered Velda and the kids. I paused to tell the driver to stay with his vehicle no matter what he might hear, and he nodded, knowing the last thing I'd want is my ride compromised.

The building was a nice older number with black-and-white tile floors and lots of woodwork. Just beyond the vestibule there was an elevator about the size of a coffin, so we took the stairs instead. I didn't want us crammed in there or separated into two parties taking two rides up, either.

On the fifth floor, I made the kids wait by the stairwell door while I went down the hall to check out the pad. Because of all that warm and fuzzy talk in the limo, I was in a mood that maybe made me careless, and I'd damn near put the key in the lock when I heard the voices through the door.

They weren't loud voices, the wood muffled them, but I would have been able to make them out if the language being spoken were English. I couldn't tell you what tongue they were talking, but you didn't need to be a professor of dead languages to know its home was the Middle East.

Down the hall Velda was frowning at me, her expression asking if I wanted backup. Mine told her I didn't, to just hang with those kids.

The .45 was in my left hand when my right hand worked the key in the lock and I pushed through fast into a shockingly cold room. The small hallway opened onto a furnished living room, nothing fancy unless you counted the two guys with natural tans in gray jogging suits.

The mustached one at left was using a Bic to light up a cigarette for the bearded one, which meant the first guy had his rod in his waistband whereas the second one still had his piece, a big silenced automatic, in his mitt.

I was tossing the .45 from my left hand to my right, coming in low when the first shot got thrown at me, high and wild and as quiet as a cough, but then the other guy yanked his gun, a snubnose .38, and when it barked at me, I had to dive behind an easy chair.

They didn't want to shoot it out. They were cowardly killers, not soldiers with balls, and they scrambled out the already-open window, ready for a quick getaway through the passage that explained the indoor chill. I didn't see them fleeing, I heard it, running shoes pounding on squeaky iron, and when I popped up, I caught sight of the second one out on the landing. The ladder must have already been dropped down because they were no longer framed in the window when I crossed the room, their feet beating a noisy retreat down metal stairs.

I was no kid, and wasn't kidding myself otherwise. Once upon a time I'd have been out on that fire escape, ice be damned, scrambling down the stairs into whatever hell those two wanted to throw back at me. But I was faster then, and by the time I was out the window and onto the fire escape, they were down in the alley where a purple gypsy cab belching tailpipe pollution was waiting.

All I could do was fire down at them, the thundering report echoing off brick and cement, and I caught the mustached one in the head, at an angle in the back that went downward and his skull exploded in a scarlet splash. The bearded one threw another cough of a silenced shot my way and it whanged off the metal of the 'scape.

Then tires were squealing and through iron gridwork I saw the purple cab shimmying on ice as it pulled away. They had taken their fallen brother with them, leaving behind a puddle of blood and brains down in that alley with the rest of the garbage.

Velda was a good soldier. Her love for me didn't let her leave her post with those kids, down by the fire-exit door, and her jaw was firm as the .38 in her fist. But her tough expression melted when I emerged from the apartment and joined her.

I filled her in quickly.

"Should we call Pat?" she asked.

I shook my head. "Nothing to report. They took their boy along. They have special burial rites they have to perform for him if he wants to go to happyland where the harem girls are waiting."

Matthew and Jenna were in each other's arms, shivering, un-afraid to show their love but, in every other way, scared as hell.

"Back to your apartment for now," I said to Velda. "We'll call in some reinforcements."

"But not Pat?"

"No. We'll call Secure Solutions."

The innocent-sounding agency was a PI firm of ex-military and mercenaries, the only men in New York I trusted for black-bag–style ops.

She was watching my eyes. "You coming with us?"

I shook my head. "That driver downstairs will get you home safe. I'll catch a cab."

"What for?"

"To catch another cab."

The black guy who had been on the site when the ex-president was selecting a spot in Harlem to open his new office had made a wise remark when he said, "There goes the neighborhood!"

America is an integrated country, all right, except that all the integrations are separated. Not segregated, just separated. Alone, I could be looked upon as an interloper. Not a threat, but an intruder of sorts. The waiter in the corner café would serve me with no trouble, but get a curious expression if I ordered grits on the side. He might figure I was getting cute with my soul-food airs, and didn't know I vacationed down South.

But walking the slushy sidewalk with Bozo Jackson, the big bald ebony ex-cop, gave me a special status around here. Bozo wore a black-leather version of a trench coat that got the attention of even a non–fashion plate like me. He'd been retired maybe five years and, even though he didn't have a PI ticket, he did cop stuff for hire on the same streets he used to patrol.

I was okay up here if I was Bozo Jackson's buddy. I had a damn key to the neighborhood. I could sense the feeling in the knowing looks I got—not exactly friendly, but nowhere near threatening.

Right now Bozo was escorting me to a big garage next to a small dead gas station. A modest gypsy-cab outfit was run out of here, with the office in the gas station.

The little Jamaican export standing in front of a cluttered desk had an unpronounceable last name and was known by one and all simply as Pete the Toke. He wore a greasy gray jumpsuit, had a headful of Rastafarian curls, smelled heavily of the reason for his nickname, and was a handshaker of a rare type. Man, he didn't want to let go at all.

Bozo Jackson introduced me as a "friend," no name, and after a minute or two of past business with Bozo in Pete's rapid-fire speech, Pete the Toke gave me a long stare like he'd just noticed I was here and commented, "You a *white* motherfucker!"

"Well, I'm white," I admitted.

"What you friends with Bozo for? No disrespeck."

"None taken, Pete. Bozo used to be a cop. I still *am* one. Makes us brothers."

Pete the Toke frowned. He knew all about Bozo having been a cop. But Bozo bringing around a *current* cop was a whole other thing . . .

"Priiiivate," Bozo explained soothingly.

"Oh! PI, huh? Look like a tough old boy. You pack?"

"Always," I said.

His eyes were wide and sleepy all at once. "Always?"

"How do you think I lived this long?"

"Not by comin' to this part of town, you didn't. You ain't afraid 'round here?"

"Nope." I grinned. "Not when I got Bozo Jackson as a bodyguard."

"Suppose you *alone* up this way?"

"I come up here a lot. But I'm never alone."

"Oh?"

I patted under my arm and grinned again. "Always packing, remember?"

Bozo seemed mildly amused by all this. "Pete. Don't you know who this is?"

"Who is this?"

"Hell, man, this is Mike Hammer."

Pete laughed and pawed the air and laughed some more. "No fuckin' way, Bozo! Everybody knows Mike Hammer, he die long *time* ago!"

I shrugged. "First I heard of it."

Bozo pointed to the garage side and said, "How many taxis you running these days?"

"Same four. That's all a body needs."

"You know most of the other operators, don't you?"

"Sure."

Bozo hooked a stool with his foot, pulled it over and squatted on it. Now he was only a head taller than Pete. "Any nasty-ass new boys in the game?"

Pete shook his head. "Nobody's trying to take a cut out of me." He looked my way with an eyebrow up. "People know *I* know Bozo Jackson, too."

Bozo was waving that off. "Not *bad* guys, Pete. I ain't talking street tax. I mean new faces in the game. Operators."

Silently, Pete mulled the question over, then shook his head. "Just the same ol' bunch. Some sell out, but to their own guys. Some die, like Duke Harrington, but his kid wound up with his daddy's six cabs. What's this all about, Mr. Jackson?"

"Somebody," Bozo told him, "ran a gypsy jobber to a hotel in

Manhattan yesterday with a shooter who tried to knock off a couple of white college kids."

"Shit you say!" Suddenly Pete looked startled. "We don't need that kinda heat!"

"Be straight with me, Pete," I told him, "and I'll put in a word with Captain Chambers at Homicide."

Pete said nothing, mulling that.

I went on: "And earlier today, a purple gypsy beater dragged off a couple of brown-as-a-berry hit men who were after those same white kids."

"Those white kids could use some motherfuckin' *help*!"

"They're getting it."

Pete's eyes disappeared into slits that were like cuts in his face. "This ain't *wiseguy* business, is it? We ain't had that kind of trouble around here in a long time!"

"Not mob," I said.

Bozo put in: "Ragheads, Pete."

Pete blinked. "We got Muslims 'round here. I got two workin' for me, good drivers."

My eyebrows went up. "Yeah?"

Bozo said, "He means Black Muslims, Mike. This isn't a part of town that Middle Eastern types flock to."

I knew that. Which was part of what was puzzling about all this.

"If you hear something," Bozo said to Pete, "you *will* let me know?"

"If there's something to hear, Pete the Toke'll hear it all right. And when I do, so will you, Mr. Jackson." Pete paused, then shifted his eyes to me. "I believe maybe you *are* Mike Hammer."

"That's the rumor," I said.

Pete patted the breast of his greasy jumpsuit. "We don't bother people, Mr. Hammer. We stay to our own. We don't need none of this action, gypsy jobbers and white kids getting shot at by these camel jockeys."

"They aren't camel jockeys, Pete," I said. "They're ruthless, deadly people, trained to kill and to die for what they believe in. You hear something, you call Mr. Jackson."

Pete the Toke nodded dutifully.

There was another contact Bozo Jackson wanted to touch bases with. He ran a candy and smoke shop, but sold guns in the back— not that he kept any in stock where the law could snag him or some streetwise punk rob him. This was strictly a series of photo albums, where instead of vacation shots you saw pictures of available shooting irons. You could get information on any product you saw pictured, domestic or foreign, pay the full amount in cash and as soon as a day or no more than a week, the piece would be in your hand.

Bozo said, "Jellybean, this is Mike Hammer," and we shook hands. Hard. Mr. Jellybean wanted to know right away who he was dealing with. So then we were both squeezing like hell, and finally we grinned at each other and called it a draw.

In the small, spare backroom office, our host took his seat behind a metal desk and we took the visitor chairs.

Lanky Jellybean's name might have come from any number of things, from all that candy out front to his colorful disco-retro clothes, or the multiplicity of colors in his smile, an array of gold, silver, and diamond-studded-white teeth.

"Mike Hammer, no flyin' shit," Jellybean said. "You know, you got yourself a real following in this part of town."

"Yeah? I haven't had mail requesting autograph pictures."

His colorful smile widened. "Back when you tangled with those mob boys, when the younger and older generations butted heads? Ten, twelve years back? We had a regular cheering section going for you. Right around then, them guineas was tryin' to cut into our personal business here in the 'hood. We were glad to see you send 'em to hell."

"My pleasure."

He placed big hands with long powerful fingers on the desk; no jewelry on his hands and wrists, just the diamonds in his teeth. He jerked his head toward a file cabinet. "Now, what can I do for you fine gentlemens? Something new in the small-arms category?"

Bozo Jackson cut in. "We don't need a gun. We looking for a shooter."

I filled him in about the try on the Hurley kids outside their hotel.

Jellybean gave us a quiet nod and said very simply, "I know who you mean. That shooter's gone. Got out of town real fast."

We waited.

"Begins and ends there, gentlemens."

Bozo started to speak and I raised a hand. "No. Fill it in, Jellybean. We're not looking to bust your chops. If you sold the gun in question, that's strictly business."

"No offense, Mr. Hammer . . . Mr. Jackson . . . but are *we* doin' business?"

I said, "We don't need to do business, Jellybean. We're friends, remember? And friends don't sell out other friends to Captain Chambers of Homicide."

Now he got the picture. And he knew more—plenty. Bozo Jackson and I both felt it.

Wrinkles creased Jellybean's forehead as he thought out all the angles. "He came in four days ago. Stayed at the Cooper Hotel. You know where that is?"

Bozo nodded. "Residential, pretty decent, not some damn flop. Six blocks north?"

"That's the one. Said he was from Jersey City, but while he was here he bought only Chicago papers. Made old Charlie at the desk a little nervous."

"Just for buying an out-of-state paper?" I asked.

Jellybean shook his head. "No. Not just that. This character wore gloves all the time. Lightweight brown ones. Never took them off that anybody saw."

"It's cold out," I said.

"Not cold indoors."

"An injury?"

"No way. He carried a heavy little case all the time. Like a musician haulin' around his precious instrument. Old Charlie said he could smell gun oil on it."

"That would take *some* nose," Bozo remarked, eyebrows up.

Jellybean nodded. "And that's what old Charlie's *got,* too. He could sniff out a guy smokin' a joint up on the roof. Somebody with a crack pipe on the fourth floor, Charlie knows it at the desk and throws their ass out. Runs a respectable joint, Charlie."

I said, "Jellybean, that comment you made—about this shooter wearing gloves indoors? Did that come from personal observation?"

Jellybean swallowed thickly. "Mr. Hammer, you agreed with me, some things is strictly business. Somebody buys a piece from me, he doesn't want paperwork, and he sure as shit doesn't want no questions."

"*You* sold him the gun."

Jellybean sighed and nodded. "A Hammerli .22."

Bozo sat forward, frowning. "What's a guy carries his piece around in a carrying case need to buy a damn target pistol from you for?"

Jellybean held up his hands as if we'd made an arrest. "I told you, we don't ask questions on this side of the transaction." He shrugged. "I *can* tell you it wasn't cheap. Cost him a grand."

I said, "He hires a precision pistol—the kind you enter competitions with—and he doesn't kill his target? Then he books out of town? Doesn't make sense, Jellybean."

The gun dealer shrugged elaborately. "Means he won't try again. He's gone for good. To toss a grand around like that, he musta got paid good in the first place. Then when the job went bust, he grabbed the next plane out."

Jellybean looked at us one at a time, a little tic touching his left eye. Bozo, his eyes boring right into Jellybean's, said, "You sure got a lot to say without saying much, my brother."

"Bozo, I give it to you straight."

"Except for what he *looked* like. You left that out, Jellybean."

"He was dark. Not a black man, maybe . . . Latino."

"Jellybean . . ."

"Or maybe one of them Ayrabs." Jellybean frowned. Then he lurched forward. "You go around telling people I sold a gun to some damn terrorist, I get my ass in a sling!"

"He went downtown in a gypsy cab," I reminded him.

"Sure. He dropped five bills on Lonnie Hartman to rent one of his old taxis for a couple hours, and hired some kid of Lonnie's to drive it. Hell, neither Lon or that kid knew the guy was a shooter. Far as they knew, he was a damn tourist!"

"Right," I said.

"Anyway, the kid driving didn't even hear the shots go off, but right after, the guy yelled for him to get out of there, he smelled burnt gunpowder. He dropped the shooter off at Grand Central, and that was the last he saw of him. Kid got the cab back to Lonnie Hartman's garage and scrammed." Jellybean paused, took a deep breath and added, "That's what I hear. . . . Look, if this guy's some damn *terrorist*—"

I grinned at him. "Who said the guy was a terrorist, Jellybean?"

"I wouldn't sell shit to them motherfuckers, I ain't *that* evil a asshole. They *crazy*, Mr. Hammer. They fly airliners into buildings and think when they die, they go *zip* up to heaven. Live the life of ease up there."

"A lot of people believe in a life after death, Jellybean."

"Not me, Mr. Hammer. Man, I want to stay right here on God's green earth in the devil's own city. I *like* these badass streets. I like a fattie or maybe a cold beer at the end of the day. I like a ball game on my flat screen. I like some warm, snuggly cooze to curl up with. They can have their virgins in the afterlife. I'll take me some ho in the here and now."

I'd heard worse philosophies of life.

Bozo Jackson gave Jellybean a long, solemn look and eased off his stool, and we both said so long to him. On the way out, Jellybean called, "Mr. Hammer! You in the book?"

"Under *Michael Hammer Investigations.*"

"I hear anything, I give you a call. If I'm lyin,' I'm dyin.'"

I gave him my nastiest grin. "It's a deal, Jellybean. And as an expert on small arms, you'll like my gun—it's a .45, a classic from the Great War."

But behind his spare desk, the man with the colorful smile was frowning. "Ain't nothin' great about *any* war, Mr. Hammer."

"Without war, Jellybean, there'd be no armaments. And you'd be out of business."

And now the big glittery grin came again. "I ain't worried about that ever happenin', Mr. Hammer."

Out on the sidewalk, trying to wave down a cab, Bozo asked, "What now, Mike?"

"Check out that purple gypsy for me, Bozo."

I held out a hand with a C-note in it. We shook and my hand came back bare.

Bozo was frowning. "I still don't know why a pro shooter buys a target pistol for a hit."

"Maybe it wasn't a hit."

And he was thinking about that when I got into the cab—a yellow, not a gypsy. Not today.

I called Velda and had her bring the kids around to the French House, an off-the-beaten-path restaurant she knew well.

"Call a cab," I told her. "Don't go down to the street for one."

"You don't have to insult me," she said.

"Sorry. I'm just worried about those kids."

"Those kids are about the age we were when we met."

"Don't remind me."

French fries were as close as the French House came to what its name implied, serving great deli-style food in a rough neighborhood near the Times Square theater district, where squad cars passed by every five minutes. I got there ten minutes before the kids and Velda, and had almost finished off half a bottle of Miller Beer when they spotted me in the booth.

They came quickly down the aisle and slid in opposite.

Neither one looked very happy.

"Hope you nice people had a quiet afternoon," I said, as Velda settled in next to me and gave me a small smile and a big nod.

The Hurley kids looked at each other, trying to find an answer. Then Jenna said, "Remember my friend in Israel who mailed the bone back to the States for us?"

I nodded.

"Marcy's her name—she got beat up yesterday."

I frowned. "How bad?"

Jenna's eyes were moist, but her voice stayed firm. "She didn't go to the hospital or anything. But two men—she thinks they were Palestinians—grabbed her on the street, dragged her into a car and, when they were in a desolate section of the city, pulled into an alley and yelled at her and beat her terribly."

"What were they after?"

"At first they didn't say. They just yelled at her and beat up on her, slapping her, slugging her. One was in the front seat, the other in back with Marcy, and . . . anyway, she was hurt and crying and scared stiff and then they suddenly asked her in English where she had sent the package. She said, 'What package?' And the one in the front seat said, 'The one the American bitch gave you.'"

I heaved a sigh. I had given up smoking maybe twenty years ago, but I would've killed for a Lucky Strike right now. "And she told them, right?"

Jenna swallowed. Nodded. "She told them."

"Shit!" I said.

Jenna leaned forward and clutched my arm. "Mr. Hammer, I couldn't blame her. She thought they'd *kill* her if she didn't tell them. She's just a college girl from California. Getting a beating like that, it's nothing she'd ever imagined—"

"Don't sweat it, Jenna. It's not like we didn't already know people are . . ." I almost said, *After you.* Instead I finished with, ". . . interested."

"I wish we'd never found that stupid fucking thing."

Matthew touched her arm. *"Jenna . . ."*

"A bone. A stupid silly lousy hunk of bone."

I smiled. "Jenna, that big old bone makes an even bigger new symbol."

She was shaking her head. "Haven't they got enough hate for each other already over there? What do they need a stupid *symbol* for?"

A waitress came by with coffee for Velda and another beer for me, and the two kids asked for Diet Cokes.

I said, "You're dealing with people who have comparatively little compared to the Western world. They have armies equipped with antiquated equipment, and have very little personal wealth—that oil money doesn't exactly get spread around."

Jenna smirked. "Oil money doesn't *exactly* get spread around over here, either."

"Better than over there. On top of that, they have violent tendencies when it comes to religious and nationalistic beliefs. But don't for a minute think they're dumb."

They were still kids. College kids, but kids who hadn't lost all of their teenage habits, like suddenly letting their eyes flash to one another asking a silent, *Should we or shouldn't we?*

I said, "Go ahead and spill it. What *I* don't know can hurt you."

There was another sudden exchange of eye contact. Then they both looked squarely at me.

Matthew said, "One of the Israeli students assigned to help our parents out with their Dead Sea Scroll research . . . ? He called me on my cell this afternoon."

Jenna said, "His name's Jason Diamond. Seems like a nice guy. A little old for a student, maybe, but there are a lot like that in Israel. Everybody's taken time out for military training and service. Even the little kids have a degree of maturity you don't see over here."

"Probably because they've been living under tension so long," I said. "With all the suicide bombings from the crazies and the general world situation, those kids are well aware of what's going on." I paused, then asked, "But what about this Jason Diamond?"

"I can't emphasize enough that he was very nice," Jenna insisted. "Not mean or threatening."

I nodded. "What did he want?"

"It was just a phone call, saying hello, making sure we got back home safe. Nothing that, in itself, seemed significant."

Velda said, "Then why does it seem significant enough for you to mention to Mike?"

Jenna and Matthew exchanged glances, and then she went on with their story. "When Marcy called and told us what had happened to her, she said that Jason Diamond came around to see her, a few hours later, and seemed shocked to find her all bruised and frightened. He helped her with bandages and cool cloths."

"You said he was a nice guy."

"Right. But while he was helping her . . . he asked her the same thing."

"What do you mean, 'the same thing'?"

"The same thing that her *attackers* asked—where Marcy had sent the package that included some of our things. He never mentioned the Goliath bone, but . . . why else would he care about that package?"

I sat there watching Jenna lick her lips, thinking about what she was going to say next.

"Finally Marcy asked Jason how he knew she'd sent a 'package' home, with some things of Matt's and mine. And Jason told her he had overheard a couple of Palestinians talking about it."

I glanced at Velda, and she glanced at me, frowning. I said, "That was pretty thin."

"Maybe," Jenna said. "Still, maybe Marcy wouldn't have thought anything of it, even after taking a beating like that. But the thing is . . . one other time? Marcy saw Jason going into a building where the Mossad had offices."

I frowned. "You think Jason Diamond is an Israeli agent?"

"Marcy does. She'd never made him for an agent before, because he seemed too young for a thing like that. She thought."

Velda said, "Too old for a student, too young for a spy."

I said, "However you slice it, Jenna, Matthew, your parent's hired 'helper' is more than he pretended to be."

"He seemed to know about the package," the girl agreed, "if not the bone."

We ordered a light supper and the conversation resumed.

I said, "Until that bone is authenticated, everything else is speculation."

Matthew leaned forward in his seat, his eyes meeting mine. "Well, it will be authenticated soon. Probably already has been— my parents have been working on it all day."

"Even so," I said, "you can't tie it with a certainty to the historical Goliath."

"No, but the university has the latest technology at its disposal to do everything short of that. The artifact isn't all that old, relatively speaking—it was well preserved, and research bears out the probability that this *could* be part of the historical figure in question . . . and does it really matter whether it was Goliath's femur or came from a wandering diplodocus? Both the Arab world and the Israelis seem to *know* about it . . . and both *want* it."

I liked hearing him talk. He'd be a professor like his old man someday. "So what's the bottom line, Matthew?"

He leaned forward a little more, totally engrossed in his exposition. "Jenna's right, I'm afraid. It would be better if we'd never found that goddamn thing. The Israelis will see it as a symbol of defeating an Arab giant and his army. And the Arab world will want to keep it out of Israeli hands—whether to claim it as a symbol of their own fallen hero, or to destroy the thing. Who can say? We were just digging in the ground, Mr. Hammer—we didn't want to light a match and throw it in an ocean of gasoline. Remember after 9/11 and then the anthrax scare? They had all of us running scared, the American public buying up old surplus gas masks."

"Yeah, but not buying any extra filters. Damn, most of that stuff is World War II surplus."

"You didn't go out and buy any of that stuff, did you, Mr. Hammer?"

"Naw. I have my .45 Army-issue Colt automatic. Still shoots good, too. And I have about thirty boxes of vintage ammo and never had a misfire yet."

Velda smirked. "That relic'll blow up in his face one of these days, wait and see."

Jenna asked with a sweetly mocking little smile, "How is your aim, Mr. Hammer?"

"Well, my eyesight's twenty-twenty and I've never needed

glasses, if you want a hint. Otherwise go check the old newspaper files and see. I was in all the papers."

"Like the war in Iraq?" Matthew asked, something gently mocking in him, too. "Instead of frontal attacks, we've got hidden car bombs, soldiers playing the role of civilians, kids sporting and using adult weapons. Israel tries to calm things down by emptying out villages to give back to the Palestinians, and it still does no good."

"Speaking of the papers," I said to the boy, "you might ask yourself one more question."

"Such as?"

"Such as, who's going to cover your tail when the media hails you brother-and-sister lovebirds as the discoverers of the Goliath bone?"

Another glance passed between Matthew and Jenna. Quietly, he asked me, "Would they? Print that, I mean."

"You think they'd restrain themselves?" I asked.

"Then where does that leave us?"

"With the world's biggest soup bone, Matthew. And you in it— the soup, I mean."

Jenna sat forward. "Is Matthew right, Mr. Hammer? Could our discovery lead to a wider war?"

"Could be," I said. "They can't fight us with weaponry, but a small lab can turn out a sizable amount of deadly bacteria that can decimate the population like the AIDS scourge that hit Africa. Smallpox did the same thing to the American Indians. Our friendly government agency sent them contaminated blankets and never had to waste bullets to shoot them."

Velda was looking at me gravely. "Mike—the way we outnumber this enemy is ridiculous."

"But they've had a lot of time to infiltrate us with personnel looking to be martyrs. We're a diverse country and they can move freely wherever they want to. Never play this enemy down. At this point, we don't know the extent of their intelligence, their intimate knowledge of their supposed enemy."

Matthew was frowning. "Supposed enemy? You mean the USA?"

"You spelled it right, anyway—*us,* Matthew. You and Jenna and me and Velda."

Our food arrived and everybody but me picked at it. I was hungry.

"My guess," I said, between bites of corned beef, pastrami, Swiss cheese, coleslaw, Russian dressing, and rye bread, "is they have you kids pretty well covered. They know you didn't move into that apartment where the shooters were waiting. And they most likely know you left Velda's apartment and came here."

Velda was nibbling at her salad. But the two kids had wide eyes and open mouths and forks slack in limp hands.

"Oh yeah," I said, gesturing around the packed restaurant. "They know you're here. Outside, a couple of more shooters will be bracketing the door, and if you go waltzing out front, they'll cut both of you down."

Jenna, pushing her plate away, went very white and her eyes opened even wider, fear sparking in them first, then anger. She was about to sound off in my face until I held up my hand and she pressed her lips together tightly.

"This restaurant is a safe house," I said, "and the owner is a friend of mine. We built an exit to the street behind this one that comes out six buildings down. A white Ford pickup truck already parked at the curb will be your ride. The driver will take you to different quarters, where you will stay until Velda or I come and get you. You'll have half a dozen men watching you; two inside, four out. Tomorrow your clothes and other personal belongings will be delivered to you."

Matthew was frowning. Too much was flying by too damn fast. A taut expression pulled at his face, and he leaned forward on the table, the fingers of his hands interlocking. For the first time he dropped the "Mr. Hammer," saying, "Mike—we barely know you. You stumbled onto us, and I'd heard of you, of course, but figured you were just a plain old-fashioned private detective . . ."

Velda said, "Emphasis on the 'old-fashioned.'"

". . . the kind who could handle the rough stuff, but this whole business sounds like a *military* operation. How come you can operate out of safe houses like the CIA, or be the point man on a historical artifact that can have, well, international repercussions?"

"Just lucky I guess," I said. "You two ready to go?"

I nodded toward the kitchen door and six waiters came out and bunched together, blocking anybody's view. The four of us got up and followed the owner through a side door while another foursome took our places at the table. Five minutes later, we had traversed the cluttered backyards of two houses, gone into the cellar of the third, and exited through the basement door of the old tenement.

There were no more comments or complaints. Matthew and Jenna got into the Ford pickup; the unseen driver started it up and took off. I took Velda's hand, and we had a leisurely walk to her apartment building.

Very softly, as we held hands, she asked, "When are you going to move the kids again?"

"You *are* sharp, kitten. Beautiful and sharp." I let my eyes run over her gorgeous contours. "We'll move them once a day—at different times, of course. Why do you ask?"

"Because those kids are the bargaining chips, aren't they? If the enemy grabs them, they have something to trade for the bone. And both you and I know that while their parents might be sucker enough to pay the ransom price—maybe even *we* would be sucker enough—all you'd get back would be two dead kids."

"And what would happen then, Velda? Something even bigger and wilder. What else?"

She knew, all right. She said, "The sleeping giant might awaken again, like after Pearl Harbor. A country of people so goddamn mad they'd be ready to go to war against every rogue state on the planet. Like a disturbed rattlesnake, there'd be a demand for the bloodiest retaliation you ever saw."

"Right," I said. "So we need to make sure that doesn't happen."

"Mike Hammer? Peacemaker?"

I nodded, enjoying the way the neons glowed in the dusk. "Blessed are the peacemakers, doll. And back in the Old West, remember, that's what they called a Colt .45."

Chapter 5

It had started to rain.

Not heavy. Just a penetrating drizzly rain eating at the snow, working to wash away the dull slushy gray and reveal the darker gray of concrete beneath. I turned up the collar of my trench coat against it as I walked from my apartment to the office. Each street corner had its band of unprepared citizens trying to flag down taxis and I bypassed them all.

New Yorkers are a strange bunch, never prepared for anything. The Trade Centers came down around their ears; now they line up to get a tourist's-eye look where the towers once stood. No tears now. Just bewilderment. They shake their heads, then leave. To most, it was an *event*. They still haven't put the situation in full perspective. Most of them seem to think it was all over.

They never seemed to think that maybe it was only the beginning.

This was the kind of case where Captain Chambers and I spent more time together in my office than his. The morning had barely begun when he came around bearing Danish, but knowing Velda would supply the coffee. He was a tough guy who took it black, but

I was a sissy who needed a couple of Sweet'N Lows. Velda made that stuff strong—would have knocked Juan Valdez off his damn mule.

Pat tossed his fedora on my desk and handed around the Danish and napkins—he'd already made a delivery to Velda in the outer office. He settled in the comfy client's chair and made a face that didn't go with the sweet pastry he was nibbling.

"Afraid those bullet fragments are a bust, Mike. Lab boys came up with bupkis. I sent the frags on to Washington for a complete analysis, but most likely they'll be American made, standard over-the-counter ammo you can buy anywhere. At close range they can be pretty deadly."

"The gun came from a dealer in Harlem," I said.

He paused in mid-bite. "That's a little vague."

"I can give you more if and when you need it. I'm doing some poking up there that might be more effective than the official variety."

His eyes narrowed. "Bozo Jackson?"

I nodded.

Pat already knew we'd had to move the kids from the Brooklyn apartment to another safe-house. He didn't ask where, and I sure as hell didn't offer it.

He swallowed and his expression was casual but the gray eyes probing me weren't. "I had a call from my opposite number in Brooklyn Homicide. He says they had a call about gunshots at that apartment building the Hurleys own. Right about the time you would've moved their kiddies."

"I already told you, Pat, I chased a couple guys with guns out of there."

"You didn't say shots had been exchanged. You were a little vague about *that,* too."

"Some things are on a need-to-know basis, Pat."

"What, now you're the goddamn government? You didn't happen to wing a guy, did you?"

"I don't know. My age, eyesight's a little iffy."

"You're twenty-damn-twenty, pal."

"You could tell your Brooklyn friend to check the hospital ERs."

"I don't think so. Their lab boys found arterial blood and brain matter and bone."

"The Goliath bone?"

"Cut the comedy, Mike. You need to level with me."

"Do I? Anything I tell you, you have to report. If you don't, your ass could be in a sling. Haven't we worked enough cases for you to trust me on this?"

He chewed Danish. He knew I was right. He knew twenty times—hell, fifty times—I'd hidden things from him and the upshot had been the bad guys had gone down. He envied me my freedom like I envied him his resources. We'd been a great team for a lot of years, we'd just never admitted it.

"We'll leave it at 'need-to-know,'" he said, wiping his hands off with a paper napkin. "After all, the Doctors Hurley and plenty of others at that university have some pretty hot ties to the federal agencies. When you ask questions up there, they smile and give you noncommittal answers, and somehow you know the conversation has been recorded. Then an inquiry comes down from the mayor's office wanting to know what's going on."

"So you shrug and brush it off."

"That would seem to be my best option. Officially, this is a foiled subway mugging and a handbag with a couple of .22 holes poked in it. Jenna Hurley didn't have a mark on her, there were no witnesses, and she could have shot those holes in that bag herself, earlier."

I about choked on my bite of Danish. "Why in hell would she do that?"

"Somebody might think she and her brother staged this to build up publicity for the Goliath bone. They come as close to owning the damn thing as anybody."

"Nobody here wants publicity, Pat. Who'd be dumb enough to think those kids hired that subway shooter and—what, set the whole thing up?"

"Stranger things have happened."

"No they haven't. Not even in this town. And they'd say I was in on it, I suppose? Called in by the Hurley kids to plug that guy and make their story look good?"

"You *could* be accused of that."

I talked with my mouth full, just to stick it to him. "I've been accused of lots of things, pal. Nobody's made any of it stick. You want the NYPD to be constructive? Get ready for the shit to hit the fan when the media gets hold of this Goliath-bone story."

"I don't follow you."

"The damn thing might be the match that touches off the next major blast."

He made another face, pawed the air. "Like where? The Rose Bowl's been played, the Olympic Games are over, Disney World and Hollywood are heavy on alert status, and everyone stays glued to twenty-four–hour news for current information so they won't be standing in the wrong place at the wrong time."

I used a napkin on my sticky fingers. "Yeah, right. Color codes. Every time some damn politician drops the ball and wants the public's eyes off him, the color code goes up magically. How dumb do they think we are?"

"Well, you're pretty damn dumb if you think al-Qaeda can pull an impromptu 9/11. Those fanatics take a lot of time to set up a major scene of destruction and, believe me, our guys have everything covered."

"Horseshit," I said. "Right now I could orchestrate a disaster and set it up in a couple of days."

"Come on, Mike. Now you *do* sound dumb."

"Do I?" I stared at him a few seconds, then grinned.

Pat's eyes got cold as he tried to sort out the possibilities. "Okay . . . so you have that kind of evil mind. I'll give you that. But who'd finance it?"

"Minimum layout," I stated offhandedly.

"How big a crew?"

"Two," I told him.

"Small-time, then . . ."

"No. Major destruction. Millions of people affected."

Pat rarely swore, but this time he made an exception. "Fuck you, Mike. You're all talk."

I said nothing. He knew I was a lot of things, but all talk wasn't one of them.

Then he said, "Care to tell me how you'd do it?"

I nodded again. "One man in a truck loaded with cheap explosive—fertilizer-based, like the Oklahoma bombing—drives onto the middle of a major bridge, fakes a flat, pulls over, gets out, and a following car picks him up and they exit the scene. A timer sets off the bomb a couple minutes later, and down comes Choose-your-bridge."

"Which bridge would you suggest?"

"How about the George Washington right here in the town so nice they blew it up twice? Or the Golden Gate, maybe? Neither one is a military target, but either one sure would raise hell with lines of communication nationally, and the publicity would satisfy all those unwashed masses overseas who hate the United States on general principle."

For a few seconds, we sat there quietly. Then Pat said, "You've been thinking about more than just knocking down a bridge, haven't you?"

When I didn't answer right away, he went on, "That bone is bugging you, isn't it?"

"Yeah," I admitted. "There was enough hate in this world already without that damn thing turning up."

Pat's eyes got a little cool, and for a few seconds he studied me. His fingers made silent little taps on the desktop. He took a couple of sips from his coffee cup, then put it down.

"Pal," he told me, "you are a goddamn troublemaker. Always have been. Here I am, almost ready to retire and there *you* sit, finally ready to marry that beautiful dame . . . and yet you take time out to play with a big can of deadly worms again."

"Velda!"

She appeared in the doorway to the outer office, a long-stemmed vision in a trim gray suit. "Yes, Mike?"

"Captain Chambers called you a 'dame' again. Is that sexist, or . . . what's that other term?"

"Anachronistic, Mike." The lush lips formed a glowing smile. "But I like it. Coming from Pat, it's always a compliment."

Pat glanced back at her. "You deserve better than this bum, Velda."

"They don't come better than that bum, Pat." And she was gone.

The captain of Homicide sat forward in his chair. "What comes next, Mike?" Before I could answer him, he held up his palms for silence. "Don't tell me. You're going to use that damned bone as bait, knock a few bad guys off, and make a point."

"How could I manage that, Pat? They got that relic under lock and key over at NYU."

"So thought Brink's before the gang nailed all their money. So said the Brits about those millions of pounds safe in that mail train until those hoods very neatly stalled it out and took off with the cash. Some show."

"What's your point, Pat?"

"You can't keep that bone locked up in a university research center. Sooner or later there'll be a surgical strike from some foreign interest, and this country will be tied right into the next big Middle Eastern mess. They got nukes over there now, Mike! Christ, what did you get us all into . . ."

"Want to help me steal it, Pat?"

That hit Pat like a poke in the belly. "Come on, I'm a cop. You think I want to mess up my retirement?" His mouth twisted into a grin but I didn't make any nasty remark. Pat was too square a cop to play dirty.

I said, "The only hope is to defuse this thing by getting that bone out to the public—the *American* public."

"What, a museum display? You don't think some terrorist cell would knock over anything any museum had to offer? Even the Smithsonian? Why don't you just stick the Hope diamond in Macy's window, and hope nobody breaks the glass?"

"Maybe I will."

His brow knit and his eyes narrowed. "You got something knocking around inside that empty space between your ears, don't you, buddy?"

I grinned back at him and nodded again. "That's on a need-to-know basis, too, Pat."

He sighed, got up, slapped on his hat, and pretended to be mad as he stalked out.

He never was much of an actor.

I wandered out into Velda's domain to freshen my coffee and found her seated at her desk opening a modest-sized package. I kissed the back of her neck and she turned her head toward me as she flipped open the top of the cardboard box.

"Mike, did you order this?"

She knew what it was and so did I. It had been packaged in its green metal box sometime before 1945 and still had that smell any old Army vet could remember. I put my finger under the latch, pulled it open so the cover flipped back, and there were all those boxes of .45 caliber cartridges that had stopped an insurrection a long time ago and could ream out a terrorist organization right now.

"Mike, you have to stop ordering this ancient ammo. It's just not safe."

"Sure it is, kitten. That kind of ordnance lasts a lifetime."

"This kind of ordnance can end a lifetime. You'll get a misfire or even some unstable old slug that will blow that precious .45 of yours up in your hand."

"A lot you know about it. Worst thing likely to happen is an explosion that bulges up the barrel."

Her brow furrowed. "I can think of something worse—*any* of that happens, and the other guy with a gun blows your head off."

"*What* other guy?"

"The other guy who isn't ordering ancient ammo out of some weird sense of sentimentality!"

"Are you done, kid? 'Cause I didn't order the stuff. Has it got a return address?"

"Oh. Well, it came from New Jersey."

"You already checked on the sender, right?"

"Sure."

"And nobody home?"

"Public housing."

"Untraceable, right?"

"Right," she told me. "Maybe it's a fan afraid you're going to run out of ammo."

"I doubt it," I said, "but I appreciate the sentiment."

She arched an eyebrow. "Or it could be the kind of 'fan' who rigs a slug to blow up in your face."

"Velda . . . we *had* that conversation. . . ."

She returned her attention to the green metal container. "Come on, Mike. This is a *message*—you know that, don't you?"

"Sure." I shrugged. "I just wish I knew what it was saying."

"Maybe they want you to shoot somebody, lover boy. Details to follow."

"With a cartridge box of .45s? I could shoot a whole lot of some-bodies with that little after-Christmas present. Hell, all I need is one shot per target . . . well, maybe two."

She was shaking her head. "Mike, you're not the randy young PI you used to be."

"No. I'm the randy old PI of today." I leaned down and kissed the back of her neck again. "This thing is getting a little dicey, isn't it?"

"Terrorist cells from half a dozen rogue states? The Israeli Mossad interested? What's dicey about *that*?" Slowly, she turned her head to look up at me. "You scared, Mike?"

"Not yet. I'm still on the fringes. I haven't put myself in the middle yet."

"How *do* you feel?"

I thought about it a moment, then told her, "I'm curious. I never bodyguarded a bone before. It sounds like a Halloween joke, but it's a deadly serious affair with international repercussions. One shooter maybe tries to take out both kids and snag old Goliath's femur in that subway, but before that Jenna gets herself shot at when she and Matt don't even have possession of the damn thing yet . . . and indications are that a pro was brought in to pop her."

"Did Pat put a tracer out on him?"

"Sure, but that's outside the NYPD's realm. This isn't some standard pro, not some freelance hit man. It's a shooter tied in with al-Qaeda or some other terrorist organization."

"Mike . . ."

"What, doll?"

"Somebody laid out a lot of bucks to bring in an out-of-town shooter, didn't they? It's not like al-Qaeda doesn't have somebody already in the New York area who could hit those kids."

I sat on the edge of her desk and looked down at her. "You're right. Go on."

She was staring into her thoughts, and her words came out careful, deliberate. "He'd be a damn good shooter then, wouldn't he? Good enough to bother importing."

Velda got up from her chair, unwinding the sensuous way a cat does, twirled halfway around, and looked over her shoulder at me like the pinup girl she could've been.

But the point she made was pure female PI: "Maybe he didn't *want* to kill her. Maybe those shots into her handbag were well-aimed. If he was supposed to kill her, he would have aimed for her head."

This time I beat her to the next step.

Snapping my fingers, I said, "Those .22s were deliberately altered! A light load with minimum penetration power."

She was getting herself some coffee. "I don't care what anybody says, Mike. You aren't stupid."

"Thanks a bunch."

She strolled back, sipping. Then she asked, "You think that shooting could be some kind of snow job?"

"Anything is possible. But what for?"

Velda thought about it briefly, then suggested, "Scare tactics? Put pressure on the parents, Mike?"

"Now we're back to that damned bone again." I shook my head. "I have to get control of the thing. I can protect that thing better than those college clowns."

Her expression was a smile that got stalled somewhere. "Mike, stop—don't go off half-cocked about this. Before you know it, the Feds will weigh in and, until then, the university seems up to the job of—"

"That's not enough," I cut in. "Too many people already know or can guess where the Goliath bone's being kept, and any place can be broken into. Any faction interested in possessing that thing could power their way into the university, and can make it happen."

Velda's frown deepened. "Mike—what do you have in mind? And please don't make me sorry for asking."

I said, "The Hurley kids can be our key to the box that bone's being kept in."

"What?"

"Let's call them and we make an appointment to drop by and pick them up and see their folks at the university again."

Velda didn't know exactly what I was getting at, but she knew not to argue with me in this frame of mind. She did her job and put everything in motion.

The khaki-clad security team that met us at the NYU research facility door did everything but a cavity search on the four of us. My .45 went into a black canvas bag along with Velda's .38 and a couple of small spray-perfume vials, Matthew dropped in a pocketknife, and Jenna some nail clippers.

"Entering this building," Matthew said with a weary smile, "is like boarding an airliner for D.C. every single day."

The guard with the canvas bag disappeared into another room and came back a few minutes later, empty-handed. But not alone—eight more guards in khaki trooped out from who-knew-where and soon all dozen of us were squeezing on that elevator to take the ride down to the corridor of stainless-steel doors.

Then the jury's worth of us, four strategically surrounded by eight, walked to the gleaming door behind which the remnant of Goliath now resided. We stood in that circle and experienced the tingling sensation as we were photographed and X-rayed or what-ever the hell, and when we entered the room, four of the guards came with us, the other four staying on the other side of the closed door.

Doctors George and Charlene Hurley in their matching lab coats were at work at the same metal table where the Goliath bone had first been displayed like a decorative piece of driftwood, the relic surrounded now by half a dozen lipstick cameras on tiny tripods as if the Lilliputians were making a movie about Gulliver. On a flat-screen computer monitor, one of the images sent by those cameras revealed an angle on the bone overlaid with a measuring grid.

Petite Charlene was seated at the keyboard before the flat screen, and big, rangy George was just behind her, looking over her shoulder.

They didn't seem at all annoyed by our intrusion, and George Hurley grinned and came over, sticking out a big hand for me to shake. "I trust our security measures didn't put you out any?"

Matthew, at my side, said, "Little over the top, isn't it, Dad?"

I answered before his father could. "No. These boys are Special Forces. Government help already, George?"

There was a fleeting exchange of looks between Hurley and his wife that said they'd probably heard from any number of government agencies.

A small conference table down at one end was one of the few nonmetallic surfaces in the lab. Charlene rose from her computer and ushered us over, slipping an arm around her daughter as we went.

Charlene played hostess, offering coffee or soft drinks, but got no takers. She was a lovely woman with a sweet heart-shaped face and a halo of blond curls and a beauty that required little or no makeup—George Hurley was a lucky man. Damn if she didn't remind me of someone, but I couldn't quite place the resemblance. It would come to me.

There are times when you have to get something across fast, and I knew a couple of the tricks. It's only a look, but they got the gist of it.

This time I looked straight at Matthew Hurley and said, "You do remember that chunk of dead protein over there is more than a scientific trophy, don't you?"

The Hurleys exchanged expressions that seemed vaguely embarrassed. Charlene, sitting next to her daughter, took Jenna's hand and squeezed.

"Nothing means more to us than the safety of our children," Charlene said. "A scientific slant on history is our calling, Mr. Hammer . . . Mike. But our family is, well, our *family*."

I looked at Hurley. "You on the same page as your wife, George?"

"Of course I am." His smile seemed a little forced. "And we're grateful to you for everything you're doing."

But I'd kept the parents in the dark on part of what had been going on. They didn't know why yesterday I'd moved Matthew and Jenna out of that apartment in the building they owned, and the kids had been instructed not to say anything about it to them over the phone.

So I gave the Hurleys a quick rundown on the incident, speaking softly so those guards down at the other end of the stainless-steel bone sanctuary couldn't hear.

When I'd finished, both George and Charlene Hurley were as white as their smocks.

"Mike," George said. "You . . . you *killed* one of them?"

"Unless he has a spare skull I did, and the only extra bone around is Goliath's over there. Yes, we've racked up another death. But we would've racked up the death of these two kids if I hadn't been around."

Hurley shook his head. "Well, of course, we're very grateful, Mike. What else can be done to protect them?"

"That's what I want to talk to you about. In the short term, I can move the kids on a daily basis from one safe house to another. I have some people who do contract work for me that would make your Special Forces babysitters here look like mall cops."

If the guys in khaki down there had heard me, they had better poker faces than those guards in the funny hats outside Buckingham Palace.

Charlene, still clutching her daughter's hand, said, "That's the short term. What about the long term, Mike?"

I shrugged. "Up till now nobody has bothered to establish ownership of this artifact, although there are a few entities seemingly connected with its discovery. The state of Israel, for one. Certain Arab states and/or groups may also stake a claim."

Velda said, "Till now we've been concerned with protecting your kids from kidnapping or some other harm. As for the Goliath bone, all we've done is get it into your hands where it can be kept under armed guard."

I asked Hurley, "What have the government people you've spoken to been saying? What have you been advised to do?"

"So far," he said, "it's been strictly a matter of support—these guards and other heightened security measures designed to keep our lab in twenty-four–hour lockdown. After all, the university works quite closely with the government when the need arises."

"And the need, from time to time," Charlene added, "can arise on both sides, theirs and ours."

"Well," I said, "somebody down there in Washington is pretty damn sharp. When that bone was given a name, they saw right away the implications of what that thing could become in the so-called War on Terror. Me, I don't believe in declaring war on nouns—I'd prefer to take on a person like Bin Laden or a group like al-Qaeda or maybe a whole damn country if I'm feeling ambitious. But I'm not on the marketing side of killing. I'm just another old soldier. And right now I'm in a battle in the war to protect Matthew and Jenna Hurley."

"Obviously we're all in favor of that," Hurley said, and exchanged a confused glance with Charlene.

"I don't know if I see where you heading, Mike," Charlene admitted.

"Who has ownership of the bone?" I asked them.

For a few seconds they both hesitated, each deciding whether to defer to the other. Then George Hurley said, "Well, most likely these two." He gestured to his children.

"There are laws," I reminded him, "against removal of artifacts from some historical areas."

"So far there have been no formal claims or protests," he remarked.

"Oh, they'll start, all right. Right now all the talk is on the lower levels, but when things start to escalate, the attacks will go beyond men with guns to courtrooms of so-called international law, not to mention that other kangaroo court, the media."

George Hurley's jaw was firm. "I believe our government will stand behind us here at the university."

"If the politicians think it'll make them look better to turn this discovery over to the Israelis or Saudi Arabia or whoever has the most political clout or oil or connections, they'll sell out your university *and* these kids without a twinge."

Matthew, sitting next to me, said, "Is it so bad, Mr. Hammer, if Israel winds up with the bone? We could negotiate terms that give my parents control over the research."

I said, "Has it occurred to anyone here that the Goliath bone is valuable . . . and I'm not talking about historical or symbolic value. Money. Good old American dollars. George . . . Charlene . . . these kids of yours are about to go out into the world and start their lives."

From the corner of an eye I saw Matthew tense up, afraid I'd tell his folks about his stepsister and himself.

"They have ambitions to follow in your footsteps," I went on, "but building a life on a little nest egg of, say, a few million dollars, would that be so bad?"

Hurley's eyes made damn-near-perfect circles. "Are you saying—sell this to the highest bidder?"

"I'll be honest with you, George. I haven't quite worked it out yet. I just know these kids ought to come out of this thing with more than assorted attempts on their damn lives."

Next to me, Matthew Hurley took a deep breath that seemed to make him grow taller. "Why don't we turn it over to the USA, Mr. Hammer? Let the rogue nations come after the Goliath bone. There's nothing this country can't handle."

"Fine," I said. "Check back with me after they rebuild the Trade Towers."

My burst of cynicism startled the boy. "There are efforts in progress right now to make that area a national monument."

"A multimillion-dollar piece of property in downtown Manhattan isn't going to house a flagpole and a statue. Listen, Matt . . . Jenna . . . the choice is yours."

Jenna said, "I'm not sure I'm . . . *we're* . . . ready to make that decision."

"That's fine. I don't think you should right away, myself. But I do think we need to get that bone out of this facility."

Charlene let go of her daughter's hand and sat up straight, her eyes and nostrils flaring. I almost had it for a moment, who she reminded me of . . .

She said, "Mike! Whatever selfish reasons any government

might have for laying claim to the Goliath bone, George and I want to study it only as a historical and archeological treasure."

Hurley's eyes were unblinking and hard. "I have to agree with Charlene, Mike. We agree that it belongs to the kids, but in a greater sense, it belongs to everyone."

"Well, everyone doesn't get a say in this. The bone can't stay here because, for one thing, this lab is for all intents and purposes a Federal one, meaning Uncle Sam can grab that bone and run off with it any time he feels like it. And for another thing, a terrorist cell could come into this place and, after a firefight with those guards, waltz out with the damn thing themselves."

"I don't think so," George said tightly. "These are top men. Special Forces. You said it yourself."

"Well, what if it's a terrorist cell that wants to put a stop to the Goliath bone before Israel can grab it and shake it in their faces. They might blow this whole joint up, including you, the guards, and that overgrown thighbone."

Hurley studied me for several long seconds, like I was another scrap of parchment with ancient scribbles on it. Finally he said in a flat tone of voice, "What are your intentions, Mr. Hammer?"

Not "Mike" now—"Mr. Hammer."

But it was Matthew Hurley who caught the ball. He said, "Dad, Mike is right—that is *our* relic. Jenna and I are the sole owners of that grossly enlarged femur. Where it came from and to whom it once belonged is pure speculation, but its discovery belongs to us. We're as interested in its history as you are, but its disposition is rightfully ours."

The parents looked from Matthew to Jenna, who nodded firmly. Good kids. My kind of clients.

I thought Matthew's father might turn on him like a snake, but

Hurley's face softened and he gave a slight shrug and told the boy, "Damned if you don't sound just like me when I was your age. Okay, son—what have you got in mind?"

"Ask Mike."

Hurley turned to me. "Mike?"

"Mike" again. Nice to see that Dad and Mom put their kids first and science/history second.

I said, "I'd like to have three copies made of that bone."

The Doctors Hurley gaped at me.

"By copies," I said, "I mean exact duplicates. I know you have the facilities right here to perform that kind of work, and in museums I've seen some of the results that satisfy the casual viewer. But the kind of duplication I'm talking about can be handled by only a few experts, and they aren't tied into any university."

This time Charlene responded, and her response had a certain haughtiness. "Oh? And where would these so-called experts be?"

"Hollywood."

Now they were all gaping at me, except for Velda, of course.

"You must be joking," Hurley said. "Matthew, are you going along with this?"

Matthew swallowed. I gave him a hard-eyed smile. Then the kid grinned and said to his dad, "Yeah. Whatever Mike says."

I told the Hurleys, "Tomorrow have that bone ready to be turned over. Spend the rest of today and tonight going nuts with your research—knock yourself out. In the meantime, I'll be with the group taking the pickup and will sign off for the transfer. Either Jenna or Matthew, the owners and discoverers of the bone, will be with me. The reason we're here is to establish ownership of that bone, and you've already certified that fact. Hell, it's all in the family, so nothing's out of the bag. Let's keep it that way."

"We're to pretend we still have the bone?" Hurley asked.

"Yes. I plan to play an elaborate game of button-button-who's-got-the-button with the factions after this thing. And you'll be getting the original back eventually. Till then, who's to know, as tight as you're locked down here?"

Hurley swallowed and said, "You want me to lie to the government?"

"You're not under oath. Hell, don't lie—just mislead. Anyway, no governmental agency has put a hold on that bone, have they?"

"Mr. Hammer," Hurley said challengingly, "the United States government has sponsored the works of this institution to the tune of countless millions of dollars. You're asking me to risk that."

"You're risking your own reputations, maybe, for the sake of your kids. Not the university's."

I glanced at Jenna and Matthew. Just a flick of the eyes. Their expressions seemed mildly amused, as if they were enjoying the moment. For a second it occurred to me that living in the shadow of a pair of geniuses like their parents could have been a tiresome job.

Charlene, her momentary haughtiness gone, said, "George—if Mike thinks this strategy will help protect our kids, perhaps even enrich them . . . we need to go along."

I said, "Look at it this way, Dad—your kids found the buried treasure. Let them benefit."

I stood and so did everybody else.

"Tomorrow," I told the white-smocked parents. "The pickup will be at nine in the morning. Have Goliath bubble-wrapped and boxed, keep a copy of the papers you will sign, and when the duplicates are ready, you'll get his leg back. And don't screw around with this. Old Goliath isn't just a historical relic—he's the unholy grail."

Chapter 6

We made like sardines again on the elevator—Velda, the kids, the security team, and me—and took the one-floor ride up to the anonymously modern lobby of the NYU research center, where I asked the khaki-clad guard at my side if I could speak to the head of security.

He was a blue-eyed buzz-cut young soldier who with one hand could kill most people. With me, it would have taken two hands. When I was his age, he'd have been in trouble.

"Sir," he said, "I'm not authorized to do that."

"You're not authorized *not* to do it, either," I said with a grin. "I must be a VIP to warrant this attention, right? So trust in the other seven of you that they can handle me and one woman and a couple of college kids till you get back."

He almost grinned himself, but, after a moment of hesitation, he said he would call it in, then stepped away from us and spoke into the button mike on his jacket lapel.

When he returned to my side he said, "Mr. Rogers will be right down."

"So that's whose neighborhood we're in."

I got him that time. The kid grinned and said, "Yes, sir, it is. But he doesn't have my outstanding sense of humor, sir."

"I'll keep that in mind."

The blue-eyed guard stayed right with us until I heard elevator doors *snick* open then *snick* shut and Mr. Rogers strode into the lobby, and he wasn't wearing a sweater and sneakers. He wasn't in khaki, either, merely the kind of black business suit with black tie that you usually only see Feds, morticians, and hipsters wearing.

He was five-ten and maybe fifty-five, with just the broad shoulders to give away anything unusual about him, and only his seldom-blinking slate gray eyes separated him from a guy selling you insurance.

I knew this guy was some sort of an ex-cop from the way he walked and the characteristic expression he wore—not mad, not overjoyed, simply indifferent; not biased in any way.

The blue-eyed guard said, "This is Mr. Hammer, sir. He's part of the Hurley party—the rest are by the door there."

Velda, Matthew, and Jenna were standing on this side of the security checkpoint, the kids wondering what I was up to; Velda had long since stopped bothering trying.

Mr. Rogers didn't hold out his hand to shake mine. This was business, and business on his turf. It was a rough business and a private turf, and a man like Rogers kept his hands ready for more than a pointless ritual between strangers.

He spoke carefully in a mid-range, toneless voice. "Mr. Hammer, you're a private investigator, I understand."

"Want to see my ticket?"

"Not necessary. Dr. George Hurley has already cleared you. He's made it clear I'm to cooperate with you."

"Nice to hear."

"But I don't answer to Dr. Hurley. So you'll understand that you don't have carte blanche here at this facility."

"Wouldn't expect it. I'm glad to see you run a tight ship."

A tiny flicker in the slate-color eyes indicated he was processing that remark for sarcasm or condescension. When he came up empty, he said, "Well, then, Mr. Hammer—what can I help you with?"

"Could you spare me a few minutes? No more than five."

He studied my face just a little more thoroughly than the Hurleys downstairs were studying the Goliath bone. Then he nodded. Once.

We moved away from the guards, Velda, the kids, and the security checkpoint. He gestured to a sleek pine modernistic bench by the tinted glass wall of windows, and I sat. Then he sat.

I said, "How tight *is* security? I saw you hesitate when I complimented you on the security situation here."

There was another slight pause before he answered me. Then: "As tight as they could make it."

Now my nastiest grin blossomed. "But not as tight as *you* could make it."

His lips twitched slightly and his eyes darted briefly toward Velda, Matthew, and Jenna, but they were too far away to hear what he was saying. His eyes looked into mine and he was satisfied with what he saw there.

He told me, "Police work—security operations—have to be absolute if they are to be functional."

He might have been giving a sermon. I think he knew he was preaching to the choir.

I nodded vaguely around the high-ceilinged lobby. "How easy would it be to break into this place?"

"Not easy at all."

"But it *is* possible?"

"Probably for an expert, yes."

"You're not just talking about a commando action, or a terrorist bombing?"

"No. I'm not."

"There's a hole in the wall somewhere, isn't there?"

His smile was so faint, it almost wasn't there. "What makes you think so, Mr. Hammer?"

I let him see another nasty grin and shook my head. "Because there always is. A university building is not designed to be a military guardhouse. It has *guards,* all right, but it is purely a civilian structure, and it always has at least one hole in it."

The seconds ticked by while our eyes stayed locked. Finally his head bobbed slightly and he said, "I think I *will* take a look at your ticket, Mr. Hammer."

In seconds I had my leather folder out, the one I use on rich clients, where the state license from New York was displayed over the permit to carry a concealed weapon. He didn't have to read it. Mr. Rogers *knew,* and a slow smile took some of the hardness out of his face. This time he held out his hand and we shook, a private cop and an old ex–city cop.

"Why'd you want to check my ticket?" I said. "You recognized me from the start."

"Maybe I wanted to see if you were still licensed after all this time and after everything you've pulled. Haven't seen much about you in the papers for maybe, what—ten years? Not till that subway shooting the other day, anyway."

"Maybe you got some beer-drinking buddies you want to tell you met Mike Hammer. Be sure to let 'em know I'm even uglier in person."

That actually got a chuckle out of him. "I retired out of the two-seven as a captain before I took this job. Heard about you, Mr. Hammer, over the years—never had a chance to meet the wild man himself before. Really did have to check your creds, though—there are a lot of look-alikes on the streets these days."

"Nobody looks like this but me, pal."

"Maybe not. But you'd be surprised the sophisticated stuff that's been pulled. There was a heist here just two months ago."

"Here? No kidding."

"Whatever it is the Hurleys are studying right now, Mr. Hammer, is only one of the many precious artifacts housed within these walls in my time on this job."

"What got snatched?"

"That's not for public consumption."

"Do I look like the public?"

His sigh was small but large with weariness. "Somebody heisted a moon-rock specimen out of here."

"Had to be an inside job."

"Most likely, but who do we put the finger on? Do you think the university would allow a real investigation involving their precious academics? People like the Hurleys are superstars in their fields—Nobel Prizes come cheap around here."

"You got a suspect?"

"Hell, I *know* who did it."

"Too high up the ladder here to expose?"

He shook his head and, in the same quiet tone, told me, "Not even a full professor. Probably wanted it for his personal collection.

Intellectually brilliant and a specialist in his area, but a moral midget."

"You'll get the rock back, then? You've let him know that *you* know, right?"

"Right. I was a cop long enough to know how to play the intimidation game without going over the line. Very soon that precious chunk of green cheese will show up in an obscure place where it could just very *possibly* have been overlooked."

"So he didn't have to use the hole in the wall."

"No."

"But somebody, someday, could."

"Yes."

"Can I see it?"

"Of course," he said, and stood.

Velda stayed with Matthew and Jenna while Mr. Rogers and I exited under a canopy and down the sidewalk out onto the street, turned right, walked to the corner, and turned right again. Trucks came in this way, and one was still at the loading dock, a pair of burly jumpsuited guys moving a series of wooden crates from the tailgate into the building.

On each side of the dock stood a university guard in navy blue, both young, muscular-looking and armed. These were not the khaki-clad Special Forces types that had been brought in to supplement the existing security staff with the need for heightened security the Goliath bone represented. But they looked efficient enough.

"What are they carrying?" I asked Mr. Rogers.

".38 Police Positives."

"Light weaponry, these days," I offered.

"Enough to keep the riffraff away. Besides, it's university regs. They're not interested in lawsuits."

I shook my head, amazed by their stupidity. "What, do they think a .38 caliber can't kill you dead?"

"I won't pretend to understand the civilian bureaucrat mentality, Mr. Hammer. But they would never allow something as deadly sounding as a Glock or an AK-47."

"How about a good old-fashioned .45?"

"Now there's a man's piece," he said, and laughed. Who said he had no sense of humor? "If the slug doesn't do the job, you can always knock the bastard's brains out with the butt."

We were bonding.

He pawed the air and smiled. "Come on around that truck, Mr. Hammer." His voice dropped to a whisper. "I'll show you the Trojan Horse walkway into this place."

The door was a painted metal face set into the brickwork with the flush look of old-time stability, a closure that would resist the impact from a small tank. It was hinged from the inside so there was no way you could get the door off. The brickwork that surrounded it was thick, pure granite that no intruder would want to mess with.

"Where does it lead, Mr. Rogers?"

"To a damned latrine. A pair of toilet bowls, two sinks, and a ten-foot long urinal. Made for the construction workers when they built the place."

I started grinning.

"What's so damn funny?"

"Wouldn't happen to also be an inside door in that latrine that leads into a corridor of the building? Maybe covered over, probably with sheetrock and painted . . . that nobody knows is there? Or hardly nobody."

His forehead frowned and his mouth smiled. "You've seen the original blueprints, have you?"

"No, but I've been to the rodeo a whole bunch of damn times. Am I right?"

His nod was almost imperceptible.

"Why don't you ask me what else I'm not supposed to see?"

"Sure." His hands were on his hips; his eyes were narrowed. "How would you get in?"

"That's an idiot door," I told him. "It was built a century ago and locked with an idiot lock. Under that paint job is a plugged keyhole you can't see, but it's right where a keyhole should be. You want me to open it now?"

"Wise guy," Mr. Rogers said. But he was grinning now.

"Have you suggested a reinforcement?"

"The Board of Directors live in the past, Mike. They pooh-poohed the idea. The door was tight, didn't even rattle, no access has ever been attempted, and they were running on a budget."

"They got enough money to X-ray my ass when I come calling on that lab downstairs." I shook my head. "Any other soft spots?"

"Not that I know of. Why the Twenty Questions, Mr. Hammer?"

"Because we're in a war, friend. The enemy has racked up a solid score so far, and they're looking to take another bite out of the Big Apple."

"Well, shit, if they get near here they're going to run into some damn heavy fire, anyway."

"Dying is their pleasure, buddy. They shoot right up to paradise. They think."

"We'll be glad to give them a boost." Then he frowned. "What the hell would terrorists be wanting around here?"

"Why do you think you were provided those Special Forces boys to beef up your staff all of a sudden? The Hurleys are dealing with a relic of interest to a certain part of the world that would be goddamn worthless if a shitload of oil weren't bubbling beneath it."

"Mr. Hammer—"

"Make it Mike."

"And I'm Dan. Mike, this facility has superior security—"

"With you in charge, Dan, I'd have to agree."

". . . as far as it goes. The research done here involves precious—sometimes priceless—artifacts. With the exception of my temporary new staff members, we're chiefly set up for the kind of security a major museum might have. But we're not cut out for a terrorist incursion."

"Yeah. I know. But I figured you wouldn't mind getting a heads-up."

"Not at all, Mike. Really appreciate it, though I don't know what I can *do* about it."

We walked back to the main lobby where Velda and the kids waited and I told Dan Rogers I'd see him in the morning. The rugged ex-cop had a tight expression as he nodded so long, and our little group went out to the van with its Secure Solutions driver and a guard who rode shotgun. And when that guard rode shotgun, he rode shotgun.

The new safe-house was on a cross street near the Garment District, a five-room furnished apartment, one of half a dozen the security outfit maintained in Manhattan. I had the driver and guard wait down with the van and Velda and the kids, while I went up and made sure the premises were intact and empty.

Nobody with guns was waiting this time around. And the place should suit the kids since it was furnished like a damn college dorm room.

The two security guys stayed with the van for now. Eventually one of them would come upstairs to babysit brother and sister. For the moment it was just Velda and me with them. Velda and Jenna went off into the small kitchen to make coffee and rustle up some sandwiches, while I sat next to Matthew on a flimsy sofa in a living room furnished like a page in an IKEA catalog.

This was my first chance to talk to Matthew away from Jenna. I put a hand on his shoulder. "You doing all right, son? Some pretty tough sledding."

His smile was lopsided. "It is a little weird. Jenna seems fine during the day, but she cries at night."

"But you're there to comfort her, right?"

"Right. Uh . . . Mr. Hammer, I told you before, my parents don't know about us, and if they ever find out, I don't know what they'll do."

I scowled at him. "Stop thinking of yourself as a kid. You're a grown man, Matt, and Jenna's a grown woman. Your folks'll get over it."

"Dad may. But—"

"But what?"

"Nothing."

"You don't get along with your stepmother, do you, Matt?"

"We . . . we get along okay."

"Hell you do. You resent her for stealing your Dad away from your Mom."

He didn't argue the point.

I asked, "Where is your real mother now?"

"She died. She . . . she killed herself."

"Sorry, Matt. Hell, I had no idea."

"She was a teacher, too, but not in my father's area, or league. She taught high-school English. And she was devoted to Dad. But she didn't share his work life the way Charlene does."

"Charlene. You don't call her 'Mom'?"

"No. Listen, I was in middle school when Dad left Mom, and I didn't handle it very well. Mom wasn't perfect. She had a drinking problem. Who am I kidding? She was an alcoholic. She kept it away from her work, but every evening, she got awful sloppy. And when things got rocky between her and Dad, she really began to fall apart."

"So you took it out on your stepmother?"

"Yeah. I suppose I did. As I got older, I realized I'd been, well, a real jerk, and tried to make up for it. But no matter what I try or say, she's never warmed up to me. Oh, she's nice to my face, but I know she says terrible things about me to Dad, behind my back."

"How do you know?"

"I just do. She's terribly two-faced. She pretends to be nice, and then puts me on the spot with Dad in any number of sneaky ways . . . hard to explain."

"Not really, Matt. It's an old story. Jenna knows how you feel?"

"Yeah, and it's . . . kind of a sore point between us. She doesn't want to hear me rag on her mother, and I guess I can't blame her."

"And you think when your stepmother finds out about you and Jenna, the shit'll hit the fan?"

He nodded. "That woman could really drive a wedge between me and Dad. She's tried before, but I've always managed to stay pretty tight with him."

I patted his shoulder. "Fathers and sons have their problems. But nothing can come between them, not if they really *are* tight."

His eyes pleaded with me. "What do you think I should do, Mr. Hammer? Tell Dad? That assumes I can get him off *alone* somewhere—Charlene's *always* around."

"If it was me? Soon as Goliath is history again, I'd grab that girl and run off with her."

"Elope?"

"You really think your folks'll want a big wedding? 'Matthew, do you take your sister for your lawful wedded wife?'"

His eyes widened, then rolled. "Good point, Mr. Hammer. Good point."

The green metal cartridge case sat on Velda's desk, the lid open so the smaller cardboard containers that held fifty rounds of .45 ammunition each looked like an ornamental display. A chemically fragrant smell hung over the brass-and-lead ampoules like a perfume of death.

On the side of the metal case were stenciled white letters and numbers, denoting where these babies were destined for. But that was back in 1945. The year of manufacture was there, too. Maybe a great researcher could track this antique back to the last owner, but I didn't have the time nor the aptitude to go that lengthy route.

For a long while, Velda sat perched on the edge of her own desk, watching me camped out there in her swivel chair. When she thought I'd spent enough time looking at a damn box without doing anything about it, she blurted, "Don't you have *any* idea who sent that, Mike?"

And that was when I knew.

It was somebody who had access to cartridge cases of old but unused .45s.

It was somebody who knew me pretty damn well.

It was somebody who had something to tell me and wanted to make sure I was interested enough to trace it out.

When I first knew him, Dick Mallory had been a wheeler-dealer kid tossed out of the Army on a bad-conduct charge. He had then managed to grab off loads of surplus military equipment when Vietnam was winding down. In one week, he had parlayed nine hundred bucks into ten thousand, and tripled that a week later. Two months later, he had opened three outlets and was on his way to being a millionaire. Unfortunately, he drank. And he gambled. And he got in with the wiseguys of Manhattan and supplied them with artillery he never should have had in his inventory.

So the NYPD nailed Dick Mallory and sent him up for a bunch of years, and when they set him loose, he went back to his old business. This time he catered to hunters who had converted military equipment to sporting gear. It was an idea I had given him half-jokingly over beers, and it was working great until he started up his old ways on the side. When Pat arrested him for selling a dozen sound suppressors for common handguns to known underworld figures, I loaned Dick five hundred bucks for an attorney who didn't do him any good.

Velda said, "Is that a thought I see on your face, Mike, or just gas pains?"

"Let me make a call." I pulled the phone over and dialed Pat's office. There was a two-minute wait that I drummed my fingers through before he said, "Captain Chambers here."

"Hiya Pat. I need a favor, and fast."

"You always do. What's up?"

"Do a rundown on Dick Mallory for me, will you?"

"That low-life scum? Isn't he still inside?"

"That's one of the things you can find out for me, pal. It's pretty important."

His suspicion leached over the phone wires like steam. "Where do you tie in with an incarcerated gunrunner, anyway?"

"Beats me. He sent me a present with no return address, and I'd like to thank him for it."

"And I'm supposed to believe that?"

"I'm not yanking your chain, Pat. Dickie bird sent me something, and I'd at least like to know what he's up to. Plus, I'd like to get that five hundred bucks back."

"What did he send you, Mike?"

"Aw, it's not big enough to bother you with, Pat. Captain of Homicide and all."

"Sure. I'm above such things. I have other matters to attend to, like tracking down info on the scumbag likes of Dick Mallory."

"So we're on the same page, then?"

"Go to hell." Then he told me wearily, "I'll call you back."

I hung up and looked up at Velda, whose nyloned legs were crossed and lovely as she sat on the edge of that desk, an alluring distraction. She had opened one of the cartridge boxes and was rolling a .45 slug between her fingers.

"Somehow that seems dirty," I said, "the way you do it."

She gave me one of those lush smiles. "Then I haven't lost my touch?"

"Put it back," I growled.

She replaced the bullet as the phone on her desk rang. I answered it myself.

Pat said, "Mallory is in Bellevue. Somebody knifed him as he was leaving the joint. Guy seemed to know when Dick was being released and was waiting. Stuck in the shiv, jumped in a waiting car, and took off."

"Some welcoming committee. Dick just lay there with a shiv in him?"

"No, the perp yanked it out and took it with him. Luckily, that blade didn't hit anything vital, but left one hell of a wound. Mallory got to his feet just as a visitor from the city came up in a taxi, and he grabbed that, but the driver saw him gasping and gagging in the backseat, saw him wipe his bloody hand across his face and then dumped his ass off at the hospital. He's there right now."

"Thanks, Pat. I owe you."

"You think?"

They had Dick Mallory in a semiprivate room with a wrinkled old man in the next bed; the old boy's breath rasped like a warm-up to a death rattle. Dick had a prison pallor and stark white hair and was a lot thinner than I remembered him; he was maybe twenty years younger than me and looked a good ten years older.

I took the padded chair beside the bed and stared at him and, when I let out a little cough, he opened his eyes, watched me for half a minute, then let his mouth split in a grin. "Got my mail, eh?"

"Where did you get that stuff? Man, those babies are antiques."

"Got a warehouse full of that vintage ammo. Oldies but goodies. I called my manager and told him just what to pick out and just where to send it."

"Why the subterfuge, Dick?"

"Hell, man, maybe I just wanted to see if you were still good enough to figure things out."

"It wasn't too hard, Dick. I'm a detective, remember? And now I'm here."

"You're here, Mike."

"*Why* am I here? I'm asking *you*, Dick, not the sky."

I got another grin out of him. Bigger this time. "Payback time for that five hundred bucks, maybe."

"It didn't do you much good at the time," I reminded him.

"Sure it did. Showed me I had one real friend, at least. Who didn't judge me. Who knew, for all my faults, I was loyal to my friends. Like you, Mike. Nobody ever had a better friend."

"You can throw me a dinner when you get out."

"*If* I get out, Mike. You still friends with that Captain Chambers?"

"Yeah, sure. That's how I tracked you down."

"Would you ask Chambers to put a cop on my door, till I'm out of the woods?"

"He'll want a reason, Dick."

"You listen to what I have to say, Mike, and see if you don't think I got a reason."

I guess anybody who had a guy waiting at the prison gate with a shiv ready had a good excuse to want a guard on his hospital-room door.

"Okay, Dick. I'll talk to Pat. Now give me the big *why*."

His face got somber. "Mike, you are on a very special, really god-damn *bad* hit list. Badder than this they don't come. You know that? Anybody clue you in yet?"

I shrugged. "It's not the first time."

"No, but it could be the *last* time."

"So who wants me?"

His smile was slight, his eyes narrowed. "You've never been in the joint, have you, Mike?"

"Only as a visitor."

"They got groups in there, you know." He saw me frowning and added, "Racial groups, I mean, and political groups. They stay separated. Black power, white Nazis, yellow yakuza. They keep to themselves except when there's trouble. Lots of hate inside, Mike."

I nodded again, wondering just where he was going.

He continued, "Remember back in the '60s and '70s, when so many blacks got on board the Muslim train?"

Again, I didn't answer him with words. He could see the interest in my eyes.

"To me, Mike, it was always horseshit, some damn fad to set them apart from whitey." He sat up a little in the bed, grimaced, then got settled and his eyes fixed on me, glittering. "But then in come some *real* believers. Muslims from the other side of the world. Man, these guys were something else. Really put some life in their group. Before long the black Muslims had thrown in with the brown ones, and they were all running the damn show in there. Don't ask how they did it, but they recruited some of the nastiest sons of bitches in the yard. They made laws and rules, and if you broke them, you got the hell beat out of you, if you were lucky, and dead, if you weren't."

"You ever catch any grief, Dick?"

"Man, I stayed away from everybody. I worked the prison library, and all I did with my spare time was read. They usually didn't bother with loners like me. A couple of these boys kept talking to me, though—said they could tell I was smart, because I liked books. They said wild things, like how they were going to smite the infidels and rule the world, and all that kind of garbage."

"You take any of this serious?"

"After the Trade Towers got knocked down, and that plane dived into the Pentagon, you bet your ass I did. Didn't never join them, though, not even just pretending. A lot of the cons got real interested, but all this holy-war crapola scared the hell out of me. I understand wanting money and power, but killing and dying 'cause of your *religion*? That's some scary shit, Mike."

I asked him, "Were these guys American nationals or immigrants?"

Mallory shifted into a more comfortable position. "A lot of them only spoke one foreign language or another—I think a couple of varieties were goin' down. Others had an accent."

"From what *country*, Dick?"

"Syria, I think. Some were Saudis, though."

"You didn't bring me here to tell me the Arab Muslims have their own gang groups in prisons now, did you, Dick? Because I knew that already."

"No. No, this is something else." His voice lowered, as if he were afraid the raspy old coot in the next bed might be a spy. "A while back, one of their foreign lawyers came in to see Ali, the head Muslim inside? And whatever that shyster told him set Ali on fire. He had a big meeting in the yard with all his pet followers and damned if they didn't catch fire, too. I thought we were gonna have a full-scale riot. Jihad on the cell block. Enough to make a guy go straight."

"What was it about?" I got in.

Dick was damn near breathless. "It wasn't until one of our own guys got the message, because he could speak their language, too . . . and told us that somebody had found . . . I *swear* this is what he said, Mike . . . 'the great bone of Goliath.'"

"When did you hear this, Dick?"

"Two days ago. I got out just two days ago. What does it mean, Mike? Is it some kind of code?"

"No."

"Are they talking about the same Goliath dude they told us about when we were in Sunday school?"

"The same."

"And did two kids find it?"

"Right. College kids. This you heard inside, Dick?"

Mallory nodded, twice. "And these kids shipped it back to the States?"

"Right."

"And *you* helped them, Mike? You . . . shot one of the Muslim cats? That all for true, Mike?"

"You got it."

His eyes narrowed into slits and he told me, "They're gonna kill you, Mike. They know all about you and are planning to get you out of the action before they make their next move."

"Oh?"

"They're going to get that bone, Mike. It's the most important thing in their lives. It's going back to where it belongs."

"And they figure they have to kill me first."

"You don't want to know how many of these Muslim prisoners want to kill your ass, Mike. You got your hands on their bone, baby. Inside the joint a lot of the cons know you—hell, you even helped put some of them there. They told the Arab cons you wouldn't be a pushover . . . but those bastards couldn't care less. You were going down, along with whoever was with you, and they, the Muslim gangers? They were on the way up."

"Like to paradise?"

"That's how I took it."

I grinned at him and said, "Those guys are going to be in the pen for a long time, aren't they?"

Dick thought a second, then nodded.

"Unless they want to be the cheering section, what can *they* do?"

"They believe their people will free them, that's what."

"You believe that, Dick?"

"Hell, no. Their people'll let them rot in there. Is there a shortage of crazy-ass Arabs in the world so that you need to bust some out?"

I changed the subject. "So who knifed you, buddy?"

He twitched a humorless smirk. "Just some guy, some dark-skinned prick."

"Black or Arab?"

"Arab. But he was dressed American."

"He may *be* an American. Could you identify him?"

"Hell, no. I only had a quick look at him. Mostly I just saw the blade—it was long and sharp and flashed in the sunlight."

"Why did he try to nail you, you think?"

Dick Mallory closed his eyes for thirty seconds or so, thinking, then opened them abruptly. "That's why I called you, Mike, more than anything. Why I resorted to, like you said, subterfuge. One of the black Muslim fellas inside used to work for me on the outside. This guy knew I was your friend. And here I was getting out."

"You figure they figured you might warn me."

"Just like I did, yeah." He shivered. "I spent my last night worried I'd get a shiv between the ribs before I had a chance to see the other side of the walls. I skipped meals. I didn't even take a damn shower. And I got out without getting wasted, all right . . . but it didn't take them long to reach me after I got out, did it? Hell, right outside the prison gates. First damn day back on the pavement."

I stood. "Thanks for this, Dick."

He gave me a ragged grin. "So we square, Mike? I give you five hundred worth?"

"Oh, yeah, Dick," I said. "With interest."

At a quarter to five in the morning, the phone rang. It was a small, muted sound that didn't jar you awake, but was like a small scratching on your back.

Without waking Velda, who had fallen asleep on the sofa beside me in my apartment, I picked up the receiver and very quietly said, "MHI alerted."

"Got the voice mail, pal," was the answer.

It was Paul Vernon, my archeologist buddy in Los Angeles, who in a celebrated career had assembled the bones of some of the specimens of dinosaur remains found in the great museums of the world. Right now he was doing some work in the tar pits in Los Angeles for USC.

I asked him, "You tied up?"

"Those remains in the tar down there aren't going anywhere— why? Dinosaur turn up in Manhattan?"

"Just me. How would you like to work on making duplicates of the most significant find of this new century?"

"How . . . significant?" he asked me softly.

"You'd never believe it."

"Try me," he probed.

"How about all that's left of a certain big lug who died in the Valley of Elah some time ago?"

The pause just hung there.

Finally he said, "We talking . . . NBA big?"

"Yeah, if NBA guys were built like NFL linemen."

"Holy . . ."

"Yeah, holy something. Listen, Paul, I need duplications. Can do?"

"No problem, pal." He paused again, just briefly, then asked, "How quickly?"

"As fast as possible without compromising the job," I told him. "How soon can you get here to pick up the item?"

He didn't question my asking him to come cross-country to make the pickup personally.

"There's planes leaving L.A. for New York all the time," he said casually. "I'll snag the first one. Where do you want me to meet you?"

"The office," I told him. "Still at the same old stand. Hackard Building, remember?"

"Sure do. By the way, who am I supposed to be?"

He didn't have to be told he'd need a cover.

"Make like a messenger, Paul. You'll be handling a package . . . a big one."

Chapter 7

The day was cold but sunny, the snow dissipated by the rain. My trench coat had the winter lining out as my way of trying to trick winter into an early spring. But my breath still smoked like I hadn't given up that filthy habit half a lifetime ago.

The Secure Solutions vehicle was parked at the rear doors of the university's research facility, just a plain white Ford van that attracted no attention on the street, but "plain" applied only to its exterior. Its walls were fireproof and bulletproof, and its mechanical attributes would have kept it in competition on a drag strip. The driver and two helpers were armed and under their uniforms were the kind of physiques that came from regular professional workouts in major gyms.

Dan Rogers said to me, "Mike, what do you need an army tank like this for?"

"Peace of mind," I told him. "Last week Secure Solutions delivered eighty million dollars' worth of cut diamonds to a major jewelry firm. A hijack attempt came up empty. All the rocks got to their destination."

Rogers frowned. "Did I read something about that in the papers?"

"If you mean a story about four diamond thieves getting shot to shit, you probably did."

The open rear doors of the van that fitted into the dock obscured the operation. The pine box that contained the remains of Goliath slid unnoticed into the truck, the driver nodded at me, and I walked up with Rogers behind me and we both could see the unmarked backup vehicle through the window behind the driver's seat.

I took the clipboard, signed it below six other signatures of persons who had handled the box in transit, had Rogers sign, and handed the clipboard back.

The driver, a husky guy about thirty, looked at me curiously and said, "Mike, you sure get us into some oddball situations."

Rogers asked him, "You know Mr. Hammer?"

"Sure. Last delivery we made for him was a body in a fifty-five–gallon drum that'd been dumped in the East River."

"Johnny DeAngelo," I said with a nod. "You should remember him, Dan."

"Yeah," the driver added. "Our divers found him, and we hauled him out of there. Quite an operation."

The university security chief was squinting at me like maybe I was a desert oasis. But he said to the driver, "How the hell did you find that drum, son, in all that water?"

"Oh, Mr. Hammer knew right where to look."

The driver went back to his work, and Rogers smiled slyly and said to me, "Sounds like there's a story there."

"That was also in the papers," I reminded him. "How that body was found, and DeAngelo's uncle got nailed for it."

"That's not the story I meant."

I heard a horn honk, and my attention went to Velda in the driver's seat of my car, with her fingers clenched at the wheel. She nodded for me to come around and powered down the window, and I leaned in like a carhop.

"Something glinting on that rooftop, Mike," she said, and the direction her eyes were cast encouraged me to take a seemingly casual glance that way.

"Binoculars?" I asked, smiling at her like we were just having a friendly chat.

"Or sniperscope," she said, smiling back but with her dark eyes anything but smiling.

Rogers betrayed nothing in his posture, but his voice let us know he'd gone into tightly coiled mode. "You want me to round up those Special Forces boys? Or pull some of this Secure Solutions outfit off the line?"

I straightened and yawned. "I don't think so. You know every building on that block, right? So you can get the two of us up on top of that building?"

"I can do that."

I went over to the driver of the van and told him not to pull out yet.

"But we're ready to go, Mr. Hammer."

"I need to take care of something first. Wait for my word."

"You got it."

I went back to my car where Rogers waited at Velda's rolled-down window. "Let's take a little spin," I said.

I got in on the passenger side, Rogers climbed in back, and Velda pulled out. New York traffic is never cooperative, so by the time she had dropped us off in the alley behind that building, over five minutes had passed. Since I was the only potential target of value—everybody else on the scene was either loading that truck or working security—no sniper would have any reason to start picking anybody off.

Not that terrorists were likely to be fussy.

Still, my guess was we had a watcher on our hands, that we'd find a character with binoculars, checking out that truck and maybe informing somebody by cell phone that something important was getting offloaded at the university research center. Something that required babysitters packing heavy firepower.

The building across the way was a hotel. We were in the lower recesses, where the maids, maintenance men, and food-service personnel inhabited their own stark personal world, a maze of featureless cement hallways that Rogers seemed to know like the streets of his hometown. We encountered security staff who knew my guide well, and who saw to it that we had a service elevator to ourselves and a key card that would unlock any door.

The rooftop had a pool that this time of year was covered with a tarp dotted with clumps of snow that had survived the rain, with an apron of cement free of deck chairs, stored inside somewhere.

Standing at a galvanized-wire fence with his back to us, our man was small, wearing a hooded black sweatshirt, blue jeans, and running shoes. He was using binoculars, all right. They were in his left hand as he gazed through them down onto the scene of the van loading, but a cell phone was in his right.

We had to walk around the covered pool to make our way to him, but when he heard us, the tarp still yawned between us. He whirled, eyes wild, though his hands went up immediately, binoculars and cell phone along for the ride.

"I am tourist!" he yelled. "I am tourist!"

"Maybe," I said, gesturing with the .45. "But don't you go anywhere . . ."

He obeyed as we came around to him. Rogers took the guy's binoculars and cell phone away. He was young, maybe twenty, and the black hair on his face was really just peach fuzz. This boy who hated Western culture was in a hooded Knicks sweatshirt, baggy Levi's, and Nikes.

"Not going to hurt you," Rogers said, and patted the kid down. "He's clean, Mike."

"Don't kill me," our prisoner said. "You don't have to kill me!"

I must have been getting soft, because I damn near felt sorry for the kid. He'd been sold a bill of goods his whole life, and now here he was in the hands of the infidels.

They might be scraggly. They might be pawns of a hideous religious zealotry. But they weren't stupid. There were thousands of them in this country, and a lot of them were moles. This damned terror campaign had been well planned out. There was more than one group orchestrating things, and there were always contingency plans and plenty of money available to them.

I said, "We'll turn him over to Immigration and let them have their fun with him."

"I'm not afraid to die," he said, changing his tune. But his fuzzy chin was trembling.

"No?" Rogers said. "'Cause of those virgins waiting for you, right? But if we cut off your wedding tackle, what good will a bunch of virgins do you?"

The security chief was just razzing the guy, but it hadn't been smart. The kid panicked and shoved Rogers, sending him off the deep end onto that snowy tarp, where he got wrapped up in it, sinking into the empty pool.

My .45 was in hand but I didn't want to shoot this kid and, anyway, we might find something out from him. But he was in the worst kind of state—scared shitless about what would happen if we hauled him in, and fearless otherwise.

He came at me screaming, and clawing, and I batted him away with the .45, carving a bright red gash in his dark cheek. His eyes were wild as he prepared another charge, and that's when he saw himself looking down the long dark corridor to nowhere that starts at the end of a .45.

And froze.

For a moment I thought he might start to cry.

"Don't make me do it, kid," I said.

He heard the mercy in the words but saw the hardness in my eyes. And I guess he didn't want an infidel taking him out, because in a blur of motion, he scrambled and slipped over that wire fence and off the building and fell with a cry that might have been *"Alllahhh!"* or maybe it was just a terrified scream.

I heard him hit with a metallic crunch followed by the hysterical bleat of a car alarm and when I got to the wire fence to look down over, I could see him, thirty stories below, splayed across what not long ago had been a mint-condition late-model Thunderbird.

Rogers made an absurd swimming motion as he crawled across and up the sunken tarp, and I leaned down and held out a hand to pull him from the empty pool.

"What the hell happened?" he asked.

"Something terrible."

"What?"

"Perfectly good ride got ruined."

Most people don't understand the complexities of the federal government. In a matter of minutes the Feds can assemble every item of a person and his lifestyle, punch it into computers, and come up with a detailed analysis that would give them an insight into anything they wanted to know.

There is no such thing as privacy anymore. Everyone's existence is completely open to bureaucratic scrutiny and what Uncle Sam doesn't know, his minions can suppose, and that supposition can be designated as fact.

Don't try to lie. They already know the answers. Embellish the facts and they'll nail you to the wall. The only way you can beat them is to keep your mouth shut and play dumb. Not real dumb, just casually dumb. It isn't easy, but it works.

The two bright-eyed, rosy-cheeked young men in dark suits, smart shirts, and foulard ties who sat opposite me in the client's chairs had introduced themselves and shown their Homeland Security credentials without being asked. They weren't being polite. It was supposed to intimidate me.

So I took my .45 out from my shoulder holster, laid it on the desk while I tugged out my wallet, and flashed them my New York State PI's license. They just gave it and me the fish eye, but the way I slid the old, well-oiled Colt .45 back in its leather gave them something to think about.

At least they were polite. Harvey Leland, the one with the tight curly hair, started the conversation: "This young man this morning—can you give us the details?"

"Have you spoken to Captain Chambers?" Of course I knew they had.

Leland nodded.

"Well, I don't have anything to add. If the cops have it, you're going to want to confiscate that kid's cell phone and give it the full treatment. He was getting ready to report to somebody."

"What was that young man doing on that rooftop?"

"You'd have to ask him. *If* you could ask him."

"You were at the university when you spotted him."

"Actually, my secretary spotted a glint of glass on the rooftop. We were visiting the Hurleys. After the subway incident, I've taken their kids under my protective wing."

The one with the GI haircut said, "All right, then, Mr. Hammer. Let's *start* with the subway incident. What made you think the man you shot at in the subway—"

I stopped him right there. "I didn't shoot at *him*. I shot at his gun, and hit it."

The youthful forehead creased. "Wouldn't that have been a difficult shot?"

"Not for me." I nodded toward the trophy plaques on the wall. "If I'd wanted to kill the son of a bitch, I would have taken him out with a head shot. If you've done your homework, gentlemen, you know I'm capable."

For a few seconds, neither had anything to say.

Harvey Leland coughed gently into his palm, then asked, "Did you know Matthew and Jenna Hurley prior to this individual trying to rob them?"

"Trying to *rob* them? He was running after them with a gun in his hand—a gun with a sound suppressor. This was no casual robbery, gentlemen. That guy was damned determined to get those kids."

"Why, do you suppose?"

Did they know about the Goliath bone? Surely through the federal connection to the Hurleys and the university, the word was known in Washington. Were they trying to entrap me?

"I'd just wrapped up another, unrelated case," I said non-committally.

The GI haircut Fed spoke up again. "The Hurley boy was carrying something."

"Yeah, he was."

"Did you know what he had with him?"

"Hell, I didn't know *him*. How would I know what he was lugging around? I called my friend in the NYPD, reported the incident, and we all spent much of the night at headquarters answering questions. Fully. Recorded in reports you've no doubt heard and/or read. This is old news, gentlemen—what else do you want?"

I wasn't giving them anything without direct questions. If they wanted to know what I knew, they'd have to reveal some of what they knew.

The two young agents exchanged a glance and stood up. In a way, I suppose I was an enigma to them. At the moment, they hadn't gotten a handle on anything here, but they or others like them would be back. They'd run all the details down in their minds, feed them into their computers, add in what else they found out, and they'd be back.

We shook hands once again and they left.

Velda emerged from the outer office. She stood there framed in the doorway in a white blouse and black skirt that made no attempt to be sexy, but didn't have to on that woman.

"Anything?" she asked.

I shook my head. "Fishing expedition on their part."

"How about you?" She arched an eyebrow. "Haul anything onto the deck?"

"No. But my gut says they know all about the Goliath bone . . . and yet they don't bring it up."

"What do you make of that?"

"Based on the benefit of my many years of experience, doll, I can tell you with complete confidence . . . I have no damn idea."

She smiled, shrugged, and went back to her post.

God, they'd been young. An old soldier like me had no business getting tied up in something that should have ended in the Valley of Elah a long, long time ago. I had tangled with the hoods of several generations, the creeps that had been taking civilized society apart for their own greedy benefit. I had shot some of them and some of them had shot me, but now I was standing on another battlefield, where the stakes were so much higher and all the enemy guns were loaded up with bullets whose noses spelled my name out all in caps.

And after all these years, here I was finally about to get married. And Velda? Not only did she not object to this new war, but she was ready to back me up, all the way. . . .

I picked up the phone receiver and punched in Pat's number. When he heard my hello, he asked, "Did the boys in the suits stop by?"

"We had a short talk."

"You know," he said, a chuckle in his voice, "they didn't even know who you were. Never heard of you, son."

"Fame is fleeting, Pat."

"Got time to squeeze in a late lunch at Betty's?"

"Sure."

Only there was no Betty's. That was code for a place where Pat and I could meet when things were running too damn hot to chance having anyone hear our conversation.

A couple of scarred-up chairs, a card table, and Pat Chambers were waiting for me in the back room of a squalid little barbershop that a bookie had operated out of till somebody shot him for betting he could get away with not paying off.

I'd brought two coffees along from the corner Dunkin' Donuts, and we sat there grinning at each other.

"Still at it, at our age, Mike?"

"The fun never stops, Pat."

"Someday it will. You wait and see." He sipped his coffee. "Like you thought, those .22s held a light load, Mike."

"Got to hand it to the D.C. lab boys, anyway."

"They are the best."

"Slugs domestically manufactured?"

"Plain old, plain old. Can get 'em at any gun shop."

"No lead to the shooter, I suppose?"

Pat shook his head. "The information went into the system and, if there are any matches, we'll know eventually."

"That's comforting."

He frowned. "Mike, those Homeland Security boys aren't the only interested parties in this mess. I heard from the FBI today, too. There's talk of a joint task force."

"To what end? As a sop to the public?"

He shrugged. "More like a statement to the terrorists. Counting that guy you may or may not have shot in that alley, we've got three dead Middle Eastern types and a still-at-large shooter with a .22 target pistol."

"Come on, Pat, he flew the coop."

"Well, he's not in *our* coop." Pat sighed. "Not that our saber rattling means anything to this enemy. They have their own agenda, obviously."

"Pat, what's the scoop on these government agencies?" I sipped coffee and, when he didn't reply right away, I said, "Those Homeland Security boys were awfully cute today. They didn't get much out of me out for fear I'd get something out of them."

He shrugged. "We see these spooks floating around. But my corner of Homicide isn't very involved with their kind. We get cases where we know the victim and the perps are already indicated. Now and then these Feds and spy types move in and take over—like today after that Arab kid of yours did the swan dive."

"You get anything on him before they swooped in?"

"Just that he was an illegal immigrant. Jordanian."

I shifted in the hard chair. "Pat, these Homeland kiddies didn't mention the Goliath bone. They *have* to know about it by now. But they just danced around."

"My take is these Washington spooks don't buy into it."

"What? Why the hell not?"

"They dismiss it. It's just some old artifact. Who's to say it's really Goliath, anyway?"

"That's bullshit, Pat. They're playing it down, but they know what's at stake. So nobody can prove absolutely that bone belonged to Goliath—so what? Who can prove Christ rose from the dead? Who can prove Allah wants 'infidels' like us wiped out? Proof doesn't come into it. It's faith."

Pat drew in a breath. I knew him well—he was trying to decide whether to share something with me. I gave him a look, but he just half-smiled and shook his head.

"Mike, there is this guy I know with Army Intelligence. Arab

American who's infiltrated various Islamic groups that we've been keeping under surveillance."

"Finally somebody's getting smart."

"He says that in the last forty-eight hours, there's a lot of loose talk about suitcase-size nukes. This Goliath bone of yours—"

"Of mine!"

"—this Goliath bone of yours, if it stokes the fires, God knows what we're looking at. Full-scale war in the Middle East maybe, spilling out of Iraq and into every damn where."

"Suitcase nukes, huh? Too bad they have so much trouble lining up suicide bombers, or we might have a problem."

Pat's eyebrows went up. "Two A-bombs stopped a war with Japan. One suitcase nuke could start one with some rogue state."

"They'd have to get 'em in here," I said. "We have border guards, aerial surveillance, dogs trained to sniff out any damn thing—"

"Yeah, if you're smuggling pot. Can the wishful thinking, Mike. How many thousands of miles of borders do we have to patrol? Immigrants, drugs, weapons—all that stuff comes across our patrolled lines every damn day. And you don't even want to know about cargo containers and the ports! Not if you want to sleep tonight."

I was smiling but it was glum. "I don't think sleep is what's called for. These terrorists are scattered, but they're organized. Not like us, but like wolves. They kill and destroy without concern for the consequences, and their coloration keeps them hidden."

"Sounds like somebody I know."

"I'll take that as a compliment."

Pat's gray eyes were studying me like I was a one-man lineup. "Can I ask you something, Mike? And get a straight answer?"

"Shoot."

"What was going on this morning at that NYU research center? What was a van from your playmates Secure Solutions doing there?"

"You'd have to ask the university."

"No, I'm asking *you*. You're up to something. You *moved* that damn thing, didn't you?"

I grinned at him. "What damn thing?"

"The bone, Mike. The Goliath bone."

I stood. "Come on, Pat. You know it's just some old artifact. Who's to say it's Goliath, anyway? . . . Don't thank me for the coffee. It can be your treat next time."

The first flight Paul Vernon had been able to get was a red-eye, but at least the plane landed on time. He was ambling from the gate area into the terminal when he saw me wave and picked up the pace to join Velda and me, flashing his infectious smile.

A handsome devil with a full head of salt-and-pepper hair and a purely pepper beard, he was wearing jeans and the long-sleeved gray USC sweatshirt that was his Californian's idea of being ready for a New York winter. Fortunately for him, that winter had lately thrown in the towel, trading snow for rain.

Lugging his little carry-on bag, he held out his free hand for me to shake and said, "Sure glad to see you, old buddy. Nice to see a monster that still has some flesh on its bones. . . . This must be Velda."

She smiled and gave him a kiss on the cheek, as if they were old friends, which they were, from hearing so much about each other over the years.

The three of us walked together, Paul in the middle. It was so early the restaurants and newsstands hadn't opened for business yet, and the airport was fairly underpopulated, not yet quite awake.

I asked, "Take you away from anything important?"

"Hell, no. All those bones in the tar pits have names, and the specialists have a good month's work to clean and sort them out. I'll have all the time I'll need, if this is half as interesting as you indicated." He winked at Velda and told me, "How did you ever rate such a beautiful assistant?"

"The beauties of this world always love the beasts," I reminded him. "Didn't you ever see *King Kong*?"

"All three versions . . . I suppose she carries a concealed weapon, too."

"She carries quite a few concealed weapons."

"She ever shoot anybody?"

Velda's mouth tightened in a small smile; she was getting a kick out of being talked about.

"Only rival beasts," I said.

It had started to rain again. At the office we were the first ones there, except for the doorman, who was keeping dry under the entrance canopy. He nodded good morning, and I told him my guest would possibly be going out later to ship something for me and was not to be bothered with any inspection rigamarole.

Once upstairs, with the office door locked behind us, I went to the closet and lifted the false bottom of the compartment in the floor and removed the original Goliath bone, which had fit snugly within. That compartment had hidden many things over the years, from money to machine guns, but this was its first historical relic.

I laid Matthew and Jenna's discovery, plump with bubble wrap, on Velda's desk. I didn't unwrap it. I took in Paul's awestruck expression and nodded at him to do the honors.

Until now, Paul's decorum had never slipped in my presence, but this was a rare moment in a life that was no stranger to discovery and wonder. His breathing had grown noticeably heavy, his eyes taking on a glaze while his tongue flicked nervously across his lips.

I didn't say anything.

Neither did Velda.

We were both getting a kick out of this archeologist who'd seen it all and then some behave like a kid with a big fat birthday present to open. Slowly, he undid the tapes, then unwound the bubble wrap and unveiled a white cloth swaddling that he did not remove before his hands ran over the contours of the Goliath bone like a lovesick fool caressing the curves of a fully clothed lover he'd not yet seen naked. Then, with an intake of breath, he flipped open the wrapping and his eyes widened in sheer amazement.

I let him have several minutes of visual inspection, including the use of the magnifying glass from Velda's desk, as well as gentle touching of the white surface, before I said, "What do you make of it?"

Finally he told me in a very soft voice, "It's a real bone, all right."

"Yeah, a bona fide bone. Jeez, Paul, I could have told you that."

His eyes continued to travel the bone's contours. "It's a femur from a Homo sapiens that had to be at *least* ten feet tall."

"What are we talking, Bigfoot maybe?"

He shook his head almost irritably. "We have no evidence that Bigfoot exists or ever did. But this bone has all the earmarks of being of human origin. I've never seen anything like it before. No one has."

I grinned at him. "You know whose bone that is, Paul?"

He swallowed thickly. "There's no way to prove it, Mike."

"I said, do you *know*?"

He swallowed again and nodded. "When you mentioned the Valley of *Elah*, I knew. When I was a kid, my mother read me the tale, not from the Bible, but from a storybook with pictures—colorful paintings that depicted the grandly uniformed giant threatening the opposing army, scaring the crap out of them with nobody responding to the challenge until a young boy stepped out with a sling and took care of that giant bully with one little pebble from a stream. I said to my mother, a little *kid* did that? And you know what she said to me? She said, 'He had *help,* Paul. He didn't do it all by himself.'"

I waited for his distant look to fade and then, all business, I asked, "How well could you duplicate that artifact?"

He frowned. "Well, I can't give you perfection . . ."

"What *can* you give me?"

For a full ten seconds Paul was lost in deep thought, calculating how he would proceed. Finally he turned to look first at Velda, then at me. "This is not to be repeated to anyone. You *understand* that?"

"Give me a break, Paul. Haven't you filled in the missing parts of prehistoric skeletons for top museums all over the world?"

"Yes. We've taken old bones, not from the same species at all, but reshaped them to fit the intended purpose and placed them on exhibit for the general public's pleasure. It's a common practice and pays well, too. The spectators can't begin to spot the false parts from the true."

"I need better than that, Paul. I'll settle if I have to, but—"

He held up a hand. "Mike, I can make a dupe so real an expert would have to examine it very minutely to tell what it really was. And it would have to be a *top* expert."

"How would you manage it?"

He shrugged. "There are many old bones—mammoths, for example—large enough to carve out a replica. The procedure I won't bother to explain to you, because it involves craftsmanship by hand as well as laser and computer tech. Suffice to say I can render the faux artifact chemically so that only under acute and expert detection could anyone discern its true age. The size would be exact, the surface totally consistent with longtime burial, the shape the same as the real thing. Getting the surface color exactly right could be the hard part, but who the hell would know? There's nothing to compare it with."

Then I asked him the most improbable question of all. "How long will this take, Paul?"

"For one duplicate?"

"For three."

He just laughed. "Do I have to work alone?"

"Yes."

"Please tell me this isn't a freebie, Mike. Getting close to this particular relic is a rush, almost as exciting as meeting Velda here . . . but I'm going to really have to burn some midnight oil."

"I'll split our take from our clients with you," I said.

"What will that amount to?"

"Maybe a million. Maybe nothing."

He laughed again; scratched his beard. "Sounds about right. No fraud involved?"

"No fraud that would involve you. Or that you would find offensive. But you'll have to take my word."

"Your word is all I need, Mike. They'll be done when they're done. The first one will take at least two weeks. The others, less time."

"Are you *sure*?" Velda said, impressed.

"Well, to be sure, I'd have to check my records to see how long it took the *last* time I made three duplicates of Goliath's femur. Let's just leave it at that—I'll let you know when I'm done."

I checked my watch. "Hope you had a good time in New York, Paul. About time you headed home, isn't it?"

He chuckled. "I guess so."

From his little carry-on bag, he removed the brown shirt and slacks that looked enough like the real UPS thing to fool just about anybody. While he changed in my office, Velda and I repacked the Goliath bone in its swaddling and its bubble wrap and put it in the big brown box marked SAMPLES that we had waiting. Velda was doing the honors of taping it shut when Paul emerged, looking like a delivery man right down to the little cap.

I made a call. Velda already had the coffee going, and she microwaved some cinnamon rolls for us. We sat around her desk and drank and nibbled and chatted like we had all the time in the world. Then the phone rang and we were on.

As big and heavy as that box was, Paul carried it like a pro. I was just a guy who happened to get on the elevator with him (and who happened to have a .45 under my left arm) and also happened to follow him through the lobby past the doorman out onto the street and possibly temporary sunshine where the brown UPS-style van driven by a Secure Solutions guard was waiting.

The box and Paul both went in back, and the van went off to fight the traffic war. No real rush—the charter plane in New Jersey waiting for Paul would not take off without its only passengers: Paul Vernon, that Secure Solutions guard, and the Goliath bone.

Back upstairs, Velda raised an eyebrow. "Without a hitch?"

"Without a hitch."

"Hell of a way to send off a corpse, Mike."

"Better than old Goliath got in the Valley of Elah, kiddo."

She got me a fresh cup of coffee, and I perched on the edge of her desk as she sat behind it and crossed those sleekly nyloned legs.

"Is Paul up to this, Mike? I don't mean the duplication part. I mean . . . that's a valuable relic, and half the Middle East is after it."

"Just half?" I sipped coffee. "Don't sweat Paul, Velda. He's a Desert Storm vet who carries a firearms license recognized in most states. As a sideline, he does very specialized insurance investigation involving museums and academic institutions."

"You know where he's going to do the work?"

"Nope. I don't want to, either. When he needs us, he'll call."

As if on cue, the phone gave its subdued buzz. I lifted it and said, "Yeah?"

"Mike?"

I knew immediately who it was and it sure wasn't Paul. I sat up. "Mr. Jackson. Got something for me?"

Bozo Jackson said, "Better get your white tail up here, Mike."

"If you just want to talk, Bozo, this line's secure."

"Talk is cheap," he said softly. "So is a certain other thing."

"Give me thirty minutes," I said.

Chapter 8

Clouds had rolled in and I didn't know whether snow or rain was coming, but I knew for sure it was damn cold. My hands were deep in my trench-coat pockets and I was missing the lining as I walked along 125th Street with Bozo Jackson. Landmarks like the Apollo Theater and the Hotel Theresa had been joined by the likes of Ben & Jerry's and Starbucks, and I guessed that was progress.

Bozo's hands were deep in the pockets of his black leather topcoat, too, but I had a feeling the cold wasn't why—the lump in his right-hand pocket was more than just his hand, and his hard keen eyes roamed up and down the street, making sure nobody was taking too much interest in us.

I asked, "What's up, brother?"

"Maybe nothing. Maybe everything. Roger Cosmo was found in his crib this morning—OD'd on smack."

"That's a goddamn shame. Who the hell is Roger Cosmo?"

His sideways glance included an arched eyebrow. "The kid who drove that gypsy cab that carried a certain shooter to midtown

Manhattan. To take a potshot or two at a couple of white college kids, remember?"

"Oh. Wasn't that Lonnie Hartman's cab?"

"Yeah. The *late* Lonnie Hartman."

"Jesus, Bozo. Dropping like flies around here. What happened to Lonnie?"

"Somebody traded him a .22 slug behind the right ear for his wallet outside his apartment house last night."

The sky growled, lightning flashes making sudden veins in the dark clouds.

I said, "That turns the trail cold on our midtown-hotel shooting."

"Cold as hell. Cold as Lonnie, Mike. Cold as Cosmo."

"Was this Cosmo kid a junkie?"

"Supposedly reformed. Weaned off the stuff onto methadone, and clean for over a year. But, yeah, he had a history, so the local five-oh at the twenty-eighth precinct can write it off easy."

I shook my head. "Like they can also write off Lonnie Hartman's murder as a straight armed robbery. That .22—hell, you're not saying . . ."

We turned the corner onto Lenox Avenue. "I'm *more* than saying, Mike. That shooter is back in town. Back in Harlem."

"Just because Hartman was killed with a .22, that doesn't mean the hotel shooter's made a return trip. Come on, Bozo, you know pros don't do it that way."

"Don't they?"

"Money behind him wouldn't want his ass spotted. They'd just pay him off and hire another gun. These sons of bitches are disposable, interchangeable."

Bozo's breath was billowing in the cold. "Mike, you talking about *our* kind of hoods—black and white." He saw me scowling. "I'm

talkin' 'bout another color altogether. The shade that blows themselves up just to kill somebody else."

"You said he was back. Fill it in."

"He's not at the same hotel. Got a room at Suzie Squires' place,
this time."

"Man, that's a fifty-dollar-a-bang sex house! They charge by the
hour what most joints go for a day."

Bozo's massive shoulders lifted and fell. "Maybe he's practicing
up for his virgins. Anyway, he's on the top floor."

"Who steered him there, Bozo?"

"Beats me. Probably asked a cabbie in a gypsy job—they get
kickbacks."

"Who else knows about this?"

"You and me."

"*Just* you and me, Bozo?"

"Just you and me that counts, Mike. I put the word out. Everybody looking and nobody talking . . . except to me."

"You got *some* respect on this street, man."

"Damn skippy. They can gentrify these streets all they want, but
scrape a fingernail across this white veneer, and the gleaming black
shows through."

"So does the street have any idea *why* you put the word out?"

"No way. My say-so is good enough reason."

"Usually they don't want to mess with the white man's business."

"This motherfucker's no more white than me."

"Can you keep him covered, Bozo?"

"You want him *questioned*? The Harlem way?"

"No. Just keep an eye on his ass and keep me posted."

Bozo grinned at me. "As a favor, Mike? I don't mind doin' you favors, but these boys are a whole other brand of dangerous."

"Five hundred a day, 24/7, till further notice."

"Man! You must be rollin' in it."

"Maybe I got my Social Security check in the mail."

Bozo laughed at that a little harder than I wanted him to. Then he asked, "You gonna take this shooter down, Mike?"

This time I gave him my own grin, where he could see my teeth between my lips. "Not here, old buddy. I wouldn't want to clip any of your people. But I'll get him where I won't have to make up any excuses."

We were at our destination now. I hadn't known where Bozo was leading me till we got there, the candy and smoke shop run by Mr. Jellybean. The store had a CLOSED sign in the window.

"Don't worry about that," Bozo said with a dismissive wave. "Jellybean's got a side door on the alley for his *real* business."

"Why are we here, Bozo?"

"'Cause Jelly called me this morning. He's got a line on that purple gypsy cab."

Which was all well and good, only the side door was ajar. I saw Bozo tense and then I slipped a hand inside my trench coat and withdrew the .45. The click of its hammer was a tiny sound that filled the world of the alley. Bozo's hand was out of his topcoat pocket and a snubnose .38 was clenched in his fist.

I motioned for him to push the door open for me.

And I went in fast and low, doing a toplike spin with the .45 fanning around at any available target, only the sole available target didn't need shooting.

Jellybean had already been shot.

The gaudy gun dealer in the spartan office was seated at his desk as if ready to do business, leaned back in his chair with a frozen smile whose parted lips revealed the gold, silver, and diamonds that would never flash in a grin again. In his forehead was a small dark dot, like he'd come from India not Harlem. Only that dot bore no religious significance, other than the mark of the end of a mortal existence.

Bozo came into the small space, and I nodded toward the front of the store. The big ex-cop went out there to check it, then was back within thirty seconds to say, "Clear."

"Size of that entry wound's consistent with a .22."

"Damn, Mike—what kinda hell did you bring to Harlem?"

"Wasn't me, Bozo. I'm just working cleanup crew right now. Somebody else is making the mess."

"Do we call your pal Captain Chambers?"

I thought for a moment, then said, "No. He'd tie this in with everything that's gone down, and then the Feds would be on it. You want the Homicide Bureau and Homeland Security and FBI and all that other alphabet soup crawling around up here?"

"Fuck no."

"Eloquently put. Let's give Jellybean a little privacy and slip out. You touch anything?"

"My mama raised only one fool, and that was my brother."

"Good. You make an anonymous call to the Twenty-eighth Precinct, when you get a chance. Those boys will have half a dozen good reasons why a crooked-ass gun dealer got capped."

Just not the right one.

Driving back into lower Manhattan, I let the pieces run through my mind. This was no street rumble. This was no grand heist like the Brink's job. While the bodies piled up on the local level, this thing had international overtones that would make three killings in Harlem seem petty. From the point of view of a guy like me, a foundation of absurdity underpinned the whole damn thing—a scattering of sand dwellers throwing rocks at the monstrous democratic governments, smashing their edifices, terrorizing their populations and putting fear into everyone in the Western world.

I got out my cell and speed-dialed the office.

When Velda picked up the phone, I asked her if she'd like a hamburger. She hated hamburgers but she said sure and added, "Usual place?"

"Right on, doll."

All of the chatter was simply subterfuge. Our phone had been tapped before, and in cases that didn't involve Feds and foreign agents. What the exchange meant was to meet me at Chico's coffee shop two corners away.

I got to Chico's first, ordered two coffees, a Reuben for me and BLT for Velda. She came in just as the food was set down and patted my hand the way near-marrieds do. It felt good.

Quietly, she said, "My best girlfriends keep asking me what the holdup is this time."

"And what do you tell them?"

She let a tiny grin flit across her mouth and said, "Just that it doesn't take much to see that the desires of two little people don't amount to a hill of beans in this crazy world."

"Here's looking at you, kid," I said, toasting her with my coffee.

"So we set a new date."

"Yes."

Her eyes sparkled. "When?"

"The day this case is over. But there's one catch."

"Oh?"

"I got to still be alive."

"I'm not accepting *any* excuses . . ." Her fingers tightened on mine, saying a lot more than her mouth did. Then the tip of her tongue eased out between her lips, made a wet pass on the fleshy red mounds, and disappeared within her impish smile.

"Why do you do that stuff in public?" I asked softly.

"To see you squirm," she answered. When I shook my head, she added, "Now what can we talk about here that we can't discuss in our office? I'm sweeping for bugs every time we step out, you know, and now I'll have to do the same when I get back."

"Sweeping. My little homemaker."

"I'd say 'go to hell,' but I can see it in your eyes, Mike. This thing's ramped up a notch."

I nodded, and filled her in on the three Harlem deaths, and the shooter holed up with some high-priced hookers.

She nibbled at her sandwich as I reported. Then she said, "We had a call from a Mr. Barry Axler."

"Do I know him?"

"No. But he's the personal assistant of the deputy consul for Israel."

"Another country heard from. What does he want?"

"To set up a meeting for his boss with Mike Hammer."

"I think we can arrange that."

"I already have." She checked her wristwatch. "It's in forty minutes."

"If the Israelis want a meeting, then they're hip to Goliath. Who leaked it? Obviously some of the Arab factions are tuned in. But how did Mr. Axler's boss get the info?"

She shrugged. "We both know all about double agents and counterintelligence."

"May be simpler than that. Rumors probably started back at the site of the discovery."

Nodding, she said, "The Israelis have a far more sophisticated intelligence service than any of the Arab nations."

Velda knew her stuff in this area; she'd done a stint with the CIA behind the Iron Curtain many years ago. You don't think I'd hire just any assistant, do you?

"You're right, Velda. The Mossad would have jumped on this like a tiger on a rabbit. They'd grasp at once the implications of such a discovery, what it could mean to whoever had the bone as a trophy, all the incredible political implications. To us it's only an artifact. To somebody else it's a religious symbol. By itself it has no power, but in the hands of true believers, as they say, it could be an inspiration for a national uprising."

"Arab or Israeli?" she asked.

"Yes," I said.

With the fate of the world hanging in the balance, there was no reason not to share a piece of cheesecake.

She had a few bites of her half, then asked, "What if the Israelis ended up with it, Mike? What then?"

"Nothing. They'd do a big PR buildup and then would probably lock it in a museum under armed guard."

"But it would be under constant threat then, wouldn't it?"

I nodded.

"Suppose they just destroyed it? Announced it as the symbol of their greatest victory, then symbolically and literally crushed that enemy again? Leaving nothing to be stolen, nothing to fight over, nothing to keep under lock and key."

I shook my head. "None of the groups vying for this would go that way. It's just too important a find—a physical reminder of a historical event so incredible it left its mark on the whole world."

"And it could spark something even bigger today," she said. "Bigger and much, much worse."

"War used to be two groups of men hammering at each other out in some field till the other side surrendered or was defeated. Now it's airliners flying into buildings and suitcase nukes and dirty bombs."

And from one ancient battle, only a giant femur survived.

But that was all that was needed to start another, much more horrific war.

At the Israeli Consulate's office on Second Avenue, I waited in a small-but-tidy reception area decorated with lovely photographs of the Holy Land, the kind of peaceful vistas that betrayed the blood soaking the surrounding sand. I didn't have to wait long at all before a tall gray-headed gentleman of about fifty came out to meet me. This was an annex of the embassy in Washington, D.C., maintained for visiting Israeli dignitaries, general PR, and affairs of state like this one, where notoriety could be handled at a reasonable level.

The oval-faced, pleasant man in a suit tailored to make his slightly pear-shaped frame look its best had certainly done his homework. He was up to speed on the news accounts of my cases, dating back decades, and to put me at ease had insisted I address him as Leon. This was a relief, because I wasn't sure I could pronounce his last name.

"If you're Leon," I said, "I'm Mike, and we have that out of the way, at least."

When he offered a drink, I waved it off and sat in one of two facing soft leather chairs—no desk barrier for Leon.

"You know why I asked you to drop by," Leon said, a leg crossed, arms on armrests, casual but commanding.

Nobody "dropped by" an embassy, but I said, "Sure. Do we need to waste time circling around each other, or just cut to the chase?"

Leon smiled gently and nodded. "Cut to the chase, by all means."

"You've heard about the discovery of what we're calling the Goliath bone."

"I have. Has it been authenticated?"

"It's a human remain. Uncommonly large and inconsistent with any known Homo sapiens, with the possible exception of an acromegaly victim."

His forehead tightened. "But this relic, this bone, shows no signs of that disease."

"It does not. The thing was found in the right spot to belong to the Philistines' star player. But further identification stops there. It *does* jibe with the Scriptural accounts."

His smile remained gentle, but his eyes were shrewd. "Mike, what exactly is your interest in this discovery? I have read the accounts of your, well, exploits. You are known for dispensing a certain Torah-like eye-for-an-eye justice."

I grunted a laugh. "Yeah, for a kid raised Catholic, I've always been an Old Testament kind of guy."

"In my faith, we reserve eye-for-an-eye punishment for God to carry out."

"Must have been my imagination, then, the Six-Day War."

That got a grudging grin out of him.

"Look, Leon—I shot the gun out of the hand of a man who was identified as an illegal Jordanian immigrant. Before he fell down the subway stairs and killed himself, he was trying to, let's say, smite the pair who brought the bone back to the United States."

"I had imagined you killed the assailant."

"I just shot the gun out of his hand. I guess Jehovah took it from there."

He laughed quietly, briefly. But he laughed.

"So, Leon, we have an age-old hunk of human anatomy that can turn the world upside down, if we let it." I paused, then added, "You *do* know that, don't you?"

For several long seconds, he stared at me. Each of us was looking at another old soldier who had been there and had come back. He said, "I'm a diplomat, Mike. More or less undercover."

"And I'm just a private investigator, not at all undercover, if a little in over my head. Not that I haven't been there plenty of times before."

"You seem to have a good relationship with the NYPD."

"Yeah, but the Federal government and I don't always see eye to eye. Anyway, your Mossad outfit must have more information on these Philistine groups than we have."

"Philistine?" He chuckled. "Interesting way to put it."

"I call them that," I said with a shrug. "Too many teams to keep track of in this league."

"Well, it's an apt name," he admitted. "Worldwide events have brought these rogue states back into having a feeling of power, though for seven hundred years they've known nothing but defeat. They do have wealthy benefactors, a multitude of weapons, and a very astute system of communication . . . and cooperation."

"A lot of these countries don't espouse the radical-Islamic-terrorist party line. And plenty of Muslims are as horrified by this zealotry as we are."

"Yes, Mike, but it's to the benefit of some politicians in those rogue states to look the other way and even actively underwrite these terrorists. And never dismiss the abilities of these warriors—never underestimate their passion and courage."

"If I'm ever tempted to, I'll just check out the skyline. Leon, could you pass a message to the Mossad for me?"

The bluntness of that surprised him. Then he shook his head. "They will go only through proper channels."

"Yeah, well, tough—if they're interested in the Goliath bone, *I'm* proper channels."

"Perhaps they have no interest."

"Then they can tell me so, through you. I don't want them pulling their secret-agent jazz on me. Somebody might get killed. And I don't mean me."

Leon's voice was mild, his expression bland, when he asked straightforwardly, "Do you have the Goliath bone?"

"I know where it is, and I represent its owners."

"Its owners? How can anyone 'own' a piece of antiquity, Mike?"

"Really? No one can own a piece of antiquity, Leon? Then it's okay if I go borrow the *Mona Lisa,* or one of those wild paintings by that character who cut his ear off?"

He smiled. "You really want me to think you're that rough around the edges, don't you, Mike? It's an interesting posture."

"People who think I'm posturing sometimes find themselves in a posture of death. Hey, I'm not threatening you, Leon—you're a nice guy. Far as I'm concerned, Israel would make a swell home for the Goliath bone. Maybe you guys would like to buy it from my clients. You can pass that along, too."

After a few seconds, he nodded and told me, "I'll make inquiries, Mike. My conversation will be very circumspect, and I may get a favorable reply. In that case, I'll call your office."

"And if you're rejected?"

He shrugged. "Then the so-called Goliath bone will have been deemed of no importance at all to Israel."

"No offense, Leon, but that is a load of crap."

"Certainly it is," Leon said pleasantly. "I told you I was a diplomat."

"Why do I sense that you wish you'd never heard of the Goliath bone, and me, for that matter?"

For a few seconds, he studied me. Then he said, "The situation in Israel is very unstable right now, even for Israel. Suicide-bomb incidents have diminished of late, but there is still unbearable tension and political infighting—just like your country, Mike, the right and left squabbling eternally and the fate of a nation twisting in the middle. A lot of the Jewish population has had to give up their homes in the Gaza Strip and other places just to try to keep the peace, but everything is on edge. One spark and the area will explode once more."

"A spark off an ancient bone," I said.

He nodded gravely. "I wish your clients had never found the cursed thing. But I should warn you—it's not the Mossad you have to fear, nor Israel proper."

"Why, is there an Israel improper?"

"We have our extremists, too, Mike."

"*Israeli* terrorists, Leon?"

"Does that surprise you, Mike, considering the terror that has been visited upon us?"

"Whatever happened to the Holy Land concept?"

"Why, do you think there are no Christian terrorists? Were the Crusades benign?"

"That was a long time ago."

"How about the bombing of abortion clinics? What about Opus

Dei? Organized religion has done enormous good in the world, Mike. But in its name, enormous harm has also often been done."

"Are you talking about individuals, Leon? Extremist Israelis or sympathizers with personal agendas?"

He drew in a deep breath. He let it out. Then he said, "There's a group called Kakh, Mike. It's been condemned by our nation as a racist movement at odds with the democratic nature of Israel. Their symbol is a fist against a star. Some say this group . . . it doesn't exist."

"But you say they do. How dangerous?"

His smile was gentle. "Let's just say, Mike, that if they decide to take the Goliath bone, they will not be making a financial offer."

I met Velda at her apartment, where she sat on the sofa with her shoes off and her nyloned legs and feet up on the coffee table. She looked bushed but beautiful, and I might have tried to make something of it if her attention hadn't been on the television with the news going. I only caught the last of the commentator's spiel, but it was enough to send a chill up my spine.

Seemed that the reputed skeletal remains of the historical Philistine giant, Goliath, had been unearthed in Israel in the Valley of Elah, site of the ancient battleground where he had been slain. In transport to the United States, a terrorist of Jordanian origin had tried to intercept the delivery of the relic to researchers, and had been shot by a private detective on the scene on the steps of a subway station.

I sat heavily next to her. "They'll never get that straight. I didn't shoot the bastard, I shot his *gun*."

Velda said, "Mike—there's all kinds of info getting out that you did *not* give to Richie and that other reporter."

"Was my name mentioned on that broadcast?"

"No, but it will be somewhere. I'm recording the other networks, and we'll hit the cable outlets, too. Every TV news organization will have their people out investigating."

"I didn't hear any police verification—"

"There wasn't any. Pat called just before the airing to make sure I saw it. The network *wanted* verification, but Pat refused because it was an 'ongoing investigation.' Mike, there wasn't even a hint of the source of the story."

"You talk to the Hurley kids?"

"Called them right after Pat called me. So they've seen this, too. And they hadn't talked to any media; neither have their parents."

"You know who that leaves, don't you?"

"Sure. Your Middle Eastern friends. They're trying to draw us out."

I laughed once, harshly. "Somebody's got a lot of clout to reach the TV networks this fast."

Velda shook her head, making the glossy tresses of her pageboy swirl about her face. "No, Mike—this is news, odd, almost fantastic news, but news. Everybody is sick to death of politics and burnt out on war coverage, but then this slice of history seems to come out of nowhere, and by tomorrow it will be on everybody's lips."

"And you know what that means," I said sourly.

"Certainly. Uncle Sam'll send those Homeland Security boys around to see you again . . . or maybe somebody new."

But the government didn't send anybody immediately. At the office, the next morning, we had calls on the machine from every major network and cable outfit, and not just the news organizations: the entertainment divisions, too.

"What's *that* about, Mike?" Velda said, behind her desk, at her computer where she was checking the online coverage of the Goliath bone. "Why entertainment?"

"Just some mice nibbling at the cheese I set out," I said.

"All these years," she said, smirking, "and I still can't figure you out half the time."

The phone made its buzz on Velda's desk and, since I was standing right there, I picked it up; the caller ID was blocked and I was curious. Before I could identify myself, a smooth baritone asked, "Is this Michael Hammer Investigations?"

"This is Mike Hammer. Who is this?"

"Mr. Hammer, a pleasure. You're a celebrity in your own right." A pause followed that I could somehow tell I wasn't supposed to fill, but I used it to hit the speaker phone so Velda could listen in.

She did, with wide eyes, as he said, "My name is Harold Cooke. Cooke with an 'e.' Does that mean anything to you, Mr. Hammer?"

That was like asking if you'd ever heard of Hollywood. Cooke was a twenty-first–century P. T. Barnum gene-spliced with Mike Todd; the man who'd first brought British musicals to Broadway, the pioneer producer who all but invented reality TV, the entrepreneur who had made Las Vegas family friendly, the Donald Trump of show business.

In short, he was pretty much everything I hated.

I said, "You're what we used to call a showman, Mr. Cooke."

This time his voice had a smile in it—the kind that said he was going to take away my candy. "That's right, Mr. Hammer. I have two films shooting, three Broadway shows running, and four major circus productions going right now—one in Europe, the others about to go on tour in the United States."

"I knew a guy who used to get shot out of a cannon," I said.

"Really? Well, my point is that I have an unassailable track record in the entertainment industry as well as a great deal of capital available to put into the right new venture . . . and if I can come up with the perfect dramatic presentation, the kind that would attract massive crowds and Pay-Per-Vue and all the home-video aftermarkets, well, millions of dollars might be involved. . . . Are you there, Mr. Hammer?"

"I'm listening."

"Do you have an inkling of what I might be referring to?"

"Does it have anything to do with the news last night?"

I counted about five empty seconds before Mr. Cooke had rearranged his presentation. Then he asked, "Is this phone secure?"

Actually, Velda was recording the conversation.

"In my business, I take all sorts of precautions," I told him. "Why? Who's chasing you? Need a bodyguard?"

"I'm assuming, Mr. Hammer, that I am not alone in ascertaining the great financial potential in your recovery of a certain artifact."

"My name hasn't been mentioned on any of these news broadcasts."

"You haven't seen the newspapers this morning, then."

I hadn't. I'd bought them all and they were waiting on my desk for me to plow through all the Goliath-bone coverage.

"Mr. Cooke, I'm not the owner of the item you're referring to."

"But you can influence its disposition, I assume."

"I represent the owners, yes. Why don't we cut the small talk? I don't do business over the phone. If you're in your Manhattan office, you're fairly close by, and I have some time available right now. So get up here."

And I hung up.

Velda's grin grew a little bigger. "Want me to stick around?"

"Damn straight."

She turned off the recorder, popped out the tape of the last conversation and slipped it away in a concealed compartment in her bottom right-hand desk drawer.

I asked her, "Think we should wait till we talk to the networks before making a deal with Mr. Cooke?"

Her eyes got wide again. "Why, are you thinking of making a deal?"

I didn't answer her.

It took the biggest entertainment mogul in America just twenty-two minutes to make it over to my office. He came himself and he came alone, and that much I could respect him for. He wore no topcoat—he'd gone from the phone call from me straight to his limo and here.

In his early sixties, he looked like what the guy in the old Arrow Shirt ads might have aged into, movie-star handsome with steel gray hair but black eyebrows over green eyes that could eat you alive and the kind of quietly regal demeanor high officials assume when they wear the robes of office.

His clothes were proper yet sharp—Velda probably knew whether those threads were Hugo Boss or maybe Armani; I just saw money in the beautifully cut gray suit and black-and-white-striped silk tie.

I was in the outer office when he arrived, and introduced him to Velda, and I watched his canny combination of courtly nod and direct eye contact, knowing most women would be charmed already.

Velda wasn't that easy.

Maybe he sensed it because he said to her, "You're almost as famous as your boss. You've been in the papers, too."

"You know how it is," she said with a girlish shrug. "You shoot somebody and there's a fuss."

He didn't quite know what to make of that, and turned his attention back to me. His smile was easy, his handshake firm.

We went into my office while Velda got us some coffee and before he even sat down, Harold Cooke got right to the point. "What I'm hearing and reading about the Goliath bone, Mr. Hammer, it's exciting. Compelling."

"Call me, Mike, okay?" I was behind my desk now. "Sit down. Please."

"And I'm Harold." He sat. "You're caught up in something that is going to seize the public's imagination. Actually, it already has."

"No argument."

Velda came in with our coffee orders and sat down in a chair just behind Cooke, who glanced back at her warily.

"Velda won't be taking any notes," I said. She wouldn't have to: We were recording the conversation. "But I like her to sit in."

I could see him process that, deciding not to object. "As I say, Mike, the public's already caught up in this—starting with your subway rescue of the Hurley boy and his sister. They aren't actually related, are they? Matthew's father is married to Jenna's mother, correct?"

"Correct. In fact, the two kids are planning to get married themselves."

He beamed. "Well, now, that's just wonderful!"

"Fan of the institution of marriage, are you?"

"A fan of public interest. This story would be on fire even without Mike Hammer in it, and now we have a brother-and-sister love story to stoke the flames."

"But you didn't stop around for my autograph."

"No. You see, Mike, when I learned who Matthew and Jenna's parents were, I made it a point to get as much information on them—and this situation—as possible. You may not consider that someone in show business might have the means to gather information comparable to law enforcement or a news organization or government institution. But in a short time my people have learned a great deal about the Goliath bone."

"And here we are."

"Here we are." He shifted in the seat, cocked his head, smiled tentatively. "You're a major player in this game, aren't you, Mike?"

"*The* major player."

"More so than your clients?"

"My clients are young and naïve. They, and their parents, have entrusted their welfare to me. I'm *not* young and naïve."

Half a smile now. "You have an interesting reputation, Mike. You score high on loyalty and honesty. But you're considered dangerous, even now, in your . . ."

"Golden years?"

He chuckled. "I'm not young, either, Mike. Or naïve. But as part of my research, I've looked into your financial status. You don't seem to own much in the way of property. You've set up virtually no retirement for you and Ms. Sterling—you two are planning to get married soon, I understand. Congratulations."

I looked past him at Velda, who was frowning.

Cooke said, "Shall we talk business?"

I let him read my eyes a while. Then very quietly I said, "Tell me, Harold, just what would you do with this artifact? You understand there is no way to verify it as Goliath's femur; it's strictly a matter of faith and circumstantial evidence."

"True."

"So, what does the world's greatest showman see in a museum curiosity, a scholarly object?"

Cooke's smile was a knowing one with forced gentility. "What I see is history come alive again. And I'm not the only one, am I? This object has incredible resonance for so many, the Arab states, Israel, among them."

"They're willing to kill for it."

"I'm willing to buy it."

I shrugged. "Then let's hear your proposal."

He had a sip of the coffee Velda had provided, complimented her on it, then said cheerfully, "You know something about me, Mike? On the phone it sounded like you did. If so, you know that my first great success, over twenty-five years ago, was to import a West End show called *David and Goliath: The Musical* to Broadway. It was a smash, ran for fifteen years, made a superstar out of its composer and set a new standard for elaborate theatrical productions."

"I saw it," I admitted. Velda had dragged me to the thing. It was the kind of show that left you humming the costumes.

"The climax of act one, of course, with David and his slingshot playing to an unseen, offstage giant, led to the crash onto the stage of an enormous figure of the 'dead' Goliath. The size of it, the impact, literal and figurative, of that huge prop, well—after that came the imitators, the crashing chandelier of *Phantom of the Opera,* the helicopter of *Ms. Saigon.* Frankly, today our then-innovative staging of *David and Goliath* would seem fairly tame."

"Just pushing over a big prop out of the wings wouldn't cut it anymore."

"No." Another sip. Another smile. "Do you believe in fate, Mike?"

"I always liked the term 'kismet' better."

"*Kismet*—*another* Broadway show! Well, when I heard the words 'Goliath bone,' I knew at once what fate had in store for me. How could the impresario who made *David and Goliath* such a benchmark success resist bringing the *real* giant to Broadway?"

I shrugged. "Go ahead—stage a revival and ride the coattails of all this publicity. You don't need my clients' permission for that."

Cooke sat forward, his green eyes glittering. "Mike, have you ever seen the animated life-sized statue of Lincoln at Disney World in Florida?"

"Sure—Honest Abe walks across the stage, goes through the Gettysburg Address with all the appropriate gestures and expressions until he's got the audience actually believing they're seeing the real person."

Cooke was nodding emphatically. "Yes! And that represents only an early version of this kind of technology. Hollywood has since developed similar, more advanced animatronics, and parallel technology has been developed to make strides in prosthetics for our Iraq War veterans."

"Right."

"Well . . . I have the wherewithal to have fabricated an animatronic version of Goliath, using the bone in question to provide scale . . . meaning we'll have a Goliath the exact size of the original. We will dress our robotic 'actor' in historically accurate garb of the Philistines, and have him strut across the stage threatening the great army of Israel, just before David makes his appearance . . . and at the last moment, right in front of a massive audience, we will display for the first time, the *actual bone* of the giant Goliath, glistening white . . . with death." He laughed and it wasn't exactly insane but it wasn't exactly sane, either. "I promise you, Mike, that the opening-night audience will be shocked completely out of their senses."

"Into what, Mr. Cooke—pandemonium?"

"No! No . . . but for a few moments in this jaded seen-it-all climate, they'll be swept up in a grand pageant worthy of Cecil B. DeMille at his most outrageous . . . and yet knowing that they've witnessed a true vision of history."

I watched his face closely as I said, "You'd have the place packed with Israeli sympathizers, Muslim zealots, persons ready to act on any scream or shout, and the greatest show on earth would become the biggest disaster in America. If there's a rush for the exits, a mob of people would go down in a heap of dying flesh. Is *that* what you're looking for, Harold?"

"Of course not. I mean only to entertain and enlighten. The unusual nature of the presentation would require heightened security measures before, during, and after."

"Anything goes wrong, Harold, you'll be a showbiz Goliath pelted with lawsuits, not stones."

He smiled and waved that off. "I may seem to be painting a problematic picture now, Mike, but every detail will be carefully studied and ironed out. Legalities will be satisfied, everything will be handled with proper decorum—history and entertainment presented with a dramatic flourish."

"And you want to arrange for the use of the Goliath bone for this specific event?"

"No. I need to own it. One day I may donate it to a major museum, but for the foreseeable future, we'll start with a limited engagement of one week at the highest ticket prices New York has ever seen. Then I'll present the same show in every major city in America and Europe. The final performance of this limited tour will be a Pay-Per-Vue event, followed by a DVD of the live performance, a CD of the new cast recording the score, then a film after that, and . . . what would you say to a million dollars, Mike, as just your finder's fee?"

I knew that was supposed to knock me off my chair, but I didn't blink. "Why, Harold? What could I buy?"

"Anything you want," he answered politely.

"But I don't want anything."

He eased out of the chair, and those expensive threads didn't even need smoothing out.

Neither did his smile, as he said, "Everybody wants something, Mike. . . . Talk to your clients."

Chapter 9

Three days passed in a blur of activity—no violence, but plenty of media attention and financial offers from museums, broadcast and cable networks, even private collectors. I had to post security in the lobby of the Hackard Building and moved in with Velda to avoid the fuss outside my apartment. I went over every offer with the kids each evening at the latest safe-house, the Secure Solutions team doing a great job keeping them safe and sound and off the radar.

They sat holding hands on a blond wafer-cushioned sofa in another of those bland IKEA-decorated glorified dorm rooms that the security boys maintained, and I pulled up a hard chair to give them the latest offers.

"I never thought about this being about money," Matthew said, shaking his head.

Jenna sighed and said, "All we've ever wanted is to follow in Mom and Dad's footsteps."

I grinned at her and then him. "That's *all* you ever wanted?"

They both blushed. That's what I liked about them: They were smart, they were in a jam, plenty educated and sophisticated, too, with their worldwide travel. But they still had a youthful innocence in an era where those qualities were in short supply.

"Well, of course, Mr. Hammer," Matthew said, "all we really want is each other. To be together."

"Our dream is do what our *parents* do," Jenna said. "Work side by side. Teaming up to do something positive in what's turning out to be a pretty terrible world."

I shrugged. "Well, you've made a major find. You stumbled on to something that the most highly trained, experienced archeologists could only dream of. It puts you in a position to have a nice big payday that will set you two up for the kind of life you're dreaming about."

They exchanged looks and smiles. Then Matthew asked, "Which offer should we take?"

"More and more are coming in. But I'm probably going to recommend Harold Cooke's."

"Has he set a figure?"

"He's set a different one each day, and I've sent him packing. But I can about guarantee he'll come up with the highest figure, and we can take the political edge off this thing by choosing him. Like the man says, 'No business like show business.'"

My cell phone vibrated in my pocket and I checked to see who was calling: Pat Chambers.

"What's up, buddy?"

"Where are you right now, Mike?"

"With the Hurley kids, at the latest safe-house."

"Look . . . something bad's happened. You may want to keep this from them until you get a handle on it."

"A handle on what, Pat?"

"George Hurley is dead. Get over here now."

I took the address, which was in the Village, gave nothing away to the kids before I left, and in under half an hour I was sharing an alley with Pat, assorted crime-scene analysts, several uniformed men, and the corpse of Matthew Hurley's father, which lay sprawled just beyond a Dumpster. At almost ten o'clock on an overcast night, spillage from neons didn't cut it and some arc lights on stands were required to put the dead man in the spotlight.

There'd been rain earlier, so the alley was damp with more than blood. Really wasn't much blood, though—the hole under George's chin had been left by a bullet that had gone in at an angle up through his brain and out the crown of his skull. I didn't need the crime-scene boys to tell me the shot had come from up close— the powder burns told that tale. I also didn't need their help to know he'd fallen where he'd been shot. The splattered abstract painting from an artist working in brain and bone matter hung on the brick wall by way of explanation.

"What the hell was he doing in this alley?" I asked Pat.

"There's a Starbucks on the corner," Pat said.

"There's a Starbucks on every corner."

The captain of Homicide nodded vaguely in the direction of the Hurley apartment. "It's the closest one to the victim's residence. His wife tells us he was supposed to meet her there. She waited for him half an hour and was just getting worried when she heard the sirens."

"Who found the body?"

"A couple of gay guys who live a block over. This is a shortcut home they often take."

"They for real?"

"Seem to be. I questioned them thoroughly, checked their IDs. This is a hit, Mike. Nothing taken. Dr. Hurley had over two hundred in cash on him and a Rolex, and he still does."

I shook my head. "This is no hit."

Pat frowned. "Are you kidding?"

"Whoever shot Hurley knew him well enough to lure him to an alley for a meeting and poke a gun under his chin."

With an irritated smirk, Pat said, "Not necessarily, Mike. A guy could've stuck a gun in Hurley's back on the sidewalk, marched back here, and plugged him."

"Facing him?"

Pat shrugged. "Kept the gore off the shooter, didn't it?"

"Any shell casings or slugs found?"

"No. Possibly retrieved by the shooter." He lifted both eyebrows. "Like a *hit man* might."

I knelt over the body. Pointed toward the entry wound. "I won't claim it's scientific, but I'd say he was plugged with a .22."

"You don't mind if I wait for the forensics report?"

"Hell, no. Be my guest." I stood. "Where is Mrs. Hurley? You send her home?"

He shook his head. "I sent one of my men with her back down to that Starbucks. She said she didn't want to go back to the apartment alone."

"I have my car. I can drive her there. Stay with her if need be."

"Knock yourself out."

Soon I'd ushered a red-eyed, shell-shocked Charlene Hurley from the coffee shop to my car, and other than telling her how sorry I was, no words were exchanged until I pulled in at a space courtesy of a hydrant in front of her apartment building.

She was holding her dark raincoat's lapels tight to her throat and staring into the water-reflective street where lights glowed and puddles glistened.

"We were just trying to get away," she said.

"Away?"

She nodded. The short near-white curls framed a lovely face nearly as pale as her hair. Again, a resemblance nagged me, but I couldn't make the connection. Didn't matter.

"You must be experiencing it lately, Mike—all these media, cameras, reporters . . ."

"Yeah. The fishbowl effect."

"Last few days, we've both been sneaking away, out the back of the building, one at a time, then meeting somewhere. A little Italian place yesterday evening. That Starbucks tonight. Only . . . George slipped out an hour before me. He said he had to talk to someone."

"Who?"

"He didn't say. He seemed rather . . . secretive, for George. We don't keep much from each other."

I touched her shoulder. "Is there someone I can call? You have relatives in town?"

"Just my children. But I don't even know where they *are*." She turned to me with eyes as wide as they were red, and her voice mingled indignation and alarm. "Do they even *know* about this?"

"I didn't tell them. No one else could or would have."

She swallowed and looked away, staring at the black shiny street again. "Oh my God. Matthew loved his father so. We . . . Matt and I have never been close, Mike. Maybe this horrible thing can . . . can bring us together."

"Good things can come out of bad things." I wish I could have done better, but that was all I had. "Listen, I can bring them over tonight. I can make that arrangement, and get you protection, too."

Suddenly she clutched my hand and leaned toward me. Her face was very close to mine, so close her perfume tickled my nostrils. It, too, was familiar, a scent I couldn't quite place.

"*Could* you, Mike? Could you tell them, and . . . bring them to me?"

I dropped her off—she insisted that she didn't need me to walk her up—and drove back to the safe house, where Velda was waiting for me with the kids.

I walked Matthew and Jenna back to the sofa and had Velda sit with them as I took the same chair and I told them. There was nothing special about it. Just hard facts delivered as softly as possible. Jenna cried in Matthew's arms but the boy didn't shed a tear—his face was frozen, eyes unblinkingly staring at me. *Through* me.

Velda's beautiful dark eyes, somber with compassion, spoke to me: *Oh, Mike, these poor kids . . . these poor kids . . .*

Fifteen minutes later, the boy was walking his sister toward the door as we escorted them. "We're taking the guard with us, right?"

"Right. You'll have three guys from Secure Solutions watching you and your mother tonight. Nothing to worry about."

Matthew swallowed and nodded. "Mr. Hammer?"

"Yeah, Matt?"

"All that stuff I read about you . . . you being a killer. A sort of . . . urban vigilante, they used to call you. That was a long time ago, though, right?"

"It was a while ago."

"So I don't suppose you could do me a favor . . . ?"

"Just ask, son."

Now the tears came; they didn't fall, just welled. "Find whoever killed my father. And kill them . . . *kill* them . . . Mike? Make it *awful*."

"Count on it," I said.

I filled Velda in on the way to her apartment building. By the time we got to her floor, we were both beat, and I could tell she was feeling blue. We'd really taken these kids under our wing, and there was something new about it for us, something damn near parental.

Velda ran her hand along the upper edge of her door, where she had placed a strand of hair. When she glanced at me, I knew somebody had been inside before us.

I eased the .45 out of the shoulder holster, jacked a shell into the chamber, and thumbed the hammer back. I watched as Velda slid the key into a well-oiled lock and worked it without making a sound. Then I eased her behind me, turned the knob, pushed the door open, and threw my coat jacket inside.

There was no answering blast of bullets, no light popping of silenced guns, just blackness—so I reached in and flipped the hallway light switch on and moved in slow, the carpeted floor muffling my footsteps. Behind me Velda had her own .38 cocked and ready, and she wasn't even breathing hard.

Both of us swept the apartment. It was empty. Whoever had been there had made a careful search, but Velda could tell an intruder had gone through her belongings. She pulled open the drawer in the table next to her bed and lifted out a holstered .25 automatic, shook it partway out of the leather sleeve, and showed it to me.

I asked, "Fingerprints?"

"No. But *my* fingerprints are smudged, probably by somebody else's latex gloves." She shoved the .25 back into its home, placed it in back the drawer, which she slid shut.

I stood with hands on hips, surveying the scene. "Well, I guess we know what they were looking for."

"And I guess we know they didn't find it, since it isn't here."

We did another sweep, this time for indications of planted electronics, and when we were done she made coffee—decaf, so we wouldn't be up half the night—and we sat together on her sofa like the old married couple we should have been by now.

I sighed. "Now we know how the discoverers of King Tut's tomb felt."

"Curse and all," she said wryly. For a long moment she studied my face. "Only this deal is a lot bigger, isn't it? Than King Tut."

"The political end of it sure is."

"How long a fuse, Mike?"

"A damn short one. So many devious minds after Goliath's bone, and they can all buy almost anything they want and if cash won't get it, strange armies of soldiers descend with their warped thoughts, prepared to do anything to get into paradise, where their personal harems of virgins are on call."

Velda let a little grin crease her mouth. "You're not envious, are you?"

"Just *one* of you is all I could take."

The little chuckle she let out was almost silent. "And now we're about to get married." She shifted that lovely frame and sat on her legs and ran her arm along the sofa behind me. "Now that Vegas is out, maybe we should settle for City Hall. That license we got last year is still good. You even passed the blood test."

"First there's another blood test I need to take."

"What's that?"

"You heard the promise I made that kid."

She tilted her head. "Should be enough, just dealing with a bunch of Islamic nutjobs—but it isn't."

"No it isn't. There's a killer out there, Velda. A smart one. As deadly as any we've ever come up against. Been keeping track? Know what the box score is? Never mind the guy who took the header in the subway, or the bastard I lobotomized out that window. Skip the jumper across from the university center. Harlem *alone* we have three kills. Now George Hurley."

"Why was Hurley killed?"

"To make his wife and kids cooperate and give up the bone, maybe."

She arched a dark eyebrow. "Did that shooter holed up in Harlem make a trip to the Village tonight?"

"I'll talk to Bozo Jackson tomorrow, kid, and find out. But that guy Leon with the Israeli consulate had it right—might be better if those kids had never dug up old Goliath. I'm thinking that big bully needs to be put down once and for all."

She shook her head and the black tresses shimmered. "Politicians, terrorists, historians, entrepreneurs, all ganging up on you—you really think they'll let that happen?"

"They have no choice, doll. Decision'll be mine. Ours."

"Not the kids'?"

"They'll have their say. We'll make sure they come out of this with everything they need."

She shrugged and black locks bounced. "You're up against adversaries who have no shortage of weapons, Mike."

"Yeah," I said. "And me with just my little old .45.. . . Of course, I'm a better shot."

That made her laugh a little. The movement of her arm was very subtle, very slow but very deliberate. She reached around, let her fingers feel for the switch on the lamp beside her and clicked it off. The darkness was soft and warm, like a cottony blanket in a cool room, with only the soft glow from the outside creeping in through the windows to gradually bring shape to the objects around us.

"Mike . . ." Velda's voice was a gentle whisper. "Do me a favor."

"What, doll?"

"Take off your gun."

We got to the office late the next morning, about nine. The camera crews and newshounds had given up on me, and I would be able to pull the Secure Solutions guard off before long. The media had a hungry mouth but was a fickle eater, and the Goliath bone's news cycle was over—for the moment, anyway.

I was feeling for my keys when Velda got hers out of her purse and went to put it in the lock. She rubbed her thumb along the metal and frowned. "Mike . . ."

"What?"

She held the key out and dropped it in my palm. "Something's on it."

It had a strange slipperiness to it and at the top of the groove was a fragment of wax.

"Been a long time since I saw this done."

"What's wrong?"

"Somebody made a wax impression of your key, doll."

"You're kidding! That went out with miniskirts."

"Well, like miniskirts, some of the old ways are the best ways." It was a single key on a rounded key ring with a white round tag that said OFFICE; to be sure, I held it against mine. Exact match. "Where's your regular bunch of keys?"

"I was too embarrassed to tell you—left them here at the office in the desk drawer, accidentally."

"Don't apologize, it's been hectic as hell."

She took the single little key back. "This is the spare I keep at home, Mike."

I grunted a laugh. "Well, your visitors didn't find the Goliath bone in your apartment last night, but they ran across something valuable. They're not dumb—they knew they could likely pick *your* lock open, but figured the office lock might be a different matter."

But the office showed no signs we'd had visitors.

Velda stood at her desk. "What do we do, Mike? Change the lock?"

"No! Hell, no. This is perfect."

She gawked at me. "Somebody having a key to our office is 'perfect'? I have no idea what you're up to."

"If you did, you'd be the boss."

She smiled smugly. "Before long . . . I will be."

The morning saw us dealing with another round of offers by phone, fax, and FedEx. Just before noon, Velda came in to ask if we were going out for lunch or if she should have something delivered, when the phone in my left-hand bottom desk drawer trilled.

Velda frowned. "That doesn't ring very often. Who has that number anyway, Mike?"

"Just some personal friends. I never give it out for business." I pulled out the drawer, lifted the false bottom and picked up the small cell phone and answered.

The rich, deep voice was instantly identifiable when it said, "Mike?"

"My man Bozo. What's happening?"

"I have that shooter for you, Mike."

"I didn't say grab the bastard, Bozo. I said watch his ass."

"Well, he and his ass was taking off, so I didn't think I had a choice."

"Got you. That was a good call. Now tell me he's alive."

"Oh, he's breathing. We made him talk some, but you'd better get here and listen up yourself."

"*Keep* him alive, you hear?"

"How alive?"

"Talking and thinking and scared alive, Bozo."

"You got it, man. You know where Lonnie Hartman's garage is?"

"Sure. But Lonnie's dead."

"Right. But some of the guys that worked for him, drivers, mechanics, they got a stake in this. They give me their garage to use plus their, uh . . ."

"Moral support?"

"Somethin' like that, Mike. Somethin' like that."

I flipped the cell phone shut, snugged it back in its hidey-hole, replaced the lid, and closed the drawer. When I looked up at Velda, she was hovering over the desk, her big brown eyes narrow and hard. "Am *I* in on this?"

I shook my head. "Bozo Jackson will have his buddies there,

and I don't want those clean-cut African American youngsters distracted by you."

"Bullhockey. I'm just some old broad to them. You don't want my delicate sensibilities damaged."

"Hey, I know all about how delicate your sensibilities are. Thing is, these Muslim 'patriots' have funny ideas about women, and I don't want any kind of shame kicking in and muddying the waters."

Her hands were on her hips, Wonder Woman–style. "I wasn't going to strip him naked and sic the dogs on him so you could take snapshots!"

"That's a relief. Look, doll, you stay here."

"I know, I know, and hold down the fort."

"Exactly. And you can start by calling Pat to keep him on the alert. In fact, have him send a couple of his undercover guys to that area. Tell him to have 'em camp out in that Soul Kitchen Diner on Lenox. No white cops. Make sure they're black or Puerto Rican."

She smirked at me. "Like *you* wouldn't be the whitest ofay in Harlem?"

"Sugar, holding Bozo Jackson's hand, I *am* a brother of another color."

I parked alongside the ancient garage, pulling the car in behind Bozo's, and got out without bothering to lock it—if I had to get away fast, I didn't want to be slowed down. Anyway, a neckless pal of Bozo's in a black track jacket and sideways ball cap was stationed outside at the back door, and he would keep an eye out for me.

I entered into a small hallway between a few small glassed-in offices. Bozo, in his customary black leather topcoat, was talking tough to two guys half his age, wearing black-sleeved white-torso bomber jackets that said HARTMAN's on the front. They had cut-to-the scalp hair to show off skull tattoos and their faces were blandly menacing, half-lidded eyes stopping just short of arrogant as Bozo chewed them out.

Finally, the two guys nodded, then noticed me. Bozo, right behind them, said, "That's Hammer. Now get back in there and behave yourselfs."

They moved down the corridor into darkness.

Bozo grinned at me. "They young, Mike. They get overenthused sometimes."

"They didn't kill the son of a bitch, did they?"

"No, no! It's cool. It's cool."

I held up my hand. "Bozo, you're on a pension, aren't you?"

His head bobbed. "Sure, did twenty-five on the job. Why?"

I gave the ex-cop a hard look. "Don't want you doing anything to lose those pension privileges, pal."

"Naw, don't worry—once a cop, always a cop. Just don't remind these young *dudes* that cop blood still runs in these veins."

"Gotcha," I told him, and followed him into the darkness.

But it wasn't all darkness. A light high up was on, sending a cone of yellowish illumination down onto the slightly absurd sight of the shooter seated in a decrepit old lounge chair, embedded in its worn creases so deep that even if his hands and ankles weren't duct-taped, he could hardly have gotten up and out without help.

He was small and dark and had a fastidiously trimmed devil's beard; he wore a red Chicago Bulls sweatshirt with its cartoon bull's head logo, black sweatpants and white Nikes. He squinted when he looked our way, but the light from the little office area was behind us and we were just shadows to him. Shadows.

Great big shadows.

Threatening shadows.

Nobody said a word. There was a *snick* and a practiced ear could tell a switchblade had come out to play and the guy in the overstuffed chair, already trembling, began to quiver.

My eyes were becoming adjusted to the gloom, and the face of the shooter took on more clarity. He hadn't been badly beaten, not yet. Bozo had held off anything but intimidation and some minor roughing up before I got there. I studied the prisoner carefully, trying to separate him from the other eight million New Yorkers, which was almost impossible until you saw the small tattoo on the back of his hand.

There are countless tattoo IDs, but this one was special—it made him one of the Rada Rey, a lifetime group of hired killers who had once worked for Saddam Hussein.

I glanced at Bozo Jackson. He wiped a hand over his mouth, and the guy standing behind the prisoner in the chair suddenly whipped out a piece of duct tape and smeared it across the guy's kisser. What it implied was worth more than cutting his throat.

His eyes screamed.

Cords in his neck stood out like tensioned cables, his face went wet with sweat, his forehead a veiny bas-relief map of agony.

Something somewhere in the big room dripped, little *boinks* that punctuated the otherwise absolute quiet. Well, that and a dull humming coming from under the strip of duct tape. That was when the guy pissed his pants. The stench of urine was immediate and foul. Bozo nodded for the others to stay put and motioned me back into the cramped office corridor.

But the smell of the garage came with me. After a few deep breaths, I said, "Do we know who he is, Bozo?"

"His papers said he was a Syrian national. He cleared customs okay, produced papers that stated he was a student assigned to NYU doing graduate work. He speaks three languages and is fluent in Arabic and English."

"How'd you get all that out of him? I don't see a mark on him. Did you hit him where it doesn't show, Bozo?"

"I didn't hit him at all. Those young dudes shook him like a rag doll some, but he ain't been hit, not once. First of all, the idiot had all kinds of papers on him. Second, a Russian hooker heard him talking on a cell phone in Arabic."

"She understands Arabic?"

"Enough to recognize it was Arabic. That's how I heard he was holed up back here in my cabbage patch."

I gave him an odd look and he added, "You *do* remember you told me to keep my eyes and ears open."

"Yeah, man. And I also remember, 'Once a cop, always a cop.'"

"Never really do leave the job, Mike." He reached behind his back and brought out an object he had under his belt and handed it to me.

I fingered the covering handkerchief back and there was the .22, a striking target gun with an angular wooden handle and a six-inch rifle-type barrel.

"For neutral bastards," I said, "the fucking Swiss can make a firearm."

"That they can, Mike. That they can."

It was loaded up with copper-tipped shells.

Bozo said, "They'll match up in the lab. Keep that baby covered—still has his prints on it."

"Sure you don't want to get back on the force again, Bozo?"

"Nope. I like it up here, doing odd jobs for solid citizens like Mike Hammer."

I told him I'd give the .22 and all the information to Pat, and he could take it from there.

Bozo bobbed his head back toward the garage. "How much heat shall we lay on this prick?"

"Nothing visible," I told him.

The ex-cop grinned. "Maybe he's a candidate for the ol' Scream Room."

"You stopped me cold with that one, pal. I'll bite—what's the Scream Room?"

"Just an old frozen-food box that's insulated with two-foot–thick walls. Hasn't been used for years—for its original purpose, that is. Which was to hold a dozen sides of beef, in the day."

Bozo started to smile when he saw me frown.

"Don't sweat it, Mike. We're civilized. Stick somebody in there, let him know what the place was a few years back, turn the unit on after we strap him to a chair, and suddenly our guest gets the idea. Like a great big refrigerator—remember the old gag, 'The little light, it stays on'? Well, there's only a little lightbulb in there, too, but it's enough so they can watch themselves turn blue."

Quietly I asked, "How many have you given the Scream-Room treatment to, Bozo?"

"Hardly nobody! One slimy child-fucker held out for almost ten minutes till the frost got his beard white. Talk about a bad case of the blue balls!"

"Damn."

"So?"

"Well . . ." I shrugged. "Okay, chill him down a little."

"Want to watch?"

I waved that off. "Just tell me about it."

"Cool."

"Yeah. Cool. Did you shake his room down, Bozo?"

"What for? If there's any cash, one of the gals in that mattress factory will get it, and you can bet he'll have nothing incriminatin' lying around. You have that .22, so what else could there be?"

"They all make mistakes, Bozo."

"This one made a hell of a mistake coming back here. He does a job, he shakes a tail feather out of town, then turns around and heads back for a couple more *kills*? What the hell's that about?"

I didn't have an answer.

But I mulled it on the way back to the office. Criminal actions don't follow set patterns. There is always an ultimate goal in mind for the offender. It could be revenge or personal power or a lusting after something the offender had always wanted—but by and large, the greatest goal is money. Cash or something equally as valuable. Power is one of those abstract goals. Sex comes into play, too, but that's power for a lot of guys, the twisted ones in particular.

What means everything to one can be as nothing to another. Sex or money or drugs and now the craziest abstract goal of all: the skeletal remains of an oversized soldier boy who got creamed by an Israelite punk who hadn't even been conscripted into the damn army.

Outside my office window, the rain had started. It trickled down the glass leaving paths through city dust. Manhattan lay under a gray blanket, the sidewalks a moving multicolor human caterpillar of umbrellas. Noise from the flow of taxicabs was almost a tired sound and you had to wonder why so many millions of people would jam themselves into a jungle of concrete and spinning wheels to do the same things they had done a thousand times before.

As usual, Velda could read my mind as she came into my inner sanctum, closing the door behind her and stopping to stand in front of my desk. "It's money, love. That's why they run the rat race. It's why *we* run it. We've all got to have it."

"Why?"

"Survival."

I made a face. "Lewis and Clark didn't need it when they explored the country in the old days."

"They had rifles and gunpowder," she reminded me, "to stave off the Indians' bows and arrows when the shiny beads and trinkets didn't play . . . Speaking of which, a pair of explorers from the government are cooling their heels out there."

"Probably not Lewis and Clark."

She smirked. "Martin and Lewis is more like it."

Then she returned to the door, opened it wide, and said, "Come in, gentlemen."

Their eyes did a quick visual check before they stepped across the doorsill. I got out of my chair, looked at both their ID folders to satisfy their legal minds.

The two young men were in their early thirties, black-suited, white-shirted, nearly identical raincoats draped over their arms; their leather ID folders said they represented the Federal Bureau of Investigation. One of them was white, with one of those short butch haircuts that tries to disguise the onset of baldness; he introduced himself as Jerome Wilson and his ID agreed. The other might have been Latino, but my first hunch played off when he introduced himself as James Jabara.

"You share a name with a Korean War hero," I said to Jabara.

He smiled, surprised. "Yes. Not all Italian Americans are in the Mafia, Mr. Hammer, and not all Arab Americans are terrorists."

"No. And they aren't all Muslim, either. First ones here were Christians, right? From Syria?"

Leland said, "You know your history, Mr. Hammer."

"Lately I've taken up a certain interest. In history. By the way, I'm an Irish cop, but you'll be glad to know the Irish are a diverse bunch that includes lawyers, bankers, doctors, engineers, bricklayers, farmers, and also probably a drunk or two. Now tell me what Uncle Sam wants to know."

My light tone didn't set them off. Velda stopped by my desk where she activated a small control box, flipping toggle switches until all but two of the red lights were lit, then pulled up a chair and sat just to one side of our guests, smiling graciously, her hands toying with a pad and pen.

I said, "I hope you don't mind our office formalities, but we like to keep an accurate record of conversations, especially when we're dealing with Washington, D.C."

Jerome Wilson kept a straight face as he said, "We're out of the New York office."

"Same peas, different pod," I said cheerfully. "I spoke to your brothers at Homeland Security not long ago. Now, what can I do for you?"

After what you might call a pregnant pause, Jerome Wilson put on a stern countenance and said, "We understand you have in your possession a certain article—"

This time there was an edge to my voice. "Cut the crap and call it the Goliath bone, like the papers and TV, why don't you? Is that where you heard about it, or do you have other sources?"

Jabara sat up. "We have been instructed to—"

"Guys, let's cool the officialese. First, I'm not your ordinary citizen. I'm in the same business you are, only one hell of a lot longer. I respect the government and all that jazz, but your agencies have as many boneheads as we have here on Broadway, and we have our share. What is it you want?"

They shared a look of consternation. Then Wilson said, "To be brief, the government would like to have possession of the artifact."

I shrugged. "And what are they offering?"

Jabara said, "We're not authorized to offer anything. There may be considerations—tax benefits, for example—but we are in no position to compete with offers from the private sector or, for that matter, foreign governments."

I grinned. "The United States government with its trillions can't compete with what these rogue states have in their coffers?"

Wilson said, "It's not that, Mr. Hammer. We can't dignify the wild assertions that this bone is authentic. The extreme reactions of certain groups, including but not limited to al-Qaeda, to this representing a fallen hero of the Islamic world—not to mention certain Israelis proclaiming it a talisman of an ancient victory . . ."

"Go ahead. Mention it."

Jabara sat forward again. "Mr. Hammer, what we would like to do is defuse this situation before it sparks even more extreme hostilities."

"I can point you to a certain vacant lot in Manhattan that says things already got hostile a while ago."

"We have had requests—nothing formal, but through diplomatic channels—from fifteen of the twenty-two Arab states requesting that the Goliath bone be turned over to them. Asking the U.S. government to intercede."

"Is that what you're going to do? Intercede?"

"If the bone were displayed in, say, the Smithsonian, amid a certain fanfare and also a context designed to cool down the factions—authorities from the world of academia who can debunk the Goliath aspect of—"

"That can't be definitively debunked any more than it can be definitely proved. Doesn't the FBI know you can't prove a negative?"

Wilson's expression was damn near pleading. "Mr. Hammer, if we could just appeal to your patriotism—"

"Knock it off. I fought a war that used up my patriotism. Get real."

"Then it's your intention to sell it to the highest bidder?"

"It's not mine to sell. I'm gathering information, including quotes plus this incredibly unappealing non-offer of yours, that I'll convey to the owners."

"Will you encourage them to consider—"

"I'll encourage them to laugh you out of town."

"The government—"

"Couldn't defuse a firecracker. Oh, you fellas on your level, you're competent enough, and I respect that. But we all know what the politicians will do with this. You've heard from Israel, too, right?"

"Yes. Of course."

"And they claim the bone is theirs."

"That's right."

"Well, they have something in common with Uncle Sam—they have no case. They have a big bundle of trouble just waiting to explode, and since the big bang really hasn't started yet, they figure they'll punt. Swell thinking. Suppose the Israeli lobbyists *do* allow this thing to go to the Smithsonian—guess where the next airliner crashes into?"

Jabara said, "Mr. Hammer, your cynicism really is not warranted here."

"It's warranted everywhere, chum. Leave your business cards on the desk. I'll talk to my clients and maybe, just maybe, I'll get back to you."

Wilson stood, but Jabara was still in his chair—on the edge of it, anyway. "Mr. Hammer, your reputation is well known. We had assumed, at this point in your life and your career, that you would leave recklessness behind. You are one man. We're a huge organization, and there are other bodies within the system ready to cooperate—the interdepartmental synergy, post–9/11, is quite remarkable."

"Yeah, synergy's a hell of thing. But it doesn't help you, not with the next big trouble just waiting in the wings. You know there's an enemy, you know what they'd like to do, you know the vast probabilities you have to deal with, but you just don't know what to do about it. The enemy can even be U.S. citizens, moles waiting underground until the call comes." I gave them a tight smile. "Something wrong, fellas? Got a bone to pick?"

Both stared at me a while, but neither had anything else to say. Jabara got up, and they nodded and left.

When the door shut, Velda cut the power to the recorder and gave me a hard look. "You were kind of rough on them, Mike."

"Naw—they got just about what they expected. Their experience may be limited, but like Jabara said, they had my history down pretty damn well before they came up here. This was just another practice run."

"Ordinary citizens are *supposed* to be scared by the FBI."

"Hell, ordinary citizens pay their salary."

For thirty seconds or so, Velda stared out the rain-streaked window, her forehead showing she was deep in thought, the rain traces reflecting on her lovely face.

I went over and stood beside her and watched the rain. Outside, the wind picked up and blew a hard burst against the glass.

I said, "The wheels in high places know damn well we won't give up the Goliath bone, and they sure don't want all the legal and time-consuming details to go through court procedures while the world is dancing on tiptoes waiting for another catastrophe to get pulled on us."

"So?"

"So it's big news. World news. It's startling and it has tremendous repercussions and can affect everyone alive."

"What's your point, Mike?"

"When everything gets out of hand, where do the countries go to get authority to make things go the way *they* want it to go?"

"Forty-second Street?"

I nodded. "Right. The United Nations building. House of the babbling idiots."

"You don't sound like a big fan."

"Damn well told, baby." She was grinning at me. "What's so funny?"

"You, my love. You're taking on the whole damn world again.

One last case before we get hitched, and it has to be this one. What's wrong with a good old-fashioned murder?"

"We've got that, too," I said, and slipped an arm around her shoulder and squeezed. "We've got that, too."

Bozo Jackson was standing near the guard in the black track jacket when I pulled up. Bozo, halfway through a hot dog, nodded hello, took a last big bite of his very late lunch, and met me halfway as I approached.

I asked him, "How's the visitor doing?"

"I think the boy's gettin' the flu, Mike."

"The flu?" .

"Yeah—he's definitely got the chills." He laughed at that, but I didn't join in. "Talk about the cold sweats, baby—this chump's got 'em."

"Where is he?"

"In an office, all bundled up, a space heater going."

"Who says you aren't a caring guy?"

"Bet your ass. But no matter how much we warm *his* ass up, his teeth just keep rattling in his head."

"Yeah?"

"Not from the cold, Mike. Terror. Sheer terror."

"He tell you anything?"

Bozo gestured grandly. "Come on in and ask him your own self."

I didn't have to ask our shooter anything. The little man with the devil beard, arms and legs duct-taped to a scarred-up old wooden chair now, was talking as soon as he saw me, getting it out of his system. He might have seen a lot of street guys under a gun, but what he had faced in Bozo's Scream Room had literally chilled his bones, and the possibility of going through it again had scared him shitless.

He poured it out: He had shot at the "white girl's" purse in front of that hotel, with orders to scare, not kill. He was a precision shooter and could do that. He had returned to Chicago, but was there less than a day when he was sent back with orders to kill the people he'd come in contact with: Lonnie Hartman and the Cosmo kid with the gypsy cabs and the man who sold him the .22, Mr. Jellybean.

"What about George Hurley?" I asked.

"Who?"

"The man in the alley in the Village."

"What man? What village?"

"You didn't do a job last night?"

"No!"

I let my eyes hold his for a full minute, seeing the trembling of his half-frozen mouth. His fingers were clenched together and his arms strained at the duct tape that tied his elbows to the spindly chair.

I asked, "Who do you work for?"

"I receive orders from a man named Kaddour. There are friends in Chicago who introduce us."

"Are you al-Qaeda?"

"No. I do jobs for them, but I am freelance. I work for any group that supports jihad."

"This Kaddour is who sent you here, and then sent you back again?"

"Yes."

"They pay you yet?"

His nod was brief. "Half."

"When do you get the other half?"

This time his eye darted from mine to Bozo's, then back to mine again. He had to swallow, but couldn't make those neck muscles work.

Finally he mumbled, "I had one more job before full pay."

"And *I* was the target."

His nod was barely perceptible.

"How much would they pay to see me dead?"

The question caught him completely off guard. His mouth moved, but nothing came out. I just kept looking at him and he said, "I would get . . . another ten thousand, plus other five owed."

I let him see the nasty grin I wore. "If we don't kill you here, you're toast when you go back where you came from. You know that?"

His head bobbed.

"Maybe we should kill you here. Let you freeze, maybe."

His tongue couldn't even wet his lips.

Beside me, Bozo was grinning. At least I thought he was grinning. That wild grimace could have meant anything. If Bozo hadn't been a retired cop, that expression would have sent my hand to my gun.

I said, "You killed a bunch of people, friend. That's called murder around here."

"I am a soldier."

"Naw, you said it yourself, you're freelance, a hired gun. But I guess you could say that about most soldiers, too, so I'm going to give you a break. You played it straight with us, so a choice is in order."

"Choice?"

"Yeah. Infidels are real big on freedom of choice. We turn you over to the cops, and there's a big trial, and you die by lethal injection. Or we cut you loose right now, and you take your chances. You've been arrested and printed sometime during your lifetime, so an ID is likely."

This time his neck moved as he swallowed and nodded.

I'll say he'd been printed: Bozo was holding up a white card with inked prints of both hands on it. He was still a cop, after all.

I grinned at the display and murmured, "Bozo—you are a sneaky rascal."

Our prisoner said, "I choose freedom."

Bozo gave me a small grin. He ripped the duct tape off the very nervous hit man and handed him the small overnight case retrieved from the warm-sheet hotel down the street.

It was still light outside, although gray with rain.

Bozo said to him, "The girls got your loot, bro. There's fifty bucks in the bag that'll get you a ticket out of here, but you're on the shoe leather now, and you may have a watcher behind you, to see if you carried out your assignment. You know what I mean?"

He knew, all right. His eyes said so.

"Move it," Bozo Jackson said.

Fingers still stiff from the Scream Room clutched the bag, and legs that had been winterized shuffled toward the door. His strained look back was trying to make sense of the situation.

He was still expecting to be killed before he got out the door in some wild manner even his employers couldn't imagine. He went out, walking backward, and we followed lackadaisically.

When he was outside, he turned and shuffled to the street. At the curb he looked both ways, then, after a moment's indecision and scoping looks back and forth, moved off toward the tall buildings of Manhattan.

Bozo Jackson said, "How long do you think he has, Mike?"

I grunted.

I could see him in a one-room apartment, wrapped in a bloody sheet with a slab of tape covering his mouth, stiff and slowly turning black, discoloring the place.

"Under a week," I said.

Chapter 10

Time could race by or hit a wall. It was like watching an outfielder stand under a fly ball with everyone in the stands holding their breath and the blasted ball wouldn't come down. It just hung there while the world breathed and waited, but nothing was happening. Nothing at all. There was quiet in the stands, the silence of the unexpected. There was no slap of the ball into the fielder's leather mitt. The damn thing just hung there.

I looked at the calendar pad on my desk. It had been almost a month since Paul Vernon had taken Goliath under his wing. I had no way to know how long the restoration work would take, but Paul was a professional and an expert. He would do the best possible job in the shortest time.

What I had put on the back burner of my concerns was the usual stupidity of politicians when they all came to a joint decision. In the meeting place on Forty-second Street where nations gather to turn normal processes into madhouse schemes, a determination was made that Goliath was an international trophy to be shared by the world. The Goliath bone had no owner—no one could claim it as their property. A committee was assembled to assert this non-ownership.

They could get in line.

In the last few weeks, the media had settled down some, after giving George Hurley's murder lots of play for just under a week. Matthew was taking it hard, Jenna didn't show much emotion, but you could tell she was keeping plenty inside, and her mother had held a very small private nondenominational service at a Manhattan funeral home. No burial—George's ashes would be scattered in the Valley of Elah, appropriately enough.

I was still shuttling the kids from safe house to safe house, but on a weekly basis now. With the bill I was racking up with Secure Solutions, the payday on that bone better be a good one. Between the hired security guys, some surveillance by Pat's boys, and whatever skills Velda and I brought to the table, no sign of anybody tailing us or watching us was hitting the collective radar. I'd moved back to my own place, now that the media crowds had abandoned both my apartment house and the Hackard Building.

The morning of the day everything came to a head, Velda and Pat were having coffee and Danish in the outer office when I got there about nine. I took the cup of joe, paper napkin, and cherry pastry that Velda handed me and suggested that she and Pat join me in my office.

"You'd better return your calls first," she said, with just a hint of something in those dark eyes.

Pat was no dummy. He knew he was being excluded from something. But he didn't mind spending a little time with Velda. A long time ago he'd admitted to me *he* loved her, too. It had rarely come up again, but there had to be a reason why he'd never settled down after all these years. Twice he'd almost married, and twice it had gone south.

Maybe he'd been hanging around being my pal all these years just waiting for me to finally catch the violent death so many evil assholes thought I richly deserved. But I didn't think so.

The scrap of paper with Velda's flowing handwriting on it included four phone numbers for me to return. Three were from news desks that I recognized and ignored, but the final one was from Leon, the Israeli Consulate rep with the unpronounceable last name.

I went through a receptionist and then the secretary named Axler and finally was able to say, "Mike Hammer here, Leon. What's up?"

His voice had an almost musical timbre, his words spoken with an ease that took nothing away from a certain innate seriousness. "Good morning, Mike. I have several interesting things to share."

"Share away."

"We have just received information from an area in the Valley of Elah."

"Are you on a secure phone, Leon?"

"No matter. What I want to share with you is not classified."

"Go ahead then."

He drew in a breath. "In the area where the Goliath bone was discovered, there is currently an excavation party of twenty. They are not Israeli, and they are accompanied by armed guards. They are in a digging frenzy, not seeming to do anything logically. Each has assorted tools, and one man seems to be directing them where to dig."

"You said the area where the bone was 'discovered,' Leon. That specific spot was never disclosed by the kids—not to the media, anyway."

"I'm sure you know that people close to the Hurleys were apparently less than discreet—assistants, drivers. And this excavation site is certainly close to their campsite, according to reports I've received from a . . . knowledgeable source."

"Mossad, you mean." It wasn't a question. I put a shrug in my voice: "Let the bastards look."

"It doesn't concern you?"

"Why should it? The Goliath bone's in safe hands where I can get right to it. I'm not worried about thieves snatching this relic."

"These are fanatical people, Mr. Hammer. Zealots of the worst stripe."

"I noticed. If non-Israelis accompanied by armed guards are digging on Israeli soil, why haven't your people moved in?"

"And set a match to this tinderbox?"

I grunted a laugh. "Since when were Israelis shy about sticking up for what's theirs?"

A long pause followed. I was tempted to fill it with another question, but I knew I had Leon in a corner. I'd wait for him to work his way out of it.

Finally he did. "What I'm about to tell you is not official, Mike. It is strictly off the record."

"No problem. You want to shift to another phone?"

". . . Yes."

I hung up and worked on my coffee and nibbled at the Danish. Maybe three minutes had gone by when the phone rang again.

Without preamble, Leon said, "Israel wants nothing to do with the Goliath bone. The government does not wish to fan these fanatical flames any further."

"Really?"

"There will eventually be a statement dismissing the notion that this artifact has any historical connection to the giant Goliath. There is a hope that the bone will come home to Israel naturally, through the Hurleys—the children and the widow—to study it and conduct research in the land where it was found. But any sense that this would be a national treasure or symbol, that is not in the offing."

"That's smart, in my opinion."

"And mine. Great minds, as they say. But not everyone in my homeland feels the same. Mossad reports rumbles from a certain faction I mentioned to you."

Even on the secure line he didn't want to say it: *Kakh*.

"I appreciate the tip."

"Mike, there's something else. Something serious. That name you shared with me a while back . . ."

He was referring to the name "Kaddour," the Chicago-based al-Qaeda operative that the Scream Room shooter had given up. I'd called Leon right after and asked him to run it past his Mossad connection, but had heard nothing.

"I was suspicious from the beginning, hearing that name," he said. "Kaddour—there was a hero of the Holocaust named Si Kaddour Benghabrit, imam of the mosque of Paris, who saved over one hundred Jews by giving them Muslim IDs to avoid arrest and deportation."

"I don't think it's the same guy, Leon."

"No. But it reflects a certain irony on the part of what Mossad believes is a double agent pretending to work for al-Qaeda, who is actually a Kakh agent."

That was a stunner. *That meant every kill the shooter had done on his jihad-for-hire may have had been inspired by Israeli terrorists, not Arab.*

"My friend with the Mossad is an admirer of yours, Mike. He has followed your cases over the years with much interest."

"I'll be sure to send him a glossy for his office. What's your point, Leon?"

"The Mossad does not normally deal in rumor, but what my contact gave me to share with you is merely that. No hard evidence. And I admit it has the flavor of a children's story."

"Let me guess—out of the *Arabian Nights,* right? Only I don't get any wishes or flying carpet."

That made him laugh. Not a guffaw or anything, just a throaty chuckle. "You are an astute judge of dangerous situations, Mike. My contact says he hears whispers of an assassin dispatched to America—sneaked in from Canada, he was told—whose target is very specific—*you.*"

"A lot have tried, Leon."

"This isn't just any assassin, Mike. The Kakh isn't the only group with a sense of irony; al-Qaeda has its own twisted sense of humor. Their number-one assassin was formerly Saddam's top torturer, known for using nothing but his hands and his considerable strength. His code name, given long before that bone was found, is Goliath."

"Yeah? What is he, big for an Arab? Six foot maybe?"

"Mike—he stands seven feet three inches."

I can't claim I loved the sound of that. "I'll alert the Knicks."

"This may be just a rumor—the idea that al-Qaeda, which is known to work slowly and methodically, would rush their top assassin into America simply to deal with one man—it frankly borders on the fantastic."

"Right. So does the original David and Goliath yarn, Leon. But I bet you believe it."

"I do, Mike. I do."

We said our good-byes. Then I called Pat and Velda in and they took the client chairs opposite me.

I said, "Looters are digging around the site where the bone was found—*not* Israelis, and backed up with firepower."

Velda frowned. "Why?"

"Looking for another stray giant bone, probably, but in the millennia since Goliath got knocked off, Mother Nature no doubt distributed his remains all over the place. Those diggers have one hell of a job ahead of them."

Pat had been sitting there quietly, saying nothing, but his strained expression said he had something on his mind. All I had to do was look at him and he said, "Here I am, damn near retired, one of the most honored public servants in the history of this city, and I have to sit and beg table scraps from a private nuisance."

"You can have all the table scraps you want, buddy. Just don't ask for a big bone."

"Mike, we got full lab results back from Washington on that .22 Hamerli target pistol you were good enough to give me. The slugs that hit the Hurley girl's handbag came from that gun, all right. Same gun shot Lonnie Hartman and Wallace Washington."

"Who?"

"Jellybean."

I grunted. "A .22 took out George Hurley, too."

"Yeah," Pat said, shaking his head as if contradicting himself. "But a different gun killed Hurley."

"I could have told you that."

"But of course you *didn't*."

"Come on, Pat! I told you at the scene that Hurley's death was not a hit, and you gave me chapter and verse why it was. Give me a break, buddy."

He shrugged and nodded. "But isn't it time you leveled about who the shooter was?"

"Did I say I knew who the shooter was?"

He just looked at me.

"Okay," I said. "A hit man from out of state. He wasn't very smart, and neither were his employers. He didn't know this city, he didn't know our people, and now he's going to be a statistic on the books, if he isn't already." I shrugged. "When he's found, he'll be dead . . . but at least I can make a physical ID on him."

"*Where* out of state?"

"Chicago."

"Just a hit man. A run-of-the-mill hit man."

"Well . . ."

"A wiseguy, Mike? That what you're saying? Outfit hitter? What family was he from?"

I couldn't help myself. I grinned. "Al-Qaeda."

"Damn you."

"Truth is, he thought he was doing the hits for al-Qaeda. Something else entirely may be behind it."

"What're you holding back, Mike?"

"Nothing."

"Oh, please . . ."

"Pat, if I tell you any more, like how I got all this information out of that shooter, you'd be jeopardizing a retired cop's pension fund, get it?"

Pat drew in a breath. "Bozo Jackson?"

"I didn't say that."

And now my old friend's demeanor shifted. He shrugged and said, "Fine. Now I'll do you the kind of favor you don't want to do me on this case."

"Yeah?"

"We're getting rumbles on the street I don't like to hear. You'd better get your tail out of town, Mike. These al-Qaeda goons are coming at you. You're just a plain loner with no backup, no social standing, and the wrong kind of connections."

"Like you, you mean?"

"When you keep me mostly in the dark, I'm no good to you."

"I still have my .45."

Pat leaned forward confidentially. "One of the guys on our burglary squad heard talk that some kind of super assassin is heading your way. You'll love this, Mike—he's called Goliath."

The word was really getting around, but my conversation with Leon was confidential, so I just said, "You believe such foolishness?"

"I heard the same thing from my Arab-American pal with Army Intelligence. And he heard that some foreign national has put up a wad of cash to go to anybody who hits you."

"Since when do you worry about me, Pat?"

"We're not getting any younger, kiddo."

"I got Velda. And I got a feeling *you'd* come through in a pinch."

"A trio of soon-to-be retirees, bucking an open contract and taking on the top terrorist assassin in the world—that's a laugh." He pointed at me. "You've been designated the key to the whereabouts of that relic. Mike, the talk is flying on this thing—a ton of meetings and action going on in some of the big mosques with reference all being made about their hero, Goliath."

"The bone or the assassin?"

"Does it matter?"

I shrugged. "Doesn't your department have units that cover all that?"

"Sure, but the number of NYPD personnel who speak Arabic is damn few. Incidentally, when you leave here, there are a couple of undesirables loitering close to the entrance and another couple I recognized stationing themselves on the corner."

"They looking for me?"

"Who else?"

"Thanks for the info, Pat. Would you mind shooting them for me on your way out?"

Pat grinned despite himself, then told me, "Al-Qaeda has money, connections, and can fade right into the woodwork, Mike. Don't play them down—there are Islamic-extremist sympathizers right here in this city. Half of them came up under Saddam Hussein before they bought their way over."

The phone rang and Velda reached over and got it. She gave the standard Michael Hammer Investigations greeting, listened, then said, "Hello, Paul. Yes, he's right here."

She gave me the phone.

"Mike?"

"What's happening?" I asked.

"The triplets and their mom were released from the hospital yesterday."

"Where are you?"

"On your side of town."

"Can you get out for the night without the neighbors spotting you?"

"Sure. I got my drinking buddies with me."

"And you brought the kids?"

"Yeah. They're behaving. All newborns should sleep this sound. Where do we meet?"

"The same place as last time. You still working for UPS?"

"No, I got a job with FedEx. Pays better. See you soon?"

"See you soon."

When we disconnected, I called the lobby to say I was expecting a big FedEx delivery. Velda's bland expression told me she'd followed all of that from just my end of the conversation: Paul had arrived at the private airfield accompanied by Secure Solutions guys, and they would be arriving with the "triplets" and "mom" in the guise of FedEx delivery men. But it all went over Pat's head.

He was leaning forward. "I got one other thing for you, and maybe this will make you take notice."

"Yeah?"

"That guy that took the fall in the subway, when you shot the rod out of his hand . . ."

We were coming full circle.

"What about him?" I asked.

"The Washington boys and their cohorts overseas finally got a complete ID on him, pulled down from a very modest tattoo he had in a very modest place on his torso."

"And?"

"And he was al-Qaeda, confirmed. One of their top-notch assassins."

"Top-notch, maybe. Clumsy, certainly."

"The informer said somebody else would be taking his place. That would likely be this Goliath character."

"That's just talk, Pat. You really think there's a modern-day Goliath, a big giant Arab, out to get me?"

His answer was indirect: "You are still carrying?"

I patted under my left arm. "Loaded with one in the chamber. All I have to do is thumb the hammer back."

Velda frowned. "It's loaded, all right—I caught him stuffing the clip with that ancient ammo his shifty old pal Dick Mallory sent him."

I waved that off. "Tell her ammo lasts forever, Pat."

He gave me a long stare. "Nothing lasts forever, Mike."

And he thanked Velda for the coffee and Danish, and went out.

The box was as tall as me and wider, stamped FILE CABINET several places on the cardboard, brought up on one hand truck wielded by Paul Vernon himself, aided by one of two Secure Solutions employees and trailed by another, both obvious ex-military police, young, tough and ready. All three wore navy FedEx uniforms that looked authentic enough, and the only thing vaguely suspicious was that there were three of them. They rode up the service elevator, but this delivery didn't require my signature, as Paul rolled the cart right in.

The two guards went back downstairs to move the truck to the building's basement parking garage, where I'd prepped the attendant-on-duty to expect them. They would wait in the van for Paul.

After locking us in the office, Velda went to get a blanket from the closet. Paul and I had a brief reunion consisting of exchanged grins and handshakes and got right to unpacking the four stacked boxes within the larger file-cabinet box. Soon four identical cardboard boxes about five feet by two feet were side by side together on the floor near the blanket Velda had spread out like a picnic was about to happen.

One by one, Paul opened each cardboard box, then lovingly lay each of the four anatomically perfect giant femurs on the blanket. All four objects appeared to be absolutely identical. Their weight seemed the same, their size too, the color a darkish, mottled gray-white.

They were as finely tuned as any artificially reproduced segment of a museum's prize dinosaur. Paul had worked on some of the most delicate artifacts ever discovered, even making duplicate parts of fossil skeletons that could barely be told from the original.

Now he'd outdone himself.

The father of these children was smirking at us. "Which is the original, Mike? How about you, Velda—can you tell?"

I said, "Impossible, Paul. You've done one hell of a job here."

"Well, you two are just the general public. But we can put it over on lots of professionals, too. The weights are all exact to that of the original, the color would fool anyone except a top-notch professional duplicator, and the feel of the surface would give a longtime undertaker the squirms."

"You sold us, Paul. Which one is the *real* Goliath?"

Paul moved along the edge of the blanket as if he might pick any one of the big bones. Finally, he knelt at the one at the far right, reaching out, putting his hands under the length of death-colored white antiquity, then cradling it in his arms before handing it to me.

You don't hold something like that without feeling yourself lost in a time warp. This wasn't New York, this was the Valley of Elah. Great armies were on either side of me, and I was privy to previously unheard murmurings from rows of armed fighters, spectators to a new moment of history, witnessing a sight never before beheld.

"Hold it up beside you," Paul suggested.

Carefully, I twisted the bone in my arms so that it was vertical, then set it down next to my foot. There was a silkiness in the feel of the thing, as if it were still wet from the body fluids that had once surrounded it. My hands could feel the slight curvatures of the mighty object, almost sensing a lifelike warmth in its length.

Paul nodded, his eyes on my own, and he indicated with a hand movement that I should lift it in place.

Velda was holding her breath.

With utmost care, my fingers folded around the giant's femur until one end was at my knee, alongside my own right thigh— only Goliath's stopped at my chest.

"Big feller, wasn't he?" Paul said with a grin.

I rested the gigantic femur back on the blanket, my hands almost reluctant to leave this great piece of historical evidence. When I touched the others, no similar sensation kicked in—they were just duplicates, copies of the real thing. Cold. Totally lifeless. But you had to handle the real thing to realize that.

Only then did I completely understand what master showman Harold Cooke had seen in the Goliath bone. No museum could ever contain the noxious aura the bone emitted. It needed thousands en masse to sense the power it had once held in reality, and was trying to assume again. It was a dead thing trying to come alive through the beliefs and obsessions of those living now.

There was an almost Satanic temper to the thing, and I knew in my gut something my head had already told me: This was one piece of history that should never have come out of the ground. It had no life, and no power at all, except what zealots might try to attribute to it.

Paul said, "What are you grinning at, Mike?"

"Nothing funny," I said.

He nodded thoughtfully.

Velda knelt over the four exhibits, carefully inspecting each grisly specimen. But while she ran her fingers along the lengths of the duplicates, she wouldn't touch the actual Goliath bone itself.

"It won't bite you, doll," I said.

She shook her head with a small motion. "I can feel the contamination on that evil thing."

I knew what she meant, but I said, "Hey, it's just a relic."

"A relic is the past, Mike. This thing is in the present."

"But it's been dead a long time."

She looked up sharply, arching an eyebrow. "You sure?"

"Want me to put a bullet in it to see if it bleeds?"

She ignored that, then after a few moments of strained silence, said, "I'm just a little nervous about this, is all."

"Don't be. A fanatic's shot at an archduke's head started World War I. This dead slob's partial corpse is trying to start World War III. And we won't let it."

Paul broke up the discussion when he said, "What do we do now? You never said what you were going to do with the dupes."

"One I'm going to sell to a showman and make some bucks for those kids. The other goes back to the university for their research purposes, and we'll stash another here in the office."

Velda rose and her eyes and nostrils flared. "You're going to hide one *here*? When we know we've been compromised?"

Paul gave me a look.

I said, "Somebody made a wax impression of Velda's spare office key." To Velda, I said, "Right, and they'll swipe one of the bogus bones and head home and be off our backs—for a while, anyway."

Velda was frowning. "But sooner or later, they'll know they've been had."

"Maybe. Which will result in one of two things: Whatever bunch swipes this phony will go running home heroes only to wind up with their heads on sticks. And/or al-Qaeda will announce to the world that they have the one, the only authentic Goliath bone—and who can contradict them?"

Eyes narrowed, head tilted, Paul asked, "What do you have in mind for the actual Goliath bone?"

"Maybe I'll keep it somewhere easy to get at."

Velda's brow knit in curiosity. "You have a safe place in mind, Mike?"

"Absolutely."

"Where?"

"I was thinking of tucking it in bed with me."

A sudden quiet met that remark, then Velda said, "For once I'm glad we waited to get married."

New York City isn't an easy place to try to follow someone. There are thousands on the streets no matter the time or occasion. When somebody said, "New York never sleeps," they were speaking the truth—all lights stay lit, the neon and flashing signs on the faces of the buildings lining Times Square pulse like life blood through the arterial streets and avenues that move with taxis and personal traffic and, like corpuscles, pedestrians.

I had made a trip to a friend in Brooklyn who did special work for me, a master craftsman where furniture was concerned. I'd ordered up a special wedding present for Velda before heading back to my car where one of the Goliath dupes nestled in its cardboard box and bubble-wrap skin in my trunk. I had already called

Dr. Charlene Hurley's cell phone and found she was working late at the university, and alerted her to have their security personnel at the back door waiting for me when I dropped by in an hour or so with a package for her.

When I got back to the Hackard Building, I went in the lobby and shook the rain off my hat. The doorman winked at me. That meant nobody had been looking for me and the elevator was empty. At my office, I checked the tiny sliver of paper by the lower hinge, made sure it was the way I had left it, put the key in the lock, and opened the door. The desk light was on and Velda was asleep on the outer-office couch. She'd make a good wife, all right—she didn't snore at all.

In my office, I picked up the phone, dialed the private number Harold Cooke had given me, and left a message for him to call me ASAP. Outside, the rain was drizzling to a stop. It didn't make any difference at all to the night people.

The office door was locked and the knock rattled the frosted glass. I heard Velda rustling out there and called, "Careful! Should be Harold Cooke, but you never know."

About ninety seconds later, a wonderfully mussed-up Velda, her .38 in hand, ushered the impeccably dressed Cooke into my office. The big handsome silver-haired showman with the money-colored eyes was smiling uneasily, glancing at the gun the big brunette was flashing.

He came over and held his hand across my desk and I shook it without standing. He was grinning. "The media never get tired of our story, do they, Mike? You know about the big discussion at the UN?"

I shot Velda a look that said to give me and my guest some privacy, and she shut us in the inner office.

I said, "Just some TV chatter. Why?"

"Seems somebody found something of historical significance on foreign soil, and the honorable members want to determine who it actually belongs to."

"Gee, I wonder what was found."

"They all seem to know," he said, "but nobody wants to say. You didn't ask me over to talk international politics, though, did you, Mike?"

"Well, in a way I suppose I did. Here's what I want to accomplish, Harold. I want to try to keep the Goliath bone out of the hands of the people who want to use it for rabble-rousing and warmongering. But I also want to turn a nice dollar for Matthew and Jenna Hurley."

A fast grimace crossed his mouth. "Pity about their father."

"Damn shame." I locked eyes with him. "I have a number in mind."

He gave me half a smile, but it was wholly sly. "Thought you might."

"Flat fee, no royalties. One document, the appropriate signatures, and you go your way, we go ours."

"Fine."

"Ten million."

The full smile blossomed. "Does that include the million-dollar finder's fee I promised you, Mike?"

"No. And I want *two* million because I have run up certain expenses."

"That sounds a lot like twelve million."

"Does it? Math's not my strong suit."

His eyes regarded me through unblinking slits. "What guarantees will you make about the relic itself?"

"No guarantee that it *is* authentic."

Now the eyes popped wide. "What?"

I shook my head. "No guarantee. You sign off. If this is the biggest fraud since the Cardiff Giant, that's *your* problem. You make no efforts to authenticate it yourself, you agree not to submit it for authentication or research purposes, and you assume all liability for any purposes you may have in mind for the object."

He let out one blunt laugh. "And all for twelve million?"

I lifted a finger. "Here's what I will guarantee: We will state in public, in no uncertain terms, that the one-and-only Goliath bone has been sold to Harold Cooke. If others come forward claiming to have the authentic bone, no matter how many experts come along in support of this counterclaim, we will stand firm: Harold Cooke bought the authentic Goliath bone from us."

He held up his hands in surrender. "All right. All right. As long as the public believes it to be authentic, whether it *is* or not is a moot point."

"That's right."

Cooke leaned forward, eyebrows up, his tone conspiratorial. "I'll make a confession, Mike—I've already taken a considerable risk on this venture. I was so certain in my gut that you would come through on this for me, I went ahead with Goliath—my animatronic star is already in the process of being crafted by top Hollywood technicians and Japanese robotics experts with the kind of skills Uncle Sam only wishes he could afford."

"So you're ready for the really big show, as Ed Sullivan used to say."

"I already have the theater rented—the St. John is standing vacant right now, you know."

The St. John was one of the few Broadway theaters actually on Broadway.

"I'll put this on one month from now! While the public's interest remains high." He gestured with two hands as if presenting an act onstage. "I have a revival company on the road doing *David and Goliath* that I'm bringing in, supplanting them with a couple of names, of course, young pop stars for the key roles of David and Bathsheba, and . . . but why I am boring *you,* Mr. Hammer? You don't strike me as the showbiz type. Can our attorneys meet tomorrow?"

"Sure."

His eyes were gleaming. "Mike, do you know what the most exciting thing in the world is?"

"Yeah. She's sitting at a desk in the other room."

"It's publicity, Mike, the kind of publicity that really, truly connects with the people. For it to work, you need the kind of attraction that really takes hold of the public: Elvis, the Beatles, David Blaine, the Super Bowl, the Super Bowl *halftime* show—"

"Ever occur to you," I said, "your star attraction is one of the most famous killers of all time—who never killed anybody?"

The money-green eyes glittered. "Ah, but he was *about* to kill. He had all the potential of terror, a towering giant who could make any of us feel insignificant. And there he stood, there he *loomed,* with an army behind him that *knew* what he could do, and a whole new order was about to be ushered in at his command." Sweat stood out on Harold Cooke's face as he recalled the ancient tale.

"Then David messed up his plans," I said.

"Yes. A boy slew a giant, and became himself a giant among

men, a king." Harold let his breath out slowly. A beading of sweat stood out on his forehead. "It's still a great yarn, isn't it, Mike?"

I ran my finger across my upper lip and felt the wetness. Damn. This guy was a storyteller, all right, a true showman.

Cooke stood and this time I did, too. "So do we have a deal?"

"I have to consult my clients," I told him. "But I'll recommend they say yes."

"They won't regret it. Neither will you, Mike."

We shook hands again and he left to go back to the wet streets of the big city.

"Someday," I told Velda, as she drifted into my inner office, "I'm going to get a place in the Adirondacks and maybe apply for a job as a constable."

"I'll make you biscuits and chocolate-chip cookies."

"That's the best deal I've made all night."

She was standing at the rain-dripping window when she asked, "Where's the *real* Goliath bone, Mike?"

"Somewhere safe, baby."

"What about the dupes?"

"Well, we've got one in the closet in the floor compartment, for somebody to steal. And the other two are in the trunk of my car."

She grinned, shook her head and the black tresses shimmered with a reflective cast from the water-streaked glass. "Great security."

"Don't worry about it. I'm going to put you in a cab and send you home. I have one more stop to make tonight."

"And miles to go before you sleep?"

"Something like that."

This time I went in through the loading-dock area, and ducked the NYU research center's front-entry security checkpoint entirely.

Mr. Rogers worked days, but he'd left word with the staffers to give me a free pass. So when I lugged the big box with the Goliath-bone dupe down the mostly deserted halls of the building, I was able to keep my .45 under my arm like a big boy.

Dr. Charlene Hurley said to meet her not in the downstairs lab, but in her third-floor office, where I'd never been. The box was awkward and a little heavy, and knocking was a chore. I got no answer, so I tried the knob and went on in.

I was a little early, maybe fifteen minutes, and at first I thought the office was empty, an antiques-furnished chamber that reeked of the kind of heavy money that could hire the best decorators who would never even think of putting anything on the walls except the finest landscapes of Middle Eastern vistas, deserts, oases, bazaars. Each piece of furniture had a small brass tag affixed to an unobtrusive spot, naming the original owner, like the large wicker chair just inside the door with a little tag saying it had come from the study of Robert Louis Stevenson.

Two massive cherrywood desks in different parts of the room indicated that both Hurleys had shared this generous space. I set the box with the Goliath dupe on the nearest of the desks, the cluttered one that seemed currently in use. The neatness of the other indicated it had been the late George Hurley's.

I heard a faint sound that, if I hadn't been in a fancy office in a university research facility, I'd have sworn was the pounding of water-pressurized needles from a showerhead. Then the sound stopped, and a door across the room toward the left opened and a naked woman came out, toweling her hair, unaware of my presence.

A nicer guy would have immediately cleared his throat or spoken up or something. But while I was working on getting my jaw shut again, I got a very good look at the petite, curvy, stark-naked frame of Charlene Hurley. I'd figured her for her late forties, and had probably been right, but she might have been twenty-five, as lush and lovely as her figure was, pale female flesh pearled with moisture, hills and valleys all well worth exploring, the blonde color of her curly head of hair matched below.

"Excuse me," I said thickly.

She looked up, the towel dropping, her eyes huge, and she made a kind of yelp and ducked back in the bathroom.

I went over to the closed door and said, "Dr. Hurley, I'm sorry. I knocked, it was open . . . I guess I'm a little early."

"I'm . . . I'm sorry." The voice was muffled through the door. "My fault. I'll . . . I'll be right out."

I went over and sat on a couch against one wall under a landscape painting of what might have been the valley of Elah and felt like a schmuck. But I'd be lying if I said the naked image seared in my brain wasn't fun to reflect on.

She came out in a knee-length terry-cloth bathrobe, padding over barefoot on the wall-to-wall carpeting, her hair still damp after towel drying. She had no makeup on, but her features were pretty enough to do just fine on their own. *Who did she remind me of?*

"Mr. Hammer . . . Mike . . ." She came over, very businesslike, extending her hand and I stood and we shook. "I *do* apologize," she said.

"No. We'll just forget it."

Like hell I'd forget it.

She smiled embarrassedly. "You see, since George's death, I've been drowning myself in work. With the kids not at the apartment, and . . . and George, George's *presence,* in every room . . .

I've mostly just been staying here." She nodded toward the couch where I'd been sitting. "I sleep there, and fortunately . . . obviously . . . I have a full *bathroom* here."

"I brought you a present." I nodded toward her desk.

She went quickly to her huge red cherrywood desk and very slowly opened the cardboard box, moving away the bubble wrap. I came over and watched her face closely as she lifted the replica out and held it in her hands—the thing was better than half as big as she was.

Consternation was evident in the tightness of her lips as she turned the femur over, and even as she picked up a magnifying glass to inspect the object even closer.

Finally she looked up at me and said softly, "An excellent reproduction, Mike."

"You sure that's not the original?"

For a fraction of a second, her lower lip drooped as she concentrated, again staring through the glass. Then her head snapped up, her eyes saying she wasn't used to being fooled. "It's a duplicate. Experts could tell. But only experts."

I didn't let her get away with it. "Jolted you a little, didn't it?"

She smiled, setting the fake bone on the desk beside its box. "A very good reproduction, Mike. One of the best I've ever seen. Whoever prepared this is—"

"A real professional," I finished for her. "Who's handled some rare and exotic pieces, even if he makes better money in other areas."

She hefted the replica.

I said, "You'll find the weight is exact. The surface feels identical to the original piece. All the markings from being buried over thousands of years are as nearly perfect as anyone could get it."

She didn't seem quite sure what to say. I watched while she rotated it in her grasp a few times. "Yes," she admitted, "I can see that."

"But you're thinking something else, aren't you?"

Her nod was almost invisible. "Reproductions don't count at all, Mike."

"Well, it was cast from the original," I said.

"And the original is what I need. What *we* need, Jenna and Matthew and I, to continue our research."

With a little nod that flicked moisture at me from her damp hair, she gestured to the couch and we went over and sat.

"That's the plan," I told her. "We're letting Harold Cooke build his *David and Goliath* revival around having the 'real' bone, but it'll be a duplicate."

"Isn't that fraud?"

"No. We'll be covered legally in the contract. Cooke couldn't care less about having the real thing—he sells lies for a living. And I'm going to allow another dupe to be stolen, probably by al-Qaeda agents."

She smiled faintly. "I see. Al-Qaeda will claim it has the real bone, and so will Cooke, and eventually all of this fuss will . . . blow over. But what about Israel?"

"I've been speaking to someone at the consulate. Unofficially, I've been told that Israel has no interest in the bone, except as an archeological treasure."

"I'm not sure I follow."

"Has a representative from Israel contacted you?"

She nodded, not caught off base at all. "I heard from a Mossad representative on the phone just this morning. If Matthew and

Jenna give the bone over to me, and I return with it to Israel and do all of the research there, the Israeli government will fund a full excavation in the Valley of Elah."

"Nothing in writing, of course."

"Of course."

"When the time is right, Charlene, we'll swap the duplicate bone for the real thing. But only when this has settled down enough that we are both secure in the safety of those two kids."

I could sense the thoughts that were racing through her mind. Thoughts of the lovely shape underneath all that terry-cloth were sure as hell racing through mine.

Finally she said, "We have a wealthy financial contributor to this university, Mike. *Very* wealthy. In view of what is happening in Jerusalem, his interest in this matter is quite high. He would be willing to pay any amount to secure this artifact. And would then hand it over to us, naturally, via the university."

"Well, that's great. But what's the catch?"

"He would want to have possession of the bone—temporarily—to authenticate it through his own sources."

I shrugged. "We may be able give it to him, when the time comes."

"I'm afraid he might want it sooner than that."

"He'll have to wait his turn. Anyway, any authentication he undertakes shouldn't cause much further delay. It didn't take you and your husband long to realize that the bone was human, and of the right era."

Suddenly she seemed uneasy.

I put a hand on a terry-cloth sleeve. "All the pieces of this puzzle are fitting in just right, aren't they? That *is* old Goliath's leg, isn't it?"

She drew in a breath and nodded as she let it out. "There's enough scientific and historic evidence at hand to support that opinion. We don't need your showman, Mike. If we allow the university's benefactor to make his contribution, and—"

"We can't take that risk, Charlene. The Philistines know about the bone, too, you know. And they have people over here in the *New York* desert—ruthless people, who'll kill instead of trying to buy it."

She swallowed; her eyes were tearing up. "Do you think I don't know that? Do you think I don't rip myself to pieces every day, thinking about the sacrifice my husband made?"

"I'm sorry. Didn't mean to—"

She cut in. "One man, Mike, even a man like you, can't hope to deal with this thing."

"How many did it take to nail Goliath?"

"Just David," she said. "Just a boy. But, Mike, it wasn't David's expertise that killed Goliath. A higher power was the agency behind it. People don't want to believe that, of course, certainly a scientist like me shouldn't. It's too simple for our highly educated minds, but it happened—it's *history,* recorded long ago but with us today, although dismissed by many as just another 'Bible story.' Until now there hasn't been any physical proof—not that it was needed—but it just hadn't been found."

"That's why I want you to tell everyone here at the university, anyone who wants to know, the media included"—and I pointed to the duplicate bone—"that *that* is a fake, cast from the original, which you believe to have been sold to Harold Cooke."

"I don't understand, Mike—"

"If you are known to have a fake, a duplicate, of the artifact, then you and Matt and Jenna are off the firing line. You're safe. All of you."

She leaned in. Her hand went to my cheek. "And then . . . when the time is right?"

"We'll make a switch. You and science and Israel can have the real deal."

"Mike . . . oh, Mike . . ."

Her lips were on mine and they were moist and warm and soft. I tried not to kiss her back. I swear I tried.

She put her arms around me and, with her face inches from mine, she said, "You've done so much for us, Mike . . . so much. . . ."

And she kissed me again.

This time I managed to push her gently away. "No. It's not right."

Her robe had fallen open and the pale flesh and the pert tips of her breasts made a convincing case for saying the hell with it and taking her back into my arms.

Her hand on my face, she said, "Oh, Mike, I've been so lonely . . . so lonely without . . . without him. How I wish he'd been strong like you. He might still be here. What I could do with a man like *you* at my side. . . ."

Somehow I got to my feet. "Listen, you're a beautiful woman, and I know what you've been going through. But I'm about to get married."

She touched my sleeve. "Couldn't you . . . could you give me this *one* night, Mike? What can it matter? We're not kids, you and me. Your Velda, she and I, we're past childbearing age, we're all just lonely people who sometimes need someone to hold them. It will be our secret. Mike . . . stay with me tonight, Mike. If not *all* night—stay . . . just for a few hours."

She rose, the robe slipping from her shoulders to puddle on the floor, and she wrapped herself around me and she kissed me, hard, demanding I give in to her.

My hands slipped down over smooth flesh and I settled them on her waist and eased her away from me.

"There was a time," I said with an embarrassed grin. "There was a time . . ."

And I got the hell out of there. I left Goliath's bone behind, but I dragged one almost as big along with me.

Chapter 11

The duplicate Goliath bone in the outer-office closet didn't over-stay its welcome—two days later, it was gone.

I knelt at the empty floor compartment, then replaced the lid. Velda had come in at 8:00 A.M., checked the hiding place and found it empty, but saw no immediate sign otherwise that we'd been visited. I'd trailed in at 8:15 and we went through the place thoroughly, finding minor disturbances only in spots big enough to have concealed the fabricated femur.

I stood and grinned at her. "They knew what they were looking for, doll."

"I hope you know what you're doing, Mike. . . ."

Velda had wanted to lay a trap or at least hide some mini-surveillance cameras. I'd insisted on leaving things wide open, an invitation to dine. Anything we rigged would have been spotted, and that might have led to getting the office trashed.

I went down to the security office where Harry Butler, a retired cop out of the Two-Two, was sitting at a modest bank of security monitors. He was heavyset enough to challenge the buttons of his generic gray uniform, but nobody should make the mistake of thinking he was over the hill.

"We had a visitor last night, Harry."

"I'll check the tapes, Mike. About what time you think?"

"We left just after seven. Velda was in this morning at eight."

"They're limited views—I only have lobby elevators and one view per floor."

"Understood. But maybe you snagged something."

"Or somebody. I'll call you." He grinned up at me. "Man, are you *ever* gonna retire?"

"What, like you, Harry?"

About an hour later, I took the call at my desk. "Anything, Harry?"

"You mixing it up with them towelheads, Mike?"

"Why, is that who you see on the tape?"

"No, that's what I see in the papers. What I see on the tape is a little white weasel. I don't remember his real name, if I ever knew it, but they call him 'Pistol Pete.'"

"Sounds like a shooter."

"No way. Sharp as a pistol is where the moniker comes from. He's a lock expert. No office, cash in advance, guaranteed closed mouth. Not easy to locate unless you got a hand in the burglary business."

"He heavy money?"

"Maybe a grand for a job like this. He get something valuable off you? Evidence or something?"

"No. We don't have any big court cases coming up."

"You want me to follow up on this?"

"No thanks, Harry, I'll take it from here."

Harry could have got himself in trouble not reporting this, but he didn't say a word. It's great the way guys in the same game get along.

My next call was to Pat. "You ever hear of a character called Pistol Pete?"

A long pause followed that I knew meant I'd stepped in a hole. "You're kidding, right?"

"It was a question, Pat. Got an answer for me?"

"What I got is a report on my desk that one of the top freelance thieves in this town, a guy the Burglary Squad has had in its Top Ten for fifteen years, was found with his throat cut in a gutter in an alley by a bar in Bay Ridge."

"Named Pistol Pete?"

"Named Peter Pistelli, but that was what his friends called him, yeah."

Possibly also what people who weren't his friends called him.

"Pat, the security in this building has Mr. Pistelli on its cameras last night, and in a wild coincidence, my office was broken into."

"Shit. Anything taken?"

I had kept Pat out of the loop about the bone clones, and now was not the time to bring him onboard. "Nope. He was just inquisitive, far as we can tell. Can't find anything missing."

"He might've shot photos of evidence in your files."

"Yeah, he might. We're doing an inventory. Listen, you mentioned something about having an Arabic speaker working undercover on the Burglary Squad? Possible source of intel on al-Qaeda types?"

"Right. Why?"

"That's my question, Pat—why the Burglary Squad?"

"Because some of these terror cells raise money doing burglaries and heists. Some of them are goddamn good at it. But if your break-in had something to do with the Goliath bone, they'd have done the job themselves, wouldn't they?"

"Maybe not. They know I've posted extra men on my building to keep an eye out with a specific racial profile in mind. Ask your undercover guy if these Arabian thieves of his have connections with other local heisters."

"You mean, would they hire some white asshole to get what they wanted, and let him take the rap for them?"

"And then cut his throat for him right after he'd passed off what he took? Yeah."

"But you said he didn't take anything, Mike."

"I was speaking hypothetically, Pat."

"My hypothetical ass. Bay Ridge has a large Arab-American community, Mike. . . . What did they get? Christ, you weren't hiding that *relic* in your damn *closet,* were you?"

"We're getting back into that need-to-know area, Pat. And I need to know whether your undercover guy considers it credible, the local al-Qaeda branch hiring Pistol Pete."

He growled a little, but said, "All right. You'll hear from me."

"Where would I be without you, pal?"

"Out hiring half a dozen operatives to cover what I do for you for free. And, yes, I know you pay my salary—"

He hung up.

Two weeks later, Pat was in a much better mood. He accompanied us to City Hall and stood up with me when I married Velda. Jenna Hurley was at Velda's side, and Matthew was a witness. We had a big wedding lunch at Le Cirque on East 58th that cost me just a little bit more than my first heap.

Matthew sat next to me, and I asked him how he was getting along with his stepmother.

"A lot better."

"But I bet you two haven't broken the news to her yet, that you'll be the next couple stepping up to the marriage plate."

Matthew grinned nervously and bobbed his head.

"Kid, I waited longer than you've been alive to nab this long-legged doll. Don't make my mistake."

Things had settled down even though the Goliath bone was still big news. Harold Cooke's press conference announcing his imminent Broadway revival of *David and Goliath,* including "a public showing of the recently discovered giant femur believed by experts to be that of the Biblical Goliath himself," had sparked a media frenzy. This was one of those rare stories that straddled the entertainment world and the international scene. The one-week engagement sold out in five hours, mostly over the Internet, with ticket prices twice the already-outrageous going Broadway rate. Velda, the kids and I would be comped, of course.

A whole second wave of PR followed the announcement of the animatronic Goliath, with TV puff pieces and in-depth newspaper articles (in science-and-technology newspaper sections) about the Hollywood, Silicon Valley, and Japanese inventors working together on "a ten-foot robot operating with thirty-two air pumps."

The excitement was only fueled by an al-Qaeda claim to have "retrieved the femur of the great hero, Jalut of Gath (his Arabic alias), from the hands of infidels." That Bin Laden himself delivered the message, in his first videotaped appearance in six months, racked up enormous free publicity for Harold Cooke on the twenty-four–hour cable news channels.

The al-Qaeda party line was that the bone was a religious artifact and would not go on public display. A statement from the Israeli government disputed that the artifact was in Arab hands, and reminded the world that authenticating the femur as having been that of the Biblical Goliath was impossible. Many nuances were explored by the media—interviews with reps of major Jewish-American organizations called the artifact a symbol of triumph over the enemies of Israel, while spokespersons for Arab-American groups were, like the Arab states themselves, divided between viewing the artifact as a symbol of Islamic heroism or an embarrassment to be denied and/or destroyed.

And Harold Cooke basked in it.

Matthew, Jenna and Charlene Hurley gave no interviews. I did a few shows and simply said Cooke had bought the authentic bone from my clients, and didn't offer up anything that wasn't already in the public record. Most of the interviews degenerated into replays of my more notorious cases, and I had plenty of canned answers ready about them.

But the heat was finally off the kids and they moved back in with the girl's mother, who called me the day after Velda and I got hitched, to offer her congratulations.

"Mike, I'm sorry about that night you came to my office . . . I was way out of line, but I hope you'll understand that I was an emotional wreck."

"You better now?"

"With the kids back, and all of us in the apartment together, we're great. But I do apologize."

"Not another word. It was as close to a bachelor party as I got."

She did me the courtesy of laughing at that.

I caught up with Pat at a little deli restaurant we liked down the block and around the corner from police headquarters.

"My undercover contact on the Burglary Squad," Pat said, "confirms the possibility that Pistol Pete could've been hired by those al-Qaeda boys. Apparently Pete was a real pro, with a deft touch, kept up on all the changes, every safe and lock that got redesigned, every old security system that got revised, and every new one that came out."

"They'd used him before."

Pat nodded. "On the other hand, the talk about that open contract on you seems to have faded. Nothing lately on the assassin, the *other* Goliath, either."

"Just talk. Big talk. Bullies from the dawn of time have been all mouth."

"So what now, Mike? Is that it for you and the Goliath bone?"

"There's a shoe or two left to drop, Pat. But for the most part, yeah, I think so."

"You don't mind me tying up some loose ends? Like putting away these assholes who cut Pistol Pete's throat, if I can find them."

"Never let it be said that Michael Hammer ever stood in the way of a law-enforcement official fulfilling his sworn duty to serve and protect the public."

Pat gave half a wry grin. "As long as I remember that Michael Hammer is a big part of that public."

I grinned back at him, and saluted him with my sandwich.

He sipped his coffee. "Why did you wait so long, Mike?"

I was about to take a bite of corned beef on rye. "What?"

"To marry her. To marry Velda."

I shrugged. "Pat, you'll never believe this, but it was Velda, all these years, who wanted to wait."

"Gimme a break!"

"I know, I know, all that kidding back and forth about me putting it off . . . but really, it was her."

He was studying me like crucial evidence in a case he'd been trying to crack for years. When his voice finally came, it was soft: "You really mean it, Mike?"

"Yeah. Someday maybe I'll tell you the whole story. But bad things happened to her, years ago, when she was with the CIA, behind that Iron fucking Curtain."

"Like what?"

"I can't really say anything else, Pat. If she wanted you to know, she'd have told you by now."

"Mike . . . are you pulling my chain?"

"No."

"Well, what's it about?"

"All I can say, Pat, is she came back from that terrible time, in that terrible place . . . not able to have children."

"My God . . . what did they—"

"Buddy, don't ask me to say more. For a lot of years, she loved me and I loved her, but she had this crazy idea that she wasn't complete because she couldn't have kids. Hell of an irony, huh? The most beautiful woman in the world, the kind of creature God put here to make sure men get the right idea and keep the planet populated . . . and she wasn't in the game."

"Mike. That's awful. My God, it's terrible. Here all these years, I thought you were just—"

"A jerk who didn't appreciate her? Naw. I was a jerk who appreciated the hell out of her, Pat. Well, we're finally past where having kids means anything. Having *each other* means everything. So we're married now, and you were my best man, buddy—not a big ceremony maybe, but nobody ever had a better best man than Captain Patrick Chambers."

I held my hand out and he took it and we shook.

"Mike . . . was this your last job?"

"Maybe. Hell, man—they don't come any bigger than Goliath."

The little one-story white clapboard beach house with the baby blue tile roof was perched on its own private peninsula fronting on the Gulf. A thirty-foot channel ran along one side, the aftermath of the state dredging it for coquina to lay a roadbed to Key West. We were a little south of Marathon, with its ten thousand or so year-rounders, and we had plenty of privacy.

The accommodations were courtesy of a doctor who felt I'd saved his life by letting him save mine. A long time ago, I'd recuperated here after a bloody shoot-out that should have left me dead. A washed-up doc had hauled me off the killing field and saved my ass, but he felt the debt was his, because I gave him back his self-worth. I'd recuperated in a glorified shack on the same tiny peninsula, a concrete-block shed that the doc had replaced with this beach house after he got back on his feet and his practice started flourishing again.

If I ever wanted to borrow his beach house for a little getaway from the Manhattan madhouse, he said, all I had to do was ask.

Finally I'd asked. I'd called him to talk about it, and we'd quickly lined up a couple weeks' worth of honeymoon time for Velda and me.

She loved the place at once—it wasn't big or fancy, but it was nice and new, with an understated seaside cottage decor, big brown tiles on the floor and white walls with rattan furnishings and framed seascape prints. The doc's pad wasn't big—the living room was good-size, looking onto a modest deck with two squat white wooden chairs; a counter separated the living room from a modest kitchen that somehow squeezed in a round dining-room table. A hallway off the kitchen led to two bedrooms and one bath and a little laundry room.

Velda immediately picked up on the unusual lamp near one of two recliners angled to face a flat-screen TV. "I like that," she said. "But it's not your style."

"Why isn't it?"

She touched the shaft of the modernistic lamp, which widened dramatically into a rounded base with a hand-painted black-and-white design of willowy 1920s beauties walking their wolfhounds. "This is art deco. You hate art deco."

"I like the Empire State Building."

"That's only because you like the original *King Kong.* Looks a little pricey, compared to the rest of this stuff, which is nice, but *this* . . ."

"That's because it's yours."

"What do you mean, it's mine?"

"That lamp. It's a wedding present. That's no antique—Artie Berns in Brooklyn made it for us."

"Oh, I *love* his stuff!" She was caressing the shaft of the thing in a way a honeymooning wife shouldn't, unless she's serious.

"Of course, it's *all* yours," I said casually.

She turned to me, the big brown eyes growing even bigger. "What do you mean?"

I shrugged. "We had a good payday from Cooke. I invested in some real estate."

"You did?"

"Doc Morgan gave me a deal on this place. It's worth two or three times what he asked, but he thinks he owes me. He doesn't anymore, I can tell you."

Her jaw dropped. "Mike . . ."

"If you don't like it, we can put it right back on the market. We'll probably double our money, though that wasn't the—"

I didn't finish that, because she was in my arms, and taking her revenge by punching me in the mouth with her lips. She started unbuttoning my sport shirt and I worked on getting her shorts unsnapped, and we inaugurated the living floor before she'd even seen the bedroom.

We sat at the kitchen table and she sipped a bottled water and I took periodic gulps from a can of Miller.

"I should be mad, Mike."

"Why?"

"You don't buy a girl a house the way you do a diamond . . . thanks for the diamond, by the way."

It was a full two-carat job. A guy in the Jewelry District had owed me, too.

"It's not a big place," I said, "but there's only two of us. We've got a spare bedroom if Pat or the Hurley kids or anybody wants to come calling. Thought we could make an office of that, too—a corner of it, anyway."

"Is this a . . . *getaway* place, Mike? How much of the year do you want to spend here?"

"How much do *you*?"

"We've discussed closing up the office. . . ."

"I talked to Pat about that."

"Pat?"

"Yeah, he retires in three months. He's going to throw in with Michael Hammer Investigations. He can carry the whole load, or we can spend however many months a year up there we feel like . . . *if* we feel like it."

"Or . . . just stay down here in the sun?"

I grinned at her. "It's why old people go to Florida, doll."

She smirked at me. "What would you *do* with yourself, Mike Hammer?"

"I dunno. I still have four or five big cases I haven't written up yet. That'll probably take me till I keel over, particularly since I don't feel real ambitious."

She reached out for my hand. "Manhattan without Mike Hammer? Can that town survive?"

"Who gives a hoot?"

That made her laugh. And I had one of those warm fuzzy moments Mike Hammer shouldn't have, thinking about how great it would be hearing that sexy, throaty laugh every day—not in an office, but in a place of our own where I could haul her lovely fanny into the bedroom and do something about it whenever I felt like it. If she let me.

We had no plans except to enjoy the white beach, the blue green water and each other. Velda sunned in the kind of little white bikini that only a husband should see, and I sat in a beach chair in a T-shirt and a pair of white shorts and sandals and drank Miller beer. I would start out in the sun and then, for exercise, move to the shade of a palm. For a complete change of pace, I'd take one of the chairs on the deck. Sometimes I'd read a paperback. Mostly

I watched my beautiful wife. At sunset, we sat on the deck together and watched gold and purple fight for control of the sea and the sky. Purple won. So did we.

This was where serious sport fishermen came, but we were the tourist trade, not catching fish but eating them at joints with names like the Cracked Conch Café and the Fishbones Restaurant; nights Velda dug the classic rock at the Brass Monkey—I'm a classical guy myself and I don't mean rock, but what the wife wants, the wife gets. No charter fishing for us, and I sure as hell didn't care to catch a Goliath grouper, one of the possibilities offered.

We did get out on the water—the doctor gave us use of his boat, a twenty-two–foot Carolina day boat, so called because of its open cockpit. The boat had no name, just the number 819, which held some military significance for the doc, I guess.

Velda was startled by my confidence with the craft, but I'd stayed with the doc down here for a long time and had got the hang of it. It maneuvered well, the kind of craft you could steer with one hand and have a hand free for a can of beer. The two Evinrudes at the tail gave it some punch, too. This beat hell out of trying to drive your car in midtown traffic.

Again, fishing wasn't the idea—just feeling the wind and spray and letting the sun wash over us, and feeling beautifully small surrounded by an infinity of glimmering water. If we stayed down here, and I was thinking we just might, I would learn about the sport. Catch and release would be my preference. I was winding down where killing things were concerned.

I had only one job: breakfast. Eggs and bacon and refrigerator biscuits were my specialty, and all I knew how to make. But I could baste her eggs just like she liked them, cooking them in the square of four bacon strips sizzling in the pan. She used to say I'd make somebody a great wife, and now I was proving it.

Two weeks went by in a lovely, lazy blur, quick as lightning, slower than sleep. We had a flight out the next day, and we were sitting in the white wooden chairs on the deck looking out at an ocean that was gunmetal gray blue shimmering with diamond moonlight highlights.

"We could not go back," she suggested.

"Doll, we have to."

"I suppose you're right. Even if Pat takes over, there are things to do at the office. There's our apartments to deal with, and—"

"And there's *David and Goliath*. We can't miss that."

She chuckled. "*I* could miss it."

She was wearing a T-shirt and no bra and bikini bottoms. At her age, her boobs should have been to her knees, and the last thing she should have been able to get away with was a bikini bottom. But her breasts were full and firm, the tips poking at the cotton fabric like the eraser ends of pencils, and her belly was flat and her legs long and lush and even darker tan now than before. She was a wonder. She was my wife.

I shook my head, sipped my beer. "Naw. We have to be there for Matt and Jenna. We promised to go with 'em. Besides, aren't you the least bit curious to see what master showman Cooke's cooked up?"

"Maybe a little. I just hope he doesn't scrimp on security."

"He might."

She gave me a sharp look. "You're kidding."

I shrugged. "If there's a small-scale riot, Israeli boosters banging on Arab protesters, guess what happens?"

"Blood gets splashed?"

"Publicity, doll. Cooke's favorite thing in the world. Publicity." I got up. "One more beer."

"You'll be up all night."

"Baby, I've been *up* for most of two weeks, with you around."

But the refrigerator was out of beer. And I noticed we were also out of biscuits and had only one egg and two slices of bacon left.

Back out on the deck, I said, "I'm walking to that convenience store—we're out of eggs, biscuits, bacon, and beer. All the real staples of life."

"No! Have some bottled water."

"Remember who you're talking to."

She shook her head. "Since we're taking the plane, we can eat breakfast at the airport. Or drive to that Hardee's tomorrow morning. Just sit down."

"Mike needs beer. End of story."

She knew not to bother arguing that point.

The convenience store was half a mile north. I walked down the gravel road bordered by exotic trees and bushes and enjoyed the cool breeze and the night sounds that almost had a jungle tinge. Some nasty little gnats were out, but I'd been sprayed. I was no fool.

I'd slipped on a light windbreaker, a dark blue, white-trimmed Yankees jacket. The word "Yankee" wasn't the smartest thing to throw around in this part of the world, but like I said, I was no fool—honeymoon vacation or not, I kept the .45 handy. Right now it was stuffed in the waistband of my white trousers, and without a jacket, that wouldn't play well in any convenience store, north or south.

About halfway there, my cell phone vibrated. I checked it: Pat Chambers. We'd talked a couple times during this trip, so he didn't indulge in honeymoon kidding, going straight to business.

"That Arab-American FBI guy, Jabara, shared some interesting intel, Mike—that name you handed over, 'Kaddour'?"

"Yeah?"

"Alias of a guy named Elias Kahane. He's not Palestinian, as he'd claimed to a hell of a lot of people on the fringe of the Arab-American community in Chicago. He's Israeli."

"Part of Kakh, Pat."

"Did you say—"

I spelled it for him. "It's an Israeli terrorist group, repudiated by Israel, but with their own ideas . . . and agenda."

"You're saying there's a Jewish al-Qaeda out there?"

"That may be overstating it. Has he been questioned?"

"Mike, I didn't say he'd been brought in. The guy was killed in Chicago yesterday."

"How?"

"Close up. A .22."

"Pat, you're going to want to get with the Chicago PD or the FBI or whoever-the-hell and check the forensics on the bullet that killed Dr. George Hurley."

"Way ahead of you, pal. Perfect match. Same weapon."

"But we have no idea who the shooter is."

"None."

Only I did. But some work would need to be done before I shared my theory with Pat . . . *if* I shared it with Pat. . . .

"How's married life treating you, buddy?"

"Let's put it this way, Pat—I'm just about to enter a convenience store to pick up some groceries."

He didn't say good-bye. Just let his laughter get cut off when I hung up.

I walked back with the sack of groceries under an arm. The little beach house on the strip of land looked idyllic, basking in the moonlight with the vastness of the ocean yawning beyond.

But something had changed.

Not anything major—a light that had been on in the kitchen was off. Now, every light in the place was off. Probably Velda had come in off the deck and shut off the kitchen lights and headed for bed.

Probably.

But it was an hour earlier than we usually went to bed, and in fact we'd talked about watching a movie on TCM in about half an hour. Maybe that was it. Maybe she had turned out the kitchen light to make the living room more like a theater for our late show.

Maybe.

I got out the .45.

Gravel doesn't make it easy to move quietly, but I had two things going for me: crepe soles and experience. I crept along the side of the darkened beach house and came around onto the wooden deck, so very goddamn carefully . . .

And through the doors I saw them . . .

. . . *the beautiful woman I was married to, nude to the waist, clad only in the bikini bottoms, duct-taped rudely into one of the dining-room chairs, her dark hair mussed, her mouth a smear of red where she'd been slapped or slugged . . .*

. . . *and the giant, the tall, broad-shouldered, dark-skinned, trim-bearded, dark-eyed, grinning Goliath, because what other seven-foot-three-inch son of a bitch would be standing in my living room, threatening my wife with a fist the size of a fucking cabbage.*

He had a wild nest of hair, a Medusa's crown not of snakes but of thick, clotted locks. Absurdly, his attire was beachcomber-like, a gray short-sleeved sweatshirt and cut-off jeans that revealed muscular tree trunks for legs and un-Biblical sandals that barely housed feet bigger than shoestore sizers.

"Where *is* he?" Goliath demanded in a thickly accented but utterly understandable bass. "Where is *it*?"

"Go to hell!" she spat at him, and blood and spittle splattered his face.

He wiped it off with a hand like a frying pan, and rubbed it onto her naked chest, leaving red streaks. Then a sausage-fingered hand clutched his groin, boastfully, and his grin shone yellow within the black curls of beard. "You will break in *two*, when I take you—"

I didn't bother to open the glass door, I just squeezed the trigger, aiming through the glass at the bastard's oversized skull.

But the .45 jammed, the slide locking back impotently, making just enough noise to attract his attention. He wheeled toward me and I tossed the gun to the wooden deck with a *clunk* and pushed the door open and ran at him, threw a tackle at him that had half a room's run behind it.

And he tossed me like a rag doll into the wall over the couch, knocking pictures off and shattering glass. Mercifully, I slid down onto the cushions. Not so mercifully, he loomed over me and grinned down with those endless yellow choppers and then huge hands with thick splayed fingers came down to grip me by the windbreaker and drag me up and off the couch and he flung me again, this time into the lamp between the recliners. Velda's gift hit the hard tiles and the sound of breaking plaster was lost in my scream as I got onto my feet and barreled at him, swinging my forearm up and into his breadbasket with all of my force.

It should have knocked the wind out of him, but it didn't faze him an iota. He clutched me by the shoulders and shook me and then that big ugly face stared into mine, eyes enormous, nostrils flaring. *"Where . . . is . . . the . . . bone?"*

Holding me up like that was a mistake, because it put my foot in perfect position to kick him in the balls. My guess is they'd be shrunken to peas, because steroids just *had* to have had a hand in building this bastard . . .

Whether golf balls or peas, the kick hurt him, and he howled as he flung me again, and this time I *whammed* into Velda in her chair, knocking her over, and I heard the wood of the thing snapping, breaking. Briefly our eyes met and hers were urgent as she looked sharply to her left, directing my vision to follow and I saw, under an end table, her .38, where it had been slapped from her hand, no doubt, by our intruder.

I dove toward that end table but Goliath was on me, both hands clutching the back of my jacket like I was on the wrong end of a dwarf-tossing contest. He hurled me hard against the kitchen counter, its edge meeting my back and things popped inside me and maybe broke and I slipped down to the floor.

Slowly I got to my feet. I held my hands up in surrender. "You want to know where it is, big boy? Let me catch my breath."

He frowned, fists balled, a few feet from me as I bent over with my hands on my knees trying to catch my breath, or anyway making him think I was. Then I dropped to the floor and swung my feet around and caught him alongside the knee. He went down, hard, as if following a sudden urge to pray.

Now I was on him, throwing fists at his face in a flurry, tearing skin, breaking his nose and sending streams of blood down out of his nostrils, tearing the flesh at the corners of his eyes. I was hurting him, but he got to his feet and batted me across the room, into the glass doors, rattling them and me, putting the deck and the beach at my back.

He lumbered over toward me, his face a bloody mess, things dripping and dangling off it, and I saw Velda behind him, on her side, scooching with the shattered chair remnants duct-taped to her, toward that end table where the .38 lay a world away.

I played the only card I had left. "It's there, Aladdin—over *there!*"

And I pointed toward the special lamp, the wedding gift whose art deco plaster base had shattered away when it fell, revealing the giant femur hidden within.

"That's the Goliath bone, buddy. *Take* it! Take it and get the hell out!"

Groggily he turned toward the lamp with its smashed base and its revealed treasure with the dull ivory surface, the femur still attached to the base enough to stand there in deathly majesty. *And that was when Velda managed to kick the gun and it spun and skittered and stopped right within my reach.*

Still on the floor, I pointed the .38 up at him. His eyes were wide now and held a strange, ghastly innocence. He still loomed over me but I didn't give a shit. I had him.

"Just took David one little pebble," I said. "And a .38 slug is smaller than that."

And I put one right between his big bleary eyes.

Just a little spray of blood and bone shot out behind him, up through his skull and toward the ceiling, where it spattered and dripped, although he didn't know that. He was still on his feet but he was deader than the original Goliath; he just didn't have the motor reflexes left to do anything except topple not so much like a tree as a big useless puppet.

I thought about putting a few more into him for the fun of it, but

this son of a bitch was very fucking dead, and there was no use be-
laboring the point.

I went to Velda, got the duct tape off her lips, and kissed them.
"You saved me, baby," I said, a hand in her soft dark hair. "You
saved me."

Breathlessly, she purred, "No, Mike . . . you saved yourself, you
saved both of us. And you didn't even have a slingshot." She
grinned at me and I kissed her again and got the duct tape off her
and took her to the bathroom and helped her clean up.

"What now?" she said, wiping her face with a washcloth, looking at me in the bathroom mirror.

"We dump them."

"Dump . . . *them*?"

"You saw the Goliath bone?"

She nodded, then pretended to frown. "A *wedding* gift, huh? A
Trojan Horse!"

"I had to get it out of Manhattan. Shipped it down here.
Thought I had this thing licked, but al-Qaeda knew they'd been
stiffed with that dupe, and they came looking for it, and me."

"*Dump* them?"

"Yeah. In the drink. We've got a boat, don't we, and you're a big
strong girl and I'm a big strong . . . well, I'm a man, anyway."

She turned and touched my cheek. "You'd better clean up, too.
You're a mess."

"What else is new?"

Even if it was called a "day boat," the craft worked fine for a
night excursion lugging two big useless items out to meet Davy
Jones. I duct-taped the big bone to the seven-foot-three-inch
corpse, which seemed fitting and functional, since it would help
keep him from floating when the body gases kicked in.

So the Goliaths—new and old—went under where neither of them could do any more harm, and maybe some good, the new one feeding the fish and the old one giving the sharks something to sharpen their teeth on.

When we headed back, my first mate was at my side as I steered the boat under the stars and moon, the splash and the spray adding touches of reality to what seemed a dream.

"Is it over?" Velda asked.

"No. We have to go back to New York, kitten."

"For the other Goliath?"

"For the other killer."

Chapter 12

We were seated in the fifth row of the venerable St. John Theatre. I had the aisle with Velda seated next to me, a stunner in low-cut white satin. The Hurley kids were next to her, blonde Jenna in a pink gown with its own impressive décolletage, looking less like a girl and more like a woman. Pity that Matthew in his rental tux looked strictly high-school prom night.

Plenty of tuxes were peppered all around us in the packed sixteen-hundred-some seater, but my best business suit was all they were getting out of me.

The theater had been built in the twenties and refurbished a couple of times, but always maintained its original classy look: recessed ceiling, ornamental panels, crystal chandeliers, blood red seats complementing pale rose walls trimmed white. The auditorium with its single balcony was wider than it was deep, creating an unusual intimacy for a house this size.

Smiling, Matthew leaned forward to ask me a question. "Think this epic'll live up to the hype, Mr. Hammer?"

"Ever see the original *King Kong,* Matt?"

"Sure. I bought the DVD when the remake came out. Real classic, still a lot of fun. Why?"

"Remember when they were about to display the huge beast in New York, keeping him behind a curtain on a stage? And all of the city's elite were there in black tie and evening gowns, waiting to get the crap safely scared out of them?"

"Sure."

"Then the press photographers spooked the big monkey, and all hell broke loose."

Jenna, amused by my ancient view of things, said, "You don't really think some . . . some *robot* that Harold Cooke had concocted by Hollywood effects artists and Japanese animatronics geeks is going to break loose and create havoc?"

"Mike," Velda said with a mocking grin, "this is not a 'big monkey,' it's a piece of stagecraft."

"Yeah? Where does the Goliath bone fit into this show?"

She shrugged her lovely shoulders. "They'll probably drop down a screen at intermission and show us a film full of close-ups of the thing with some deep-voiced narrator and a bunch of wild music going."

I shook my head. "This is Harold Cooke we're talking about, successor to P. T. Barnum and Mike Todd, a Broadway Cecil B. DeMille. That bone will be *onstage. Tonight.* Question is, how?"

Matthew said, "I think Mrs. Hammer is right—even big as it is, displaying the bone on that stage with a spotlight or something just won't cut it. But if they have video cameras and drop a screen, like at a rock concert? Then everybody will see it clearly and still get the buzz from being in the same room with it."

The kids, by the way, thought Cooke had the real bone. I was the only one committing fraud here. And maybe Velda.

I kept my voice low, not wanting to be overheard. "Listen, trust your Uncle Mike—Cooke has something up his sleeve. And, remember, he's been courting controversy."

"That's just good PR," Velda said.

"Yeah, but he's courting it among groups who hate each other and have no compunction about demonstrating that hate in all kinds of violent ways."

She was almost smiling. "So why are we here, then?"

I shrugged. "We're expected. Anyway, my worst trait has always been curiosity."

Velda cocked an eyebrow. "You have many *worse* traits than that."

I grinned past my bride at Matthew. "See how they turn on you after marriage?"

My bride laughed and said, "You really think something might happen here tonight?"

"I took the aisle seat, didn't I?"

Mrs. Hammer chatted with the kids while I took in the crowd— lots of famous faces here, including the mayor and his wife, several congressmen local and national and, of course, the top critics. There's always murmuring in a theater before the curtain goes up, but this sounded like a plane landing. This auditorium had some serious anticipation brewing.

Velda was saying to the kids, "Where's your mom tonight? You *did* tell her we could arrange a ticket, right?"

Jenna said, "Yes, but she's still jet-lagged."

"Oh?"

"She attended a dead-languages seminar and just got back this morning."

Velda smiled at them. "Sounds like things are getting back to normal. Have you told her . . . ?"

Matthew shook his head and smiled embarrassedly. "No. And if we're not careful, now that we're back living in the same apartment? We might get caught, uh . . . doing something brothers and sisters don't want to get caught doing. If you get my meaning."

I said, "We get it."

The lights dimmed.

The audience's sudden hush seemed as charged with excitement as their murmuring had.

But as the first of the musical's two acts unfolded, the night began to feel like a non-event. This was the same old overblown production, with the road company of *David and Goliath* more at ease than the two young pop recording artists who'd been shoehorned in for some star power. The show had plenty of spectacle to distract—if not please—the audience, even if the songs were about as hummable as an electric fan shorting in and out.

Laugh at the old man if you want, but I fell asleep maybe half an hour in, and was having a perfectly good snooze when a sudden trumpet fanfare made me jump in my seat—I think everybody jumped in their seats.

The theater resounded with brazen brass and the throbbing beat of kettledrums punctuated by clangs from monstrous gongs, rising in intensity as the lights came down onstage. Soon only the figure of the actor playing David remained, in pinpoint spotlight. His costume a simple shepherd's peplum tied with a rope, David held a crooked staff in one hand while a leather sling dangled from the other. The wild sounds diminished slowly until only a haunting, reedy, piping tune remained.

The auditorium was pin-drop quiet, a very sophisticated New York theatergoing audience held as if hypnotized. Velda reached for my hand and squeezed it, her palm hot and sweaty.

Despite some ill-at-ease moments earlier, the young pop star was in control now, facing an audience that he knew he *had,* his voice amplified but its tone soft and elegant, yet touched with power, and how much was him and how much the sound technicians, I could only wonder. He spoke, intimately yet commandingly, directly to the audience, as if each of them was the only other person in the room.

David told the audience that he would soon have to face the consequences of his decision to abandon all armor and go out with no shield or sword to face the giant warrior, carrying only that simple child's toy, a slingshot. The crowd of seen-it-all New Yorkers was his.

Then the lights came up and David was not alone anymore—he was center stage, with thirty Israelite soldiers at stage right, and thirty Philistine soldiers at stage left, all in heavy armor with swords raised high, as if prepared to begin a battle that a movie screen could hardly contain, let alone a stage.

The soldiers cried out at each other in hostility that strained to be unleashed into warfare. No music now, just yelling and shouting in a dissonant symphony of hatred.

Slowly, David's hand went up and the vocal cacophony ceased and again the theater fell silent.

He stared toward the stage-left wings and said, "*I came to meet* Goliath!"

A booming voice offstage rumbled throughout the theater: "*And you shall meet Goliath!*"

A monster that took me back to *Kong* again stomped out from the wings, each footstep a small earthquake you could feel in your seat, a massive, vicious-looking figure promising incredible violence, a ten-foot helmeted giant in the full battle dress of the Philistines. His teeth shone through his full black beard like the mandibles of a great white shark and his eyes rolled weirdly in his head, as he surveyed the soldiers, and the upstart pipsqueak, in front of him. The spear in his fist was like a steering oar and the armor covering him was of polished copper. He was almost twice the height of David, and though his movements were not quite human, they were not quite *not* human, either . . .

He let out a roar and took a step forward, the spear going back, poised to throw, and someone in the audience screamed. I glanced around, grinning to myself, thinking it was funny that this hokum could inspire a scream like that, only to see audience members clinging to each other, some standing, a few even clambering to the nearest exits.

Velda's nails were biting into my palm.

"Doll, it's a mechanical beast. Hey, a great show, but just a show."

She shook her head, eyes huge, as she swung the arcs of black hair, checking to the sides and behind her. "Mike," she whispered, "look at the audience!"

"Yeah, I know. They've been brainwashed by all the publicity."

"But, Mike—"

"Relax. It's make-believe, kitten."

David was ready with his sling and Goliath stood poised not six feet from him, his armored animatronic chest heaving with mechanical breath.

"Ladies and gentlemen," a voice boomed from the speakers.

Everyone onstage, including the soldiers and David and his robotic adversary, froze. And certainly everybody in the audience did the same.

From the wings strode Harold Cooke himself, in a tuxedo sharp enough for Fred Astaire.

"I do apologize," he said, genial but serious. "Breaking the fourth wall is committing the cardinal sin in the theater. But the sins of the world David and Goliath lived in override any such petty concerns. I *know* what you came to see—you came to see *Goliath*."

He strode over to the ten-foot frozen Philistine.

"Son of a bitch *is* P. T. Barnum," I whispered to Velda.

Indicating his star attraction with a dramatic sweep of a hand, Cooke bellowed, "You came to see the *real* Goliath—and now you *shall*! From the Valley of Elah, where he has lain for thousands of years . . . behold *Goliath,* the giant warrior of the Philistines!"

And with that, Goliath strode to centerstage, with a whirring of moving parts and the rush of air pumps and a clanking of armor as David backed up, though the other soldiers stayed at attention. The towering figure, with uncanny human ease, reached down and tore off the armor that had covered his right limb from hip to knee . . . *and there was the bone!*

Shining, gleaming white, glistening wet as if with some natural lubricant, fully functional and perfectly fitted into the hip and knee joints and, as disgusting as it was, the effect was startling, almost as if the flesh had been torn off in battle and you were seeing the massive femur that allowed the great warrior to carry on.

Goliath threw back his head and roared with deep disturbing laughter, and though Cooke or his director had contrived the moment, the result felt real—at least it did to the woman across the aisle from me, who fainted . . . and to all the audience members slumping down in their seats, or clinging to the stranger next to them in utter fright, and in particular those who ran for exits when the ghastly giant bared his teeth again, and looked out into the audience as if trolling for victims.

Where was Fay Wray when you needed her, to calm this beast down?

Harold Cooke was smiling, and reveling in his audience's dis-comfort the way a roller-coaster owner relishes it when record numbers of his patrons upchuck. Cooke seemed about to take his leave and unfreeze the action and let the famous story play out when four men in tuxedos came rushing out of the audience, two up the stairs at either side of the stage, in a sudden assault that looked utterly ridiculous but wasn't.

They each had a heavy tool in hand, a crowbar or a wrench, and some confederate at the theater must have conveniently left a tool-box or two where these intruders could find them, because the checkpoint getting into the theater had been better than at that NYU research facility. A diabolical yell of *"Allahu akbar!"* shrilled from the tallest one, who led the charge as they ran to the giant Goliath, their makeshift weapons about to swing at the leg joints.

Whether they were attempting to destroy this symbol of their defeat or reduce it to a mechanical pile of rubble so they could re-trieve the Goliath bone as a trophy of a fallen past hero, I have no idea, because something went terribly wrong after the first swipe of a crowbar. The electronic engineering had created an anima-tronic actor unprepared for improvisation, and the programming that made Goliath behave collided with whatever plans the men had, as everything came apart, Goliath crashing down without even a pebble being flung at him, landing facedown hard on the four attackers, creating a terrible massive percussive series of sounds from metal and bone and plastic and flesh and electronics and blood.

I was close to the stage, but still had to fight to get through the panicking crowd, who were doing their own *King Kong* impression trying to jam into the exits, sixteen hundred theatergoers review-ing the play with screams of terror.

When I got up there, I found another casualty, not apparent from the audience: a detached massive arm, including the hand bearing the enormous spear, had pinned Harold Cooke to the stage floor.

The showman should survive—the arm had just missed coming down on his head—but a lot of bones besides Goliath's were broken or even crushed.

He looked up at me past a chunk of armor with a horror-stricken expression.

"You people are right," I said. "No business like show business—I'll try to get somebody over here to help you."

Security guards were belatedly making it onto the stage.

Cooke swallowed and nodded; the perfect silver hair was crooked—damn thing had been a toupee. "The bone . . . the bone . . . destroyed?"

The femur had shattered under the weight, the Goliath bone he'd invested in just a worthless clutter of white fragments and dust.

"Yup. And *this* publicity I don't think you'll love."

Stage managers and crew members were scrambling around, security guys, too, assorted frantic people on cell phones, summoning ambulances and police. A house doctor was on hand and he was dealing with Cooke, but they'd need a damn crane to lift that arm off him.

Under the twisted and scrambled metal that had been Goliath were four men. Three were very dead. Things were seeping out of their pierced bodies, and one seemed to be broken in half. The other one was still alive, and his eyes were hating me as I grinned at him.

I knelt and said, "You fell for a gag, chum—got yourselves killed over a lousy piece of machinery. That's not even the real bone."

His dark eyes were fading.

But I had some time left with him: "The world'll laugh at you for the idiots you are. Few minutes from now, you'll be dead, but paradise is waiting, right? Think again. I'm going to make sure they bury you with a pork chop tied around your damn neck."

Then his eyes filmed over. Nobody on this stage had ever had better timing than me.

Velda and the kids were among the only audience members left when I came down from the stage.

"Mike," Velda asked, "what were you saying to that son of a bitch?"

"Aw, I was just comforting him. Anybody for Sardi's?"

A few days later, a cold rainy Sunday, I made arrangements with Dr. Charlene Hurley to quietly and discreetly swap the real Goliath bone for the duplicate in her possession. She had no way of knowing that the real relic was on the ocean's floor, buried in a watery grave with another dead Goliath. That was news I needed to break to her personally, and not on the telephone, nor in her apartment where the kids might intrude.

We set it up for 3:00 P.M., and through Mr. Rogers, certain security measures were lifted. I told Charlene that the exchange being made today needed to stay confidential, so the sophisticated scanning in that high-tech visitors' circle outside the sleek steel door of her lab needed to be shut off for the afternoon. She had said that would be no problem.

I hoped she'd taken me literally and turned that surveillance off for the entire afternoon, because I arrived an hour and a half early. And I didn't come in through the front entry with its security checkpoint: I availed myself of the way in that Mr. Rogers had pointed out to me, weeks before. I allowed half an hour, and brought some tools along, to get through the closed-off construction workers' latrine, then took the rear stairs down to the lower floor.

On Sunday the hallway of metal doors was as dead as Dr. George Hurley. I used a key card I'd been provided on one of my early trips to the lab and the steel door slid open and I went in to the big, sterile stainless-steel chamber. She was standing at one of the metal lab tables where she had four Mylar-enclosed ragged-edged brown documents spread out for examination with a magnifying glass.

The sound of the door opening had alerted her, and she was facing me as I entered, smiling at her, nodding. The door slid shut behind me. She wore a white lab coat as usual and slacks, and yet her beauty was undeniable, the big brown eyes and the golden blonde curls looking almost white under the fluorescents. Even the curves of her full-breasted, slim-waisted, full-hipped body couldn't be blunted by the scientist's garb.

"Mike," she said, her half-smile guarded, "you startled me . . . you're early. . . ."

"I figured you'd probably be here already, working. Hope you don't mind."

"No, not at all."

I was beside her now. I nodded toward the documents. "More dead language stuff?"

"No, this is Hebrew. Ninth century B.C.E."

"What's that?"

"Before the Common Era. We don't use the B.C. designation anymore."

I pointed. "What's that one you're examining?"

"A widow's petition. Seeking the rights to her husband's property, primarily a wheat field."

"Kind of fitting."

She gave me a troubled glance. "I expected you to be carrying a big cardboard box, Mike."

I shrugged and grinned. "I'm afraid I have to disappoint you, Charlene. The only relic I brought is me. And the only artifact is this—"

I slipped my hand under my trench coat and inside my suit coat and came back with the .45. I held it at my waist, casually, but pointed it right at her.

I'll give her this much. She didn't argue. The beautiful brown eyes assumed a coldness, like polished agates, and her mouth a hardness that took some of its beauty away. But there were no denials.

"Your husband mentioned that you were Jewish and that you'd spent time as a young woman in Israel in a kibbutz. But so have a lot of American Jews. So when I first heard of this terrorist outfit, the Kakh, it didn't even cross my mind that you might be part of it."

She folded her arms. Her chin came up. "The Kakh is a patriotic Israeli organization. We are not terrorists."

"The State of Israel disagrees. So do I. The Kakh was in on this from the beginning, torturing and killing that Arab driver in Israel. Then, working through your Chicago contact, Kaddour, you arranged for a shooter to come to New York, and you provided the NYU ID papers he carried as a cover. Papers or not, he had al-Qaeda written all over him—literally, in the case of his Rada Rey tattoo—and his first job was to take a controlled potshot at your own daughter. Your own damn *daughter*, Charlene!"

One eyebrow came up in a tiny facial shrug.

I grunted a laugh. "That was no miss on an attempted hit—the shooter hit that handbag, just like he was supposed to, an action meant to scare your daughter and stepson and convince your husband that the Goliath bone was too dangerous to hold on to. Would Kakh have used it for recruiting and morale building? Or would you have really let Israel take charge of it, with you and your husband doing the research?"

She spoke calmly, evenly. "My husband was a good man. But he did not share my enthusiasm, my beliefs, for a cause that I think, Mike, you know in your heart is a righteous one."

"If you expect me to equate Israel with the Kakh, I'd sooner equate the USA with the Ku Klux Klan. You're a zealot, lady, just like the maggots who took down the Trade Towers. No difference—just a different shade of crazy."

Her eyes flared, her nostrils, too. "You're *wrong*. I'm a soldier, and our cause is just."

"Did you love your husband?"

That, at least, shook her a little. "Of course I did."

"But it didn't stop you from shooting him, when he found out what you were up to—and that kill you did *yourself*, Charlene. In that alley in the Village, where he stood close enough to his loving wife for her to shoot his brains out all over the bricks."

Now the eyes settled down, half-lidded orbs watching me carefully. "Sacrifices must be made for the greater good."

"You took Kaddour out, too, didn't you? That Arab patsy that Kaddour sent here from Chicago, and then sent back again, cleaned up all your other loose ends, like those three expendable black guys in Harlem, right? But that made Kaddour a loose end himself, particularly when I got his name out of your shooter and sicced the FBI boys onto the case."

She smiled. Laughed. "Now you have me killing people in Chicago. I seem to get around."

"You do. Your daughter mentioned at the *David and Goliath* opening the other night that you've been out of town for a dead-languages seminar. I had Captain Chambers check up—that seminar was at the Drake Hotel in Chicago. Then I had some Windy City PIs I use do some further checking—the afternoon Kaddour was killed, you attended *none* of the meetings."

She unfolded her arms, put her hands on her hips, her chin still up, quietly defiant, with a beauty that still shouted. "That doesn't sound like evidence."

I raised the .45 a notch. "Does anything you've heard or read about me make you think I give a shit about evidence? You're not a soldier with a righteous cause, you're a monster who gives a righteous cause a bad name. If I were younger and quicker, maybe a bunch of people would still be alive, maybe even your husband—hell, *you* were the one who set up that attempted kidnapping of your kids! It was in a goddamn apartment building you and your husband owned! You would endanger your own kids and use them as pawns in your personal fucking chess game."

A tiny shrug was her defense. Then she added, "Only *Jenna* is mine. Matthew was George's. And if you think I don't know that they are fucking each other, you underestimate my abilities as a historian and scientist."

I gaped at her. "So, then—*Matt* would be the next Hurley to reside in a gold vase for scattering in the Valley of Elah? You're a dead-languages expert, all right—you speak the language of death fluently. Shit, I don't care what country you represent, lady. I don't care about your politics and I don't even care about that lovely body of yours, and nice try on the seduction, by the way. You got a rise out of me, but I don't go into a marriage by cheating the night before."

Her mouth curled up at both sides in a smile both beautiful and snide. "Don't be so smug, Hammer. You're the *king* of ends justifies the means. How can you condemn what my group does in a world where the Islamic extremists want not only me but my entire country exterminated?"

I shook my head. "I'm just one guy who balances the books now and then, not a group or a government. You? You're the plague. You're evil, lady. I dumped the Goliath bone in the Atlantic Ocean, but I'll make you another candidate for the Valley of Elah. Only I'll make sure they scatter you in a different part than your husband's ashes. Out of respect to him."

I thought she was there alone. I knew a little storeroom opened off one end of the big shiny chamber, but it never occurred to me some asshole accomplice of hers would sneak up behind me and try to clobber me with the butt end of a .22.

But at least I heard him at the last second, and spun, and just as the nondescript balding guy in the blue smock swung his hand up to hit me with the gun butt, I bashed him in the left temple with the heel of the fist clutching the grip of the .45, like I was pounding a nail. He was dead almost instantly, collapsing in a pile.

The .22 he dropped, though, went spinning on the cold hard floor and Charlene deftly knelt and plucked it up and, as I was turning back toward her, she slammed the barrel of the target pistol into my right wrist and my fingers popped open involuntarily and the .45 fell, and the second of blinding pain gave her just the time she needed to snatch up the .45 as well. She swapped guns with herself so that my .45 was in her right hand and the .22 she dropped in her lab coat pocket. She was smiling now, an almost-demonic smile.

"I know who you remind me of," I said.

That amused her. "Really? Who?"

"Another woman of science. Another manipulative bitch. I should have remembered—same damn perfume . . . I didn't even know they still made My Sin."

"Oh yes. It was George's favorite."

Even their names were alike—Charlene, Charlotte, and the two women's faces blurred, the whiteness of the hair and the eyes that could taste you with a glance, the mouth that could devour you, the body that was fire and velvet.

I nodded toward the sprawl of blue smock with his head in pooling red behind me. "That's your lab assistant—Bryan, right? He was with you in Israel. He's a former student, loyal as a pup to you. You were screwing him, too, right?"

She frowned with her forehead but her mouth was smiling, and her face had finally lost its beauty. "Did you *really* expect to walk in here and just kill me, you pitiful shambling dinosaur? How did you expect to get away with it?"

I edged toward her. "You'll be just another al-Qaeda victim, baby. I'll kill your evil ass, then duck back out, and show up at the appointed time to find the tragic aftermath. And now Bryan's part of it, too."

Her eyes glittered. "Oh, you think you're still in this game?"

I was almost on top of her when the gun swung up and she thumbed back the hammer, the weapon trained on my heart. "Good-bye and good riddance, Hammer."

Call it God, call it Allah, call it kismet, what happened next was a literal thousand-to-one shot when she squeezed the trigger and a random unstable vintage .45 cartridge exploded and the gun that I'd used for so many years so many times to wipe away evil exploded in her hand, a modest explosion as explosions went, no shrapnel flying, just a blossom of orange and yellow and red leaving a flower of twisted metal that fell from a hand that was mostly gone, glistening blood and shreds of charred flesh clinging to the white skeletal hand that stayed behind to leave death's own knobby finger pointing at me.

Her scream was shrill and banshee-like, its own dead language, ringing off all that stainless steel, but her wild cry of pain ended when I snatched up the mangled abstraction that had once been a gun and hammered the jagged blossom of steel into her throat, turning scream into gurgle and life into death.

A Tip of the Porkpie Hat

Mickey Spillane often mentioned having written the first Mike Hammer novel, *I, the Jury* (1947), in just nine days. His record for a novel, he said, was three days.

As a young man, Mickey displayed a frenzied, intense creativity that resulted in seven novels in five years that became the top best-sellers of the mid-twentieth century. In his last two decades, Mickey drifted into a more leisurely if no less ambitious approach. He maintained three offices at his home in Murrell's Inlet, South Carolina, often having one novel or more going in each. At the time of his passing in July 2006, he had four books under way.

Around 1999 Mickey told me that his Hammer novel-in-progress, *King of the Weeds,* would be the final in the series. He had a substantial number of pages written when September 11, 2001, sent him and his tough detective in a new direction. The idea of Mike Hammer in a New York threatened by terrorists invigorated Mickey, and he turned with great enthusiasm to *The Goliath Bone,* designed to be the final Hammer novel, chronologically. (He also intended to complete *King of the Weeds,* and had entrusted several other set-aside Hammer manuscripts to me when I visited him in 1989—Mickey said, "Maybe you can do something with these someday." Two weeks later, Hurricane Hugo hit South Carolina, destroying Mickey's home.)

A few days before his passing, Mickey—who during his illness remained cheerful, tough, and hopeful—expressed one regret to me: "I may not get *The Goliath Bone* finished." I told him not to worry; if need be, I'd do whatever was necessary to complete it (which I have done, utilizing his rough draft material and extensive notes). His reply was characteristic: "Thanks, buddy."

More thanks are due: to Otto Penzler, who shares my love and respect for Mickey Spillane; Mickey's wife, Jane Spillane, who followed her husband's advice and entrusted me with this mission; Barbara Collins, my wife, who joined Jane and me on the "treasure hunt" Mickey knowingly sent us on through his offices, files and papers; Mickey's longtime typist, Vickie Fredericks; the real Paul Vernon, who provided boating info; editors David Hough and Andrea Schulz, who were both helpful and patient; Dominick Abel, my agent and friend, who made this possible . . .

. . . and, of course, Mickey Spillane himself.

Thanks, buddy. ⌣

About the Authors

MICKEY SPILLANE and MAX ALLAN COLLINS collaborated on numerous projects. They co-edited four anthologies presenting new and/or classic stories by a variety of American crime writers, and their co-creation, the science-fiction incarnation of *Mike Danger*, was a popular comic-book series in the 1990s.

With Spillane's cooperation and help, Collins edited (or co-edited) six volumes collecting previously uncollected Spillane short stories and comics work. Occasional actor Spillane also appeared in Collins's two *Mommy* films as a criminal lawyer and was the subject of an award-winning Collins documentary.

MICKEY SPILLANE was the bestselling American mystery writer of the twentieth century. He was also the most widely translated fiction author of the twentieth century, although he insisted he was not an "author," but a writer.

A bartender's son, Mickey Spillane was born in Brooklyn, New York, on March 9, 1918. An only child who swam and played football as a youth, Spillane got a taste for storytelling by scaring other kids around the campfire. After a truncated college career, Spillane—already selling stories to pulps and slicks under pseudonyms—became a writer in the burgeoning comic-book field (*Captain America, Submariner*), a career cut short by World War II. Spillane—who had learned to fly at airstrips as a boy—became an instructor of fighter pilots.

After the war, Spillane converted an unsold comic-book project—*Mike Danger, Private Eye*—into the hard-hitting, sexy novel, *I, the Jury* (1947). The $1,000 advance was just what the writer needed to buy materials for a house he wanted to build for himself and his young wife on a patch of land in Newburgh, New York. The 1948 Signet reprint of the 1947 E. P. Dutton hardcover edition of *I, the Jury* sold in the millions, as did the six tough mysteries that soon followed; all but one featured hard-as-nails PI Mike Hammer. The Hammer thriller *Kiss Me, Deadly* (1952) was the first private-eye novel to make the *New York Times* bestseller list.

Much of Mike Hammer's readership consisted of Spillane's fellow World War II veterans, and the writer—in a vivid, even surrealistic first-person style—escalated the sex and violence already intrinsic to the genre in an effort to give his battle-scarred audience hard-hitting, no-nonsense entertainment. For this blue-collar approach, Spillane was attacked by critics and adored by readers. His influence on the mass-market paperback was immediate and long lasting, his success imitated by countless authors and publishers. Gold Medal Books, pioneering publisher of paperback originals, was specifically designed to tap into the Spillane market.

Spillane's career was sporadic; his conversion in 1952 to the Jehovah's Witnesses, the conservative religious sect, is often cited as the reason he backed away for a time from writing the violent, sexy Hammer novels. Another factor may be the enormous criticism heaped upon Hammer and his creator. Spillane claimed to write only when he needed the money, and in periods of little or no publishing, Spillane occupied himself with other pursuits: flying, traveling with the circus, appearing in motion pictures, and for nearly twenty years spoofing himself and Hammer in a lucrative series of Miller Lite beer commercials.

The controversial Hammer has been the subject of a radio show, a comic strip, and two television series, starring Darren McGavin (in the late '50s) and Stacy Keach (in the mid-'80s with a 1997 revival, both produced by Spillane's friend and partner, Jay Bernstein). Numerous gritty movies have been made from Spillane novels, notably director Robert Aldrich's seminal film noir, *Kiss Me Deadly* (1955), and *The Girl Hunters* (1963), starring Spillane himself as his famous hero.

Mickey Spillane died in August 2006, joining the ranks of Dashiell Hammett, Raymond Chandler, and Agatha Christie, arguably the only other mystery writers of the twentieth century with comparable name recognition.

MAX ALLAN COLLINS was hailed in 2004 by *Publishers Weekly* as "a new breed of writer." A frequent Mystery Writers of America Edgar nominee, he has earned an unprecedented fourteen Private Eye Writers of America Shamus nominations for his historical thrillers, winning for his Nathan Heller novels, *True Detective* (1983) and *Stolen Away* (1991). In 2006 he received the Eye, the Lifetime Achievement Award of the PWA, joining a small, distinguished list of recipients that includes Ross MacDonald, Robert B. Parker, and Mickey Spillane.

His graphic novel *Road to Perdition* is the basis of the Academy Award–winning film starring Tom Hanks and Paul Newman and directed by Sam Mendes. His many comics credits include the syndicated strip *Dick Tracy;* his own *Ms. Tree; Batman;* and *CSI: Crime Scene Investigation,* based on the hit TV series for which he has also written video games, jigsaw puzzles, and a *USA Today*-bestselling-series of novels.

An independent filmmaker in the Midwest, he wrote and directed the Lifetime movie *Mommy* (1996) and a 1997 sequel, *Mommy's Day.* He wrote *The Expert,* a 1995 HBO world premiere, and wrote and directed the innovative made-for-DVD feature, *Real Time: Siege at Lucas Street Market* (2000). *Shades of Noir* (2004), an anthology of his short films, including his award-winning documentary, *Mike Hammer's Mickey Spillane* (1999), can be found in a DVD collection of Collins's indie films, *The Black Box.* His most recent feature is *Eliot Ness: An Untouchable Life* (2006), based on his Edgar-nominated play (also available on DVD); and he wrote the screenplay for *The Last Lullaby* (2008), based on his own acclaimed 2007 novel, *The Last Quarry.*

His other credits include film criticism, short fiction, songwriting, trading-card sets, and movie/TV tie-in novels, including the *New York Times* bestsellers, *Saving Private Ryan* and *American Gangster.* He lives in Muscatine, Iowa, with his wife, writer Barbara Collins. Their son Nathan (Mickey Spillane's godson) works in the video-game industry as a translator of Japanese into English.